A PRESCRIPTION FOR POSSESSION

Van Helsing Organization Book 1

NOREE COSPER

Book cover design by Rebecca Frank.
http://rebeccafrank.design/

Editing services by Pauline Nolet. Proofreading services by Wayne Scace,
Amanda Kuzma, and Cassie Hess-Dean.

www.noreecosper.com

For my husband Jayson, who has been my constant support.

PROLOGUE

R *ome, 1536*

The iron spikes in the manacles pricked the wrists of the boy Ose inhabited, causing his very essence to burn. No mortal pain could compare to the agony that seared him to his core. His control over the body slipped again, and he slumped back in the chair to which he sat bound with sweat pouring down his face and his breath coming in small pants.

Incense clogged the air of the tiny stone basement of the church, leaving wisps of intricate and meaningless designs as remnant. The priest stood a few feet away, his head bowed so the tendrils of white hair fell before his face. He held a crucifix out before him between his clasped hands as he prayed. A circle of candles surrounded him and the priest, another barrier to prevent Ose from escaping.

Damn Vittorio. The human wasn't worth the flesh he'd been sculpted into. Ose almost had him at the threshold of giving up his soul with promises of riches until this priest had arrived in Rome. Ose had come to the church thinking to seal the contract with Vittorio. Instead, he'd been caught in the trap.

"God and Father of our Lord Jesus Christ, I appeal to your holy name, humbly begging your kindness, that you graciously grant me help against this and every unclean spirit now tormenting this creature of yours; through Christ our Lord," the priest chanted in Latin.

How dare this ape call him unclean? Their existence depended on flesh and soul, so easily manipulated and controlled. They existed only to feed their urges, their desires. He was pure spirit, pure thought. He manipulated.

"Gabriella, the holy water." The priest glanced behind him.

A small figure stepped out of the shadows in the corner of the room, carrying a glass vial. Everything about this girl spoke peasant, from the white linen dress and sandals to the calluses on her hands to the coif that covered the braids of her black hair. Her gaze burned into him as she set the holy water at the edge of the circle. The skin of her face tightened as her upper lip curled away from her teeth.

Ose smiled at her. It was a shame he was about to be exorcised. She would have proven a delight to toy with. The priest patted her on the shoulder and picked up the holy water. The droplets he sprayed on Ose seared through the flesh to his spirit.

"I cast you out, unclean spirit, along with every satanic power of the enemy, every spectre from hell, and all your fell companions; in the name of Lord Jesus Christ, be gone, and stay far from this creature of God," the priest murmured in a raspy voice.

Why should these humans have the right to cast him out? He'd walked this world in their flesh before they were even aware enough to know their Creator. Ose shuddered, his fingers contorting in a twisted claw motion, and concentrated his will on keeping control of the boy's body even as the words pushed at him to depart. It couldn't end like this. He was one of the First. How dare this human presume to have control over who he chose to inhabit?

"For it is He who commands you, He who flung you head-long from the heights of heaven into the depths of hell. It is He who commands you, He who once stilled the sea and the wind and the storm." The priest grimaced and clutched his chest.

Why must he suffer, be eternally forsaken by his brothers and Father for a decision he'd made? He'd been given the will to choose. If it had been wrong, why give any choice at all? The body convulsed, jerking him out of the chair and onto the ground. The spikes dug into the flesh as he strained against the chains.

"Hearken, therefore, and tremble in fear, Ose, you enemy of the faith." The priest fell to his knees, wheezing. "You foe of the human race—"

The priest choked; his fingers clutched at the sackcloth robe he wore as his face drained of color. He stumbled forward, knocking the candles over and causing them to roll about the circle. Ose straightened from his hunched position as the jarring of his spirit subsided and the body once again began to obey his will. He laughed at the holy man. The frail-ties of humanity. If the priest intended to die, Ose was keen to help him do so. He strained against his bonds to pull the priest closer and wrap his hands around his neck. The vial of holy water skidded across the floor in their struggle.

"Padre Ricci." Gabriella's voice rose in a panic.

"I'll be right with you, my dear," Ose said.

The padre's face flushed a purplish red, and his hands batted at Ose's fingers. The spikes dug into his wrists, and for a second, his hands fell limp on the armrests. He forced his will over the boy's body and tightened his grip. The key to his shackles had to be on the priest. Once free, he would deal with the girl at his leisure. She ran back to the corner, shifting objects around in a bag until she pulled out a journal. What could she do? She was only female.

The girl flipped through the pages. "I exorcise ye, and powerfully banish ye, commanding ye with strength and violence by him who spake and it was done; and by all these names."

Impossible. How could the girl know the Hebrew incantations of Solomon? They were supposed to be lost and replaced with lies written by the very demons Solomon bound. Ose let go of the priest, who lay back coughing. The devil dug through the holy man's robes. There had to be a pocket or chain that held the key. He had to stop the girl before she continued.

"El Shaddai, Elohim, E--Elohi, Tzabaoth, Elim, Asher Eheieh, Yah, Tetragrammaton, Shaddai," Gabriella said, "which signify God the high and almighty, the God of Israel."

The Father who had forsaken him, all because of Lucifer's plan to reach the Celestial Throne. The body shuddered, as a grip, colder than any glacier, pulled at him, and he fell forward on the priest. He struggled to maintain control. The key had to be beyond the circle. Ose pulled at the chains, and the chair scraped against the floors with a grinding squeal as he tried to drag it with him. Damn, this iron inhibited his power.

"Through whom undertaking all our operations we shall prosper in all the works of our hands, seeing that the Lord is now, always, and for-forever with us, in our hearts and on our lips," the girl said.

She'd stumbled over the words. The banishment wouldn't work, yet why was the pull becoming stronger? He collapsed, unable to move the boy's body any farther. Wisps of greenish black light flared before his eyes. The cold burned him. This couldn't be happening.

"And by his holy names, and by the virtue of the sovereign God, we shall accomplish all our work."

With Gabriella's last words, the body jerked upright. The green and black surrounded him as he rocketed from the earthly realm at a speed even beyond his own thought. The light faded into a black void. This wasn't his home in hell, where he should have ended. Instead of his legions of demons, emptiness surrounded him. Or perhaps not. A shadow pulled itself from the blackness.

"Welcome, little brother," it said.

ampton, TX, Present Day

Not five minutes in this backwater town, and I had a demon sniffing my trail. He scanned the room with narrowed dark eyes and the nostrils of his wide nose flaring. His hair lay plastered against his forehead in greasy brown locks. He towered over everyone, even the people standing, as he squeezed between the large round tables and the gathering at the bar. The frayed threads of his jeans and his leather vest matched the dress of the rest of the roadhouse.

I lifted my drink to my mouth and shifted to my second sight. Most people say the eyes are the windows to the soul. Those people can't see auras. The lights on the walls dimmed, and the air took on a gray haze, like seeing things through a London fogbank. Colors bloomed out from each human in the building, blending together in a rainbow. The demon was another matter.

The shaggy black dog the size of a pony stood semi-imposed on all fours over the form of the man. Flames blazed from its eyes as it perused the room with its nose wiggling. Was there really a dog walking through a busy Texas bar? No. Demons had no corporeal form and had to possess physical bodies, and this one chose a werewolf. *Dio*, I had a hellhound on my ass.

Talk about bad timing. Ose already had some of his minions patrolling. If it found me, it would go running to its master to let him know I was in town. My hunt was in danger of ending before it even started.

Breathe, Gabby.

I leaned forward and let my black curtain of hair obscure my face and twisted the lid of the salt shaker off. With a flick of my hand, I knocked it over, allowing the grains to spill across the table and onto the floor. The salt should cover my scent. I slid closer to the group at the next table until I looked like I belonged with them.

One of the men grinned at me, his aura a happy yellow-orange. "Hey babe."

I nodded and raised my glass before returning my attention to the hellhound. He paused by a man at the bar who had caught my attention, or more his aura did. A ghostly image of a woman leaned over him, whispering in his ear. My hand tightened around the beer mug, but the mutt moved on. I relaxed. The colors around the people in the bar faded, as did the ghost woman when my sight returned to normal. The haze remained but more from cigarette smoke than any after images.

I glanced at the front of the bar and let out a long sigh. One window and a door weren't much of an escape route. Fifty feet of inebriated patrons stood between me and freedom.

A familiar tingle ran down my spine as two of the three

men I had been waiting for walked through the door. For a moment, I flashed back to a dressing room, staring down another Romanian hunter. We'd come across the same prey, though he thought it was a vampire and I knew it was a demon. It had been the beginning of something almost magical, both thrilling and painful. I inhaled, bringing myself back to the present. This wasn't the twenties, I wasn't in Paris, and these brothers weren't Dimitri.

Both had his chiseled features and his straight nose, though their hair was more of a burnt sienna. The one in front wore his cut short, had a tuft on his chin, and a pair of square, black-framed glasses that rested on the bridge of his nose. He towered over his brother, which meant he would be a mountain compared to my small height. The other's hair brushed against the nape of his neck, and he kept it tucked behind his ears. He stood with his arms crossed, wearing a smirk to let the world know he knew everything. They cast their eyes over the room. The tall one adjusted the glasses on his face and approached the man sitting at the bar.

Several women watched them as they passed to which the shorter boy gave them a wink and a grin. A soft chuckle escaped my lips. The boys were dressed to impress. Their leather coats and slacks spoke of sophistication yet still provided enough flexibility to move if needed.

I stood and nodded at the men who'd been trying to talk to me. Rude, but it was time to work. Besides, they were too young for me. I straightened my red tank top and brushed any wrinkles from my jeans. I couldn't approach them looking like a guttersnipe.

A stool opened up on the other side of them, and I took the seat, trying to look casual while listening in on the brothers' conversation. The bartender stood in front of me, waiting for an order. I pointed to a beer and leaned back to get a better look at the third man. His back remained mostly to me, giving me a glimpse of his bearded cheek and a ponytail a shade darker in color than the other two. Brother number three. I inched forward to hear better over someone's bad rendition of "Bad Moon Rising."

"Ader." The tall man spoke in Romanian. "Your prison sentence hasn't ended yet."

"I got out for being brilliant," the man at the bar said without turning around.

"Does the warden know that?" the third one asked.

If I remembered correctly, this generation of Van Helsings had four boys. Adam, the oldest, had passed away ten years ago. So that left Esais, Adrian, and Tres. The smirking boy had to be Tres; he looked the youngest. Was Ader short for Adrian?

Ader chuckled. "The warden didn't have much of a say."

Esais, the tall one, pinched the bridge of his nose and closed his eyes. He shook his head, letting out a long sigh as he looked at his brothers.

"Honestly," he said. "First you end up in jail, and now you're breaking out. You haven't changed."

"You expected me to?" Adrian asked.

"Why are you here?" Esais asked.

"Same reason as you. Revenge."

Tres crossed his arms. "Why do you even care? You were never around when we needed you."

Adrian turned to face his brothers, causing both of them to gasp. A patch covered his right eye while the other stared hard at Tres. Esais reached out to touch Adrian's arm, but he pulled away.

"What happened?" Esais asked.

"Not important." Adrian turned back to the bar. "Who were you told to meet?"

"A woman named Gabriella Di Luca."

"Any idea what this woman looks like?"

Esais glanced in my direction with hesitation and opened his mouth.

That looked like my cue. I cleared my throat, raising my hand in a small wave. "Buna seara."

Adrian and Tres turned their heads with near identical expressions of distrust. They didn't expect someone to speak their native language here, yet here I was, a stranger invading their family circle. Tres's gaze traveled down my body, and his eyes expression and became more warming. Adrian continued to regard me with a hard, narrowed eye.

"Who are you?" Adrian asked.

"Gabriella."

"Convenient." The word dripped with sarcasm.

As much as I loved a verbal battle and the opportunity to win over someone's distrust, I preferred it when I didn't have a hellhound sniffing me out. The hairs on the back of my neck stood up, and my gaze traveled to the table-filled area farther in the room. The hellhound's wiry form had disappeared through a large door to the right, the source of the atrocious singing. Now would be a perfect time to exit.

"We need to speak, but not here," I said.

"We're not going anywhere with you."

"Ader," Esais said.

Adrian looked back at his brother. "We have no proof she is who she claims to be."

"He's right. You could be a demon," Tres said.

"You choose now to be cautious? Where was this when you were talking about revenge in a crowded bar?" I crossed my arms over my chest and raised an eyebrow. "You don't know a lot about demons, do you?"

"I've read several books on the subject," Esais said. "That question doesn't answer our doubts."

"Do I fit the description you were given of Gabriella?"

Esais cleared his throat and adjusted his glasses before nodding.

I waved my hands toward the front door. "Then, can we leave? I may not be one, but there is a demon here."

Esais and Tres turned their heads, their muscles tensing as they scanned the bar while Adrian kept his eye on me. The hellhound stepped back into the room and turned his head in my direction. His gaze locked on me, and, with a mix between a snarl and a grin, he began shoving his way through the crowded tables and chairs.

I stood. "Too late."

I picked up my beer. The amber liquid sloshed around as I tested the weight of the glass. "Get outside."

"We aren't going to fight?" Tres clenched his fists; the muscles in his back tensed.

I nodded to the five feet of space between the full tables and the bar. "This isn't the best place. Besides, he's not after you."

"What about you?" Esais's forehead wrinkled as he followed my line of vision.

"I'll be along shortly."

He sighed and pushed his younger brother toward the door. Tres's jaw tightened, and he squared his shoulders so the push bounced off with no effect. Adrian snorted and moved ahead of the other two.

"Come on. Let's see what waits for us outside," he said.

The corner of my eye twitched at his words, but I focused on my approaching prey. He wasn't thick, but the skin around his arms stretched across muscle. It didn't matter, the extra muscles were more for show. The demon added unnatural strength and reflexes without all the mass. I sat up straighter, with my heart running a marathon in my chest.

When he moved between two round tables full of people, I hurled the mug at him. He saw it coming, of course and batted it away with the back of his hand. The drink bounced off the head of a man sitting at the table to the hellhound's right. Golden liquid dripped out of the man's hair and down his neck. Perfect.

The man hefted his bulk out of his seat and caught the demon by the shoulder. The mutt's head turned slowly to the offending hand and its owner. The music and the chatter of those surrounding me drowned out the words exchanged, but it must have been insulting. The man's scowl deepened, and his fist slammed into the hellhound's face.

The mutt's head snapped back from the force of the punch. He tossed the local over his shoulder with one hand, sending the man soaring past me and onto a table full of men. Wood broke, glasses shattered, and fists flew. The cacophony of yells and flesh hitting flesh replaced the music. Predictable.

Esais pushed his brother through the front door before the fight could reach them. My heart raced as I climbed on top of the bar. The bartenders paid me no attention as they moved to break up the brawl that had spread throughout the room.

The man's friends gathered around the hellhound. He swung out his arm, and two were tossed into the table they had stood up from. Spittle flew from his mouth as he bared his yellow teeth at me with the canines longer and pointier than a normal human. I gave him a wave and ran down the length of the bar, scooping up several salt shakers as I passed. A group of brawlers looked up in surprise as I leapt over their heads. I landed in a roll only a few feet from the door. It swung closed behind me as I departed.

The gravel crunched beneath my feet as I hurried through

the parking lot. I lifted my head, letting the breeze cool the perspiration on my face. The tightness dissipated from my shoulders as I breathed in the night air.

Ah, freedom.

The brothers stood at their car watching me as I approached. Esais stepped in front of the other two with his hands in his pockets and a pensive look on his face. He took three of the salt shakers from me. I twisted the top off of the fourth and spread salt on the ground.

"Forgive me. We don't have time for introductions. Could someone start the car?" I asked.

"We're just going to run?" Tres asked.

"Get in the car," Esais said.

I smiled as I took the other shakers from him, and he moved to the passenger door. At least one of them believed I knew what I was talking about. It wasn't much, but it was a start.

"You owe us an explanation soon, though," he said.

"Soon."

Adrian watched me, not bothering to move to the car. "What are you doing?"

"The salt should confuse his sense of smell so he can't follow us, which will be pointless if we are still here." I opened another and tossed it about in the air.

He muttered but got in the car. I climbed in the backseat beside him and opened the remaining shakers. The salt drifted on the air as we exited the parking lot. Hopefully, this would screw the hellhound's sinuses so much he wouldn't be able to smell straight for a week.

"I can't believe we're running," Tres said. "What kind of hunter are you?"

"A smart one. Try to choose your battles when you can."

He pressed his lips together and glared at me through the rearview mirror. Adrian sat with his arms crossed and shoulders hunched, but a smirk formed on his lips. Esais remained quiet, as if waiting for the right moment. The bar disappeared from the back windows as we drove away. Darkened buildings passed in a blur; most had closed hours ago.

"Turn in here and head around back." I pointed to a motel we were approaching after several minutes of driving.

The motel had the doors on the outside, with metal stairs leading up to the second floor. A chain-link fence divided the back of the parking lot from the forest that seemed to be at war with this entire town. We parked. The chittering of cicadas was the only sound as I strode to the door of my room. I stepped over the line of salt and held the door open for the brothers. Adrian paused after the others had entered.

"Salt again," he said.

"It deters demons."

"Hmph." He stepped inside and scanned the room with his eye narrowed.

Esais moved in front of me and held his hand out. "Esais Van Helsing."

I took his hand and squinted until I could see the shades of color surrounding him. A gold and white light flooded my vision, causing me to avert my gaze and blink away the after-images before returning to him. The light extended to a winged figure and obscured any details. The being's hands rested on Esais's temples, indicating a gift of the mind.

While I inspected him, he did the same. It started as an itch on the inside of my brain, and I resisted the urge to lift my hand to my head. It would do no good since this wasn't physical. I gasped as my time in Paris with Dimitri flashed through my mind. We'd spent weeks searching for that demon. I almost felt his arms around me when I'd revealed my past to him. He'd been so caring, so understanding of the loss I had endured. I could almost feel the soft caress of his hand on my cheek, the heat of his kiss...

No, Esais had seen enough. That was private. I imagined a steel wall surrounding me, blocking all entrance. The digging stopped, and Esais's eyes widened.

"Buna seara." I tried to keep the surprise off my face.

I turned my attention to Tres as he followed his brother's lead. This one had issues. The emerald green of his core shifted into a muddy forest hue. It mixed with a dark pink. He had the potential to be a healer, but he stunted it by his own immaturity and jealousy. Three shadowed females surrounded him. Their hands were joined while the two on the sides held each of Tres's arms.

I nodded as we shook hands and turned to Adrian. He remained in his position by the door. His aura ranged from a deep red to an orange-yellow but mixed with dark yellow and brown. He was intelligent, with a scientific mind, but I could see a lot of disbelief and distrust in him. The woman resting her hands on his shoulders smiled at me, and she whispered in his ear. Her golden hair flowed from its elaborate design at the top of her head into small curls. Her skin gave off a pale glow, softening the edges of her face. My heart beat faster by just looking at her beauty.

Tragedy tinged all of them with the muddy red of anger. Like me, each had been touched by a spirit. However, none had the blackish red lines denoting demon taint. These boys had their issues, but they were human, for the most part.

I waved to the chairs and the bed. Esais and Tres took the two seats at the small table beside the television. Adrian remained standing near the door with his hands in his pockets. His gaze followed me as I walked to the window and looked at the perfect line of salt on the sill. We were safe for now.

I picked up the sword from the bed and let my fingers play along the golden, etched designs of the sheath. The muscles in my shoulders relaxed, and I let out a long breath.

All I had to do was touch it and close my eyes, and I could see Dimitri's face the day he gave it to me. He'd been the one to offer a trade to the collector who'd owned it. Dimitri had gone out of his way to help me and continued to do so while we were with each other. All I'd ever done was cause him more trouble.

Now, I had his descendants to worry about. If it wasn't bad enough I had let Andrei, Dimitri's grandson, and his wife die to a demon attack, I had left the same fate to Adam as well. This would not happen to the remaining brothers.

"That sword," Esais said. "It looks familiar."

"A gift," I said, "from your great-grandfather."

"Then you are that Gabriella," he said.

He knew from searching my memories. What was he playing at? "You were expecting another one?"

"Wait," Tres said. "You knew my great-grandfather? Honey, you must be the mother of all cougars."

A laugh spilled from my lips. Something about this brother made it easy to smile. Maybe this hunt wouldn't be so hard.

"So, what are you?" Adrian asked.

I stiffened. "I'm human, just cursed."

"Really," he said, "humans don't live this long."

"We should listen to what she has to say," Esais interjected. "Our great-grandfather trusted her, and she helped him many times."

"We're not him," Adrian said. "That was decades ago; she could have fallen by now."

"She stepped over the salt."

"Something she introduced."

Esais shook his head. "In the books I read, salt is a pure material that protects against evil, including demons."

Adrian turned his gaze in my direction. "How did you know there was a demon in the bar?"

"I have the ability to see them," I said.

"Yes, that's real normal." Sarcasm dripped from his words.

I tightened my grip on my sword and counted to ten. If I had been in his position, I would have suspected me, too. I pinched the bridge of my nose to try and cut off the coming headache. There had to be a way to solve this.

"Do you have holy water?" I asked. "It will burn a demon."

Esais pulled a flask from his belt. Adrian took it and poured the water over my head. I pushed my hair back and flicked the droplets off of my hand.

"Satisfied?" I asked.

"We'll trust you," Esais said.

"You can't be serious," Adrian said.

"What more do you want, Ader? She's been accommodating, but this is getting ridiculous."

"But she's—"

"That's an order, Ader," Esais said.

"Order? We're a family, not the military."

"Stop being a prick for a few minutes so we can hear what she has to say," Tres broke in.

Adrian shook his head, throwing his hands up. "This is insane." He looked to me. "Well, what great information do you have for us?"

I tried to keep the smug look from my face. "Ose has resurfaced."

The boys' shoulders straightened, and their bodies leaned forward. Tres gripped the armrests until his fingers turned white. Adrian tilted his head, his eye narrowing, but the suspecting look changed to a guarded interest. I had them now.

"Where?" he asked.

"Here in town, as is his daughter Malantha. She's the seer who killed Adam."

"Seer?" Adrian asked.

"She uses fortune-telling powers to eliminate her enemies and further her goals. From what I understand, she was the one who led Ose to your parents."

Esais ran a hand through his hair. "All because Papa wanted to create a network of hunters?"

"Ose saw it as a threat to his plans."

"He failed to get the rest of us," Esais said.

Malantha had tried to get to the remaining brothers, but thanks to Lucy Harker, they remained hidden. Of course, that would change now. Lucy and her father, Jonah, had worked to keep Andrei's dream of a network of hunters alive. They'd enlisted me when Malantha started killing hunters when she couldn't get to the Van Helsings. Jonah planned to hand the organization to the brothers when they were ready. Ose was their test.

Tres stood up and moved to the door. "Why are we waiting, then?"

Esais touched him on the shoulder. "We need a plan first."

"And more information," I said. "They probably sent the hellhound."

The boy's shoulders slumped, but he sat back down. I relaxed. The last thing I needed was for him to go running around without a clue of what he was looking for.

"Hellhound?" Esais asked.

"The demon at the bar. They're used as guardians, sometimes trackers. They like to possess werewolves," I said.

"So, what's the deal?" Tres asked. "You're a demon hunter, why didn't you kill it?"

"My sword can kill a demon, but the werewolf's healing ability prevents me from making a fatal wound. And a demon can still control the body it possesses even if it's dead, so killing the werewolf won't help," I said. "Have any of you fought a werewolf?"

Esais shook his head. "It seems we've walked in on a powder keg."

Wonderful. No experience with demons or lycanthropes, which meant these children had no weapons. I needed to start with the basics. If we faced Ose now, he would mop the floor with us with one pinky of the body he wore. In my five hundred years, I'd never fought a devil—an angel who fell from heaven—on my own. I'd only killed their offspring, the demons. I needed to rethink my strategy and pick up some more firepower.

"If you can't kill this hellhound, what use are you?" Adrian asked.

I cut my gaze to him and gritted my teeth. "I can get an alchemical compound that will take care of the issue. I'm meeting with a contact of mine, John Roda, tomorrow to get more information on Ose and his setup."

Esias cleared his throat. "I'd like to come along."

"Not alone with her." Adrian crossed his arms.

He waved his hand dismissively. "I'm a grown man. You and Tres need to set up the house anyway."

"Fine," I said. "I will meet you at Rickie's tomorrow at nine o'clock." I wrote the address on a slip of paper for him.

Esais gave me a small bow. "Goodnight then, Miss Di Luca."

Tres bowed as well on his way out the door. Adrian left with the barest of nods. I shut the door and leaned against it, closing my eyes. Tonight had gone well, despite the nasty surprise, but we had a lot ahead of us. With the Van Helsings' inexperience, it was up to me to keep all of us alive.

$$\text{❅}\quad 3 \quad\text{❅}$$

The sheets clung to my back as I sat up and sucked down the cool night air for several moments. Murmurs from the program on the television competed with the buzz of the air conditioner. The light played over the bed and table in eerie flickers of white and gray while a triangle of yellow peeked through the gap in the curtains. Right, this was my hotel room.

As my feet touched the floor and the cool air blew across my bare legs, I shivered. Water would be best to clear the scratchiness in my throat. The faucet hissed as the water filled the cup, drowning out the babble of the television. I leaned against the counter, wiped my cheeks, and stared at the wetness on my fingertips. I'd been crying in my sleep again. Strange, after five centuries, the dream could still do this to me.

Using my aura sight, I stared in the mirror at the figure behind me. It floated inches above the floor with thick black chains with red cracks covering it from head to toe. It writhed and twisted, trying to break free of the chains and, every so often, a flash of white light leaked out from behind its bindings. A length of chain extended from the figure to a collar around my neck. How long had it been since I had seen its true form? Centuries? I could barely remember what she looked like, just bits and pieces like a flash of bright light. Warmth and protection from the creeping darkness in the middle of the night. No, the Van Helsings weren't the only ones touched by a spirit. Mine had to pay the price of my curse.

"I'll free us both," I said. "I'll kill the demon bitch that has us."

Allegra. My reason for existence. She'd taken my husband, my son, my life, and left me with nothing. I remained alive as part of her punishment while she stayed beyond my grasp. If I had learned more about the spirit that had gifted me with my aura sight, would things have been any different? I had pretended it didn't exist for fear of being called a heretic. The church tended to look down on things they couldn't control, or that they could attribute to God. So, I had gone through life practically ignoring the being. Her touch had granted me the power to see Allegra for what she was, but that had just caused me to get involved in something I hadn't understood. Now, I existed in this half-life.

I gulped down the water and crushed the plastic cup in my hand. Little pricks of pain flared behind my eyes, and my heart pounded in my ears. It looked to be another sleepless night. After failing to catch me, the hellhound had run back to his masters for the night. I could spend the time tracking him down or stay here and brood.

I pulled on my clothes and lifted the hood of my jacket over my head. My hand ran over the hilt of my sword. I unsheathed it, letting the light glint off the two feet of sinuous blade. It was called a sundang and was made of iron, good for cutting the connection between the spiritual and material world. Its creators had not stopped there. Kali, the

Hindu goddess, blessed certain families with the power and weapons to slay demons. They had died out, leaving only a few reminders of a time forgotten by most, like this sword. My hand ran over the flat from the wide base to the rounded point. It wouldn't pierce, but the blade would cut through flesh like butter.

I set out with the sword strapped across my back and a butterfly knife fitted in a sheath on the inside of my pants. Laughter and heavy base from rock music coming from the rooms facing the road broke the silence that should have pervaded the motel. A row of motorcycles was parked outside. They must have come in the middle of the night. The occasional headlights of cars from the highway broke the darkness as I walked. The parking lots of the two restaurants and the jewelry shop lay bare with their streetlight flickering in some struggle for continued life. The world slept while I was denied rest.

A meteorite shot across the sky, fallen from its place in the heavens. Many would still believe it was an actual star, but it was just a piece of rock floating lost in vastness. Stars remained in a mostly stationary orbit until they died. Did stars feel the burden of eternity in the deep black? Did they yearn for warmth besides their own burning intensity?

I rubbed my arms and continued on to the bar. The bar had not drifted off to sleep like the rest. Lights flashed ahead of me and a crowd gathered around one police car and an ambulance. The demon had lost his temper and hurt some-one. *Merda*, the last thing I needed was the police sniffing around.

I slipped into the empty lot next to the bar and lay on my stomach, hidden by the high grass. As I crawled forward on my elbows and knees, the blades tickled my face. When I reached twenty feet away, I stopped and poked my head up, making sure to remain out of the light.

Two officers, a man and a woman, were talking to the large man the hellhound had thrown. He waved his left hand in the air while talking with his face so bright red that it shone like a beacon. He would have used both arms, but his right was bound in a sling.

Damn, there'd be no tracking the hellhound with this crowd. But he could have left a spy behind. Someone I wouldn't recognize as a demon, or so he would assume. Little did he know I had a gift.

I closed my eyes, and something in my head shifted, like a joint popping into place. The night was lit up with an array of reds and oranges as the crowd pulsed with anger and excitement. They hadn't had this much fun in months. Behind them, a different demon looked on with its arms crossed. Barely anything about this creature resembled a human or a particular animal. Two large, bat-like wings grew out of his back. Its head had an acorn shape with its snout extending to a point several inches past its jaw, and two spikes protruded down from the sides of the head. A hard carapace covered his body, with horns protruding from the joints.

I shivered and closed my eyes, but the image remained burned in my mind. I needed to see what human this thing paraded around in. Six feet of biker leaned against a motorcycle not unlike the ones parked outside of my hotel. Tribal tattoos covered his shaven head, surrounding his right eye, and traveled down his neck to disappear under his leather jacket.

Two in one night. Lucky me, though he was neither Ose nor the fortune-teller, since she preferred women. So where did this one fit in? The muscles in my arm cramped as I lay there, waiting. It didn't take long for the police to finish their questioning.

"Go home and sleep it off!" The police woman waved off the crowd. "We'll handle this."

A few of the men shouted and whistled, but they still made their way to their cars. Tattoo climbed on his bike and drove off with the rest. I remained still. I knew where he would end up.

The patrol car exited last, following the ambulance. Finally. I stood, stretching my arms out and rotating my shoulders. A short jog had me back at the hotel in minutes, and I paused in between two trucks to catch my breath. Warmth spread to my fingers from where the cracked asphalt had baked in the sun. The night had done nothing to cool the air, nor did it lessen the stench of oil and hot rubber that surrounded me. The demon's motorcycle rested among the others, just as I thought. Ten of them. How many were demons? It looked like I would spend the night scouting a different group than the one I had planned on.

A truck door slammed, and a woman marched to the biker's door with a shotgun in her hand. Her blonde hair bounced against her shoulders with each step. She would have been pretty if not for the scowl that wrinkled her tiny nose. She paused at the first of the bikers' doors, taking a deep breath, and widened her legs to be just even with the width of her shoulders and slightly bent—a Tae Kwon Do stance. The door gave way with a crack from the kick she delivered to it. My jaw hung open as the woman stepped inside.

Her Cajun accent traveled clear on the night air. "All right you sons a ~~of~~ bitches, I have some questions, and you're gonna answer them."

4

Shouts and curses followed the woman's words, and the curtains in the window ruffled. She had to be a scorned lover of one of the bikers. The roar of the shotgun echoed across the parking lot. She had plenty of fury but was no match for the demons, even with the shotgun.

We didn't have much time until the police showed up. I tapped my foot on the ground and stared at the doorway and the window. I would just go in, assess the numbers, and get the woman out, unless she was one of them. I took a black ski mask from my pocket, slipped it over my head, and pulled the hood of my jacket back up. They didn't need to see my face until I chose to strike.

I drew my weapons as I walked towards the door. The window exploded outward, and a bloodied biker landed a few feet from me. He groaned, struggling to get up as he favored his left arm. She wasn't doing too bad for herself.

I pulled my knife and paused just inside the doorway. The mattress had been half pushed off of the bed, and the blanket lay splayed across the floor, partially covering one of two fallen chairs. Actually, it looked as if someone had thrown the chairs. On the far side of the room, the woman stood with her back to the bathroom. Two bikers picked themselves off of the floor while a third leaned against the wall, holding his abdomen.

My vision blurred as my second sight kicked in. The reddish black lines of corruption extended from every aura in the room, including the woman's. This taint on the soul was different from demonic possession. A human could gain power without actually letting a demon ride them, and most of them did this by making contracts and selling their souls.

"How do you like the iron, asshole? Bet you want to jump out of that body now!" She reloaded the gun and aimed at one of the others.

"That's not a demon," I said.

The woman swung her gun in my direction with a glare. One of the bikers took a chance and lunged at her. With a muttered curse, she raised the shotgun and smashed him in the face with the butt. He staggered back, holding his face with a groan. I stepped back on to the porch. The door to the next room slammed open and four more bikers boiled out like angry ants followed at last by Tattoo. His gaze traveled from my feet to my head, and he sneered at me.

"Come to rob me?" he asked in a Cajun drawl.

I unsheathed my sundang as a grin came to my face. Fortune stayed with me tonight. He was the only demon. The rest were human lackeys who sold themselves for power. I could use a little exorcise to help me sleep.

"Oh, you're one of them ninjas."

"No, I am death wrapped in a small package." I swung my sword at the others. "The rest of you should pray to God for forgiveness. You still have time."

His friends hooted as they fanned out around me. They cracked their knuckles and made kissing noises. They thought I would be easy. No one respected swords anymore, but after I'd finished with them, they would. The woman's shouts carried from the room, followed by the sound of flesh hitting flesh. She seemed capable on her own. The potbellied one on the end bent his knees and kept his arms loose at his sides. He planned to rush me. If I positioned it right, I could send him tumbling into the two who would attack from the other side when I dealt with him. That would leave Tattoo and the pock-faced biker playing bodyguard.

Potbelly rushed me. I pivoted forward in my stance and slid my blade across the back of his leg to slice through his hamstring. His momentum carried him into the other two. Down they went. The pock-faced boy raised a handgun at me with shaking hands. Tattoo's sneer traveled from the tangled mass of his minions to me.

"I suppose you'd be the bitch following us since N'awlins. What the hell you want?"

"Oh, hell no." The woman stomped from the room. "Some crazy burglar isn't gonna claim my kill."

Tattoo threw his head back, his laughter echoing through the parking lot. "You girls are pretty tough to take down my boys."

He dug a cigarette out of a wrinkled pack. The lighter clinked open and made several click sounds before a flame flared to life. The world around me dimmed. Tendrils of darkness stretched out from his shadow, consuming all other light. Then, the lighter blinked out, as well.

"I hope you don't sleep with the night light on," he said.

"What the fuck?" the woman said.

"Stay where you are," I called to her. What the fuck, indeed.

"I can smell the rage on both of you." Tattoo's voice floated around me. "I think I'll be taking an added bonus home."

I froze, trying to pinpoint him, but it proved impossible

to do through all the yells of the bikers and the scrambling. The crack of a gunshot blared ahead of me. The flash of light lasted less than a second before the dark swallowed it. What the hell kind of demon possessed a power like this? The wind ruffled my hair as the bullet passed close to me. I jerked back, and my hand brushed against leather behind me. Damn, he moved fast. I leapt forward and stumbled over a body on the ground. My knee jarred as it caught the brunt of my fall.

Tendrils, colder than ice, wrapped around my ankles and wrists. The weapons slipped from my numb fingers, but I didn't hear them hit the ground. The bonds lifted me into the air and threw my back against the wall of the motel. My arms were pulled above my head, yanking the right one out of its socket. I screamed as pain raced through my shoulder. I twisted my other arm, trying to slip it free, but the bonds held me tight.

My heart sped up, and my throat constricted, making my breath come in small gasps. I had to calm down. I stilled and closed my eyes. What good were they at the moment? I inhaled, counting to ten before releasing, and rubbed my fingers together, relieved when they began to tingle.

Tattoo's body pressed against mine. His hot breath on my face reeked of tobacco and just a hint of sulfur. Most people missed the sulfur, but I'd been in this position before. This is where they became cocky.

"So, sweetness, why are you hunting us?" he asked. "Have you come for Ose, too?"

Too? So this one wasn't working for the devil. What had brought him here?

"Not much of a speaker, I see. Come on, how about you sing me a song."

I kept my voice even. I wasn't about to let some no-name demon get the best of me, unknown power and all. "Sorry, I'm a better dancer. Release these bonds and I can show you."

He laughed. "You talk a lot. Why don't you tell me about Ose. Be a good girl and I may even let you live as one of my boy's bitches."

"Interested in joining up?" I asked. "I don't think he's taking applications for street trash."

The tendrils twisted around my arms and jerked painfully, eliciting a small gasp from me.

"He is my prey." He whispered in my ear. "Looks like you want to play hard. You'll wish you'd sung by the time I'm done with you."

Sirens wailed in the distance, cutting through the panicked voices. The blackness faded, and the night returned to normal. Tattoo stood a few feet in front of me, inhaling the last few drags of his cigarette as he stared off in the direction of the sirens. He blew the fumes into my face, and I coughed, squeezing my eyes shut for a second. I started when he stumbled into me. He staggered back with a grunt, his hand going to his lower back, and he spun to the mystery woman behind him. The woman stepped back in a fighting stance with a smirk.

"Don't forget about me, asshat," she said.

"Bitch!" Tattoo said. "You'll pay for that."

"You gonna make me, Ugly?" Mystery Woman asked.

A growl rolled out of Tattoo's throat and he lunged at her. The woman moved to the side and held her foot out. Her leg came up in an axe kick that hit the back of the demon's head as he bumbled forward. My bonds disappeared, and I dropped to the ground. I landed on my feet, swallowing a whimper as I jarred my shoulder.

Tattoo backed away from both of us with a scowl on his face. "This isn't over."

He ran for his bike with his lackeys blundering after him, at least the ones who could move. I gathered my weapons, fumbling with one arm as I tried to sheathe them. The woman chased after the bikers but stopped short when Pock-face raised the gun at her. He held her there until Tattoo disappeared down the road in the opposite direction of the sirens.

I moved up behind the woman, holding my useless arm to my body. "Do you even know how to use that?"

"S-stay where you are," he said.

The woman moved, but I grabbed her arm. She swung her head in my direction with her eyes narrowed. Pock-face hopped on his bike and started it up.

"He's not the demon, and a rather pathetic biker," I said. "Too easy for you."

"And I'm supposed to listen to the masked avenger because?"

I blinked at her odd comment. "Do you wish to get arrested?"

She mumbled.

"Grab your gun, and let's go."

I led her through a hall that cut between the front of the motel and the back. No one followed us. The bikers were too busy trying to get themselves out of this mess, and the other guests didn't want to get involved. The door to my room clicked shut behind her, and I flattened her against the door with my knife to her throat.

"If you move anything but your mouth, I will bury my blade in your neck," I said. "Whom do you serve?"

5

The woman's hands twitched, and she glared at me. I pressed the blade into the tender point of her throat. She stiffened and raised her arms up in a position of surrender. I could hear her teeth grind as her jaw clenched.

"Did Ose send you after that gang?" I asked.

"Who the fuck is Ose?" Her brows drew closer together. "I don't serve any demon."

My vision blurred as I concentrated on her aura. She was a study in reds. The deep, clear reds of her strong will and passionate nature were muddied by the rage she carried with her. Blackish-red lines, glowing like blacklights, encroached inward from her outer aura. Other colors pulsed and shifted, but no deceptive ones. She spoke the truth.

I stepped back and slid my knife into my sheath. I pulled off my mask and used it to fan my burning face. She stood upright, turning her neck from side to side until it cracked.

"Your salt line's screwed to hell," she said.

"Gabriella Di Luca." I held my hand out to her, which she just stared at until I dropped it.

"The hunter?" she asked with a raised eyebrow.

"As usual, my reputation precedes me."

"Yeah, you're supposed to be this big bad demon hunter. Didn't see much of that tonight."

The more this woman spoke, the more the ache in my temples overcame the throbbing in my shoulder. I touched the side of my forehead and closed my eyes, taking a deep breath.

"And you are?" I asked.

"Marguerite Devereux."

She lifted her chin to look down her nose at me, and I chuckled. For having such a foul mouth, she acted like she was nobility. Still, something about her reminded me of stories I'd heard. Blonde hair, bad disposition.

"I remember something about a new hunter in New Orleans. Nice work on that fake medium," I said.

She shrugged again as she moved the salt back into a sort of straight line by the door with her foot. I pulled my right wrist to my stomach, squeezing my eyes shut. I gritted my teeth as I inched the arm out to the side. My arm resisted the movement, and my joints begged me to stop, but I kept going.

She crossed her arms and tilted her head at me. "What the hell are you doing?"

"Just give me a moment."

I closed my eyes and swallowed hard as I worked to pull my arm back in its socket. My stomach roiled, threatening to eject the beer I'd had earlier. I pushed out again. The muscles in my face twisted in a grimace as I fought not to cry out. My shoulder popped back into place, and I threw my head back, panting. I swayed, my legs almost giving out.

"That's better," I said. "Now, where were we?"

She leaned against the door and gave a low whistle. "That was kind of hardcore."

"Why are you here, then?" I asked.

"I've been tracking the D-boyz since N'awlins."

"D-boyz."

"I know. They don't have the brains to come up with something better."

I snorted. Typical of demon worshipers. Either they became too pretentious or didn't bother with any creativity. One thing remained the same. They all loved showing off the fact they bowed down to hellspawn and the power it supposedly gave them. There had been a few throughout the centuries that had truly been masterminds, but most weren't intelligent, and it made them easy to track, even for someone like Marguerite here.

The sirens blared from the parking lot, drowning out the low drone of the television. Marguerite stiffened, glancing to the flashing lights through the window. I gritted my teeth as an itch ran through the inside of my muscles. I would have to question the woman more later. I dug through my duffel bag, past the glass jars and linen sacks to the neat rolls of clothing. I pulled out a pajama set and stripped off my clothes.

Marguerite scowled. "I don't owe you that much."

"The police will come to ask questions." I ran my hands through my hair and tangled it more. "It works best if they think I was asleep."

"And where am I supposed to be in all this?"

"The bathtub. Can you manage to keep your mouth shut until they've left?"

Her eyes burned into me as she opened her mouth. She shut it again and formed a sour little smile. "Sure."

I nodded to the bathroom, and with a roll of her eyes, she trudged inside. She was probably planning something as revenge. She seemed the type to remember the slights more than what people did for her. My life would be much simpler if I just tossed her out and left her to her own devices against the police and demons. Unfortunately, she seemed the type to have no problem blazing forward on her own, and I wanted to know why she was tainted. I had too much work to do to add breaking her out of prison to the list.

A corner of the red and pink paisley comforter half-covered a yellowish stain on the carpet and covered my bag in its spot underneath the bed. I tucked my sword under the pillows, which left me with my knife in a calf sheath hidden by my pants. The sirens were replaced by muffled banging on doors. I sat on the bed and watched the window, my heel tapping against the floor in rhythm with my heartbeat. I started when the automatic air freshener hissed out a spray of freesia. I could say a car backfired, but that wouldn't explain the glass or shouting.

After twenty minutes, there was a knock on my door and a woman's voice. "Hello? This is the Hampton Police Department. We have a few questions we'd like to ask."

"One moment," I said in my best groggy voice. I answered the door, rubbing one eye. "Yes?"

The same woman from the bar, human and all, stood outside. She gave me a sympathetic smile. "Sorry to disturb you, ma'am, but we had a disturbance here tonight. Did you see or hear anything?"

Her obsidian hair cupped around her face, and her skin was dark as chocolate. She stood tall, with her shoulders straight, and held herself with tautness, as if she was prepared to handle any threat that opened the door. Her uniform remained neat despite the night's events.

I pursed my lips, running a hand through my hair. "Well, I heard a lot, actually. Woke me up, with all the yelling. Was that a gun?"

"Yes, ma'am, there were reports of a gunshot."

"I thought this motel was safe."

She narrowed her umber eyes, studying me for several

moments. I coughed and blinked at her as I mentally went over what I looked like: my messy hair, my sleepy blue eyes. My olive skin was probably marred by shadows under my eyes. I knew I looked tired because I felt it. Had I missed something? I had wounded one of the bikers. Was there a spot of blood I didn't wash off? She moved her head to peer into the room. I opened the door wider for a better view.

"Looking for something?" I asked with a slight edge to my voice.

She smiled at me again and shook her head. "No, ma'am. So, you didn't see anything?"

I shook my head. "Never left the room."

"May I have your name?"

"Gabriella Lucco."

"And what brings you to our town, Ms. Lucco?"

"Family business."

She handed me a business card. "Okay, ma'am, if you remember anything else, please contact us. Will you be in town for a few more days? We may have more questions."

I raised an eyebrow, palming the card in my hand. "What more would you need to ask?"

"You never know what might come up."

"I'm not sure." I rubbed my arms. "If there was an incident, then probably not long in this hotel. What others are there?"

"Well, there's the Hampton Inn downtown. But I wouldn't be too worried, ma'am. We don't get a lot of trouble here. It's been a weird night." She studied me for another moment before giving another wave and moving to the next door.

I shut the door and let out a breath. Marguerite stood in the doorway of the bathroom. I held my finger to my lips, and with a sigh, she crossed her arms, tapping her foot as we waited. The officer's voice faded into the distance. I flopped down on the bed, rolled my neck from one side to the other, and rubbed some of the soreness from my shoulder, relieving the tension that had built up.

I pulled my sword from its hiding place and grabbed my bag. I had spoken true when I said I wasn't staying here. This motel was compromised, but moving to the Hampton Inn would allow the police to find me easier. I needed to assess my options. There had to be another place to stay. Maybe John could put me up for a few nights. My heart raced at the thought.

"So Ose's some demon in town?" she asked.

"Devil, actually," I said.

Marguerite whistled. "Big game, then."

She rocked back on her heels. I knew the look on her face. The hunger for new prey burned inside me often over the years. She still had her own problems, and unfortunately, they seem to have compounded my own.

"Why are these D-boyz here?" I asked.

"I don't really care why. Not what I'm after."

"You're looking to get revenge on a bad deal?"

She glared at me. "What?"

"You're tainted. So now you're looking to back out on your contract."

"How the hell do you know that?"

"I have amazing observation powers." I pushed the clothes deeper in my bag and scanned for anything in the room that was forgotten.

"What? You got a demon detector or something?"

I moved to stand directly in front of her and held her gaze. "Perhaps, but I'm not going to share my secrets and I'll let you keep yours."

She threw her hands up and stomped to the door. "Fuck the police. I don't need this shit."

"Right, because getting detained by the police will help

your case. You might as well sit down and wait. While you do that, you can tell me about your contract."

She glared at me and slammed her body down in one of the chairs, crossing her arms and stretching her legs out straight. "It's none of your damn business."

"Very well. Good luck to you," I said. "Try not to get in the way of my own hunt."

Her fingers tapped against her arm as she stared at the television. I continued to pack. In a few hours, she would be safe to leave, but I doubted tonight would be the last time I saw her. The D-boyz and the reason they were here worried me more.

❧   6   ☙

I swirled the last dregs of coffee in the bottom of my cup as I debated ordering a refill. It would be my third. It tasted like burnt ashes, but I needed the caffeine to stay alert. I rested my head on the back of the booth seat, longing for a cappuccino from home. Italy had never been my home, though. I'd been far away, hunting one demon or another, when they officially became one country in the 19th century. I'd grown up in the kingdom of Naples. I closed my eyes, replacing the smell of eggs and grease with the scent of the sea. The roar of the waves supplanted the sizzle of the grill. I would take my son, Marco, to the beach and sing to him as I watched the sun rise on the horizon.

The bell above the door jingled, and I jumped, opening my eyes. A woman holding a baby carrier entered. She set the carrier on a table close to mine. The child, no older than a few months, waved his hands about and stared off at something no one else could see. I bit my lip and waved to the waitress as I blinked back the tears. No, Naples hadn't been my home for a long time. Still, I missed the coffee.

The bell rang again, and Esais stepped inside. I slid out of the booth and held my hand out to him. He smiled at me, and I couldn't help but return one. It reminded me of youth and sunshine.

"Mr. Van Helsing," I said.

His fingers wrapped around mine with a gentle squeeze. "Ms. Di Luca. Please, call me Esais."

"Gabby, then."

We slid back into the booth. He picked up the menu and adjusted his glasses as he scanned it. His broad shoulders filled out the white buttoned shirt but not in a muscular way. He wasn't the "in the thick of melee" type of hunter. Instead, he had a bookworm type of charm. He glanced up and caught my stare. I ducked my head, clearing my throat, and opened my own menu.

"Have you been here long?" he asked, slipping into Romanian.

"A few hours," I said.

"Why so early."

"Too much excitement to sleep," I said with a sour smile.

"Grandfather Dimitri said you had trouble sleeping." He laughed and ran a hand through his hair. "I feel like I know you thanks to his journals."

My heart fluttered and a shiver traveled through my body. "He wrote about me?"

"Often. I don't think he ever got over you."

My eyes stung. I had remained in his heart despite the fact he'd found a wife. If only. No, I had traveled down that road too often. Life for him turned out better this way. Allegra had almost killed Dimitri when we found her. My past had nearly ended a legacy before it could flourish. So I'd left, freeing Dimitri to continue the duty his father had sworn to after Dracula's defeat. Neither of us had known of the curse Dracula had laid on his family. After the birth of Dimitri's son, the vampire had risen again. Dimitri had died in battle, and I wasn't able to fight at his side. I swallowed the lump in my throat.

"I have so many questions," he continued. "I'm not sure where to start."

I pushed my regrets away and smiled at him. "You want to pick my brain?"

He nodded.

"Well, what do you want to know about most?"

"You mentioned this last night and the journals talked about your ability to see things for what they truly are."

"That's one way of putting it." Mad visions would be another. Or witchcraft, but I had not been accused of that in centuries.

"Where did it come from?"

"I've had it for as long as I can remember."

His brow furrowed. "But do you know where it came from?"

"Such gifts come from the spirits of the Eclipse, and from what I have found, there is a name for us. Your brothers do not know about yours, do they?"

His gaze met mine, and he held it for several moments. His lips parted as though to speak, but then pressed shut again. "Tres does, but Adrian is a different matter."

The waitress came with a pad in hand. "Have y'all decided?"

"I'll have the Tuesday Special," I said

"Same and a coffee," Esais said.

After gathering our menus, the girl walked off. I stirred cream and a mountain of sugar into my cup, giving him time to gather himself. Murmurs from the other patrons and the sizzle of the grill in the kitchen filled our silence.

"My home doesn't accept things that are different," he said. "I don't think I could handle my family judging me as well."

He glanced at a young man passing our table on his way out. His eyes filled with desire. Telepathy wasn't the only thing he hid from the world. One secret at a time. I patted his hand, and he jumped, looking back at me.

"The world never seems to understand. But you have a gift, and in our work, you use what you're given. And this sort of thing doesn't stay secret forever."

He smiled but pulled his hand away. "I just don't know the right time to tell them."

"You'll figure it out. If you want help, let me know."

"So what is this name we are called?"

"Emissaries."

"And this Eclipse you mentioned? Like the solar and lunar eclipse?"

"No, the Eclipse is the home of the spirits."

"Can you see it?"

"I can see where it overlaps with this world."

"Exactly how old are you?" he asked

"Don't you know that's not something you should ask a woman?"

He laughed.

I scanned the patrons and staff for the fifth time. Rainbow waves radiated around me. Blues, reds, and yellows. Joy, sadness, ambition, but no demon taint. The bell jingled as the officer from last night stepped inside and nodded hello to the waitress. I stiffened. She sat at the counter and smiled as the waitress came to fill her coffee cup.

"Long night, Nancy?" the waitress asked.

"You have no idea."

The waitress patted her on the hand. "Well, we all appreciate your hard work."

Nancy sighed. "I just wish the sheriff did."

She brought the cup to her lips and turned to scan the rest of the diner. She nodded to a couple in a booth with a smile, and they gave her little, half-handed waves. An old man walked by her and paused to pat her on the shoulder. Her eyes landed on me and filled with recognition.

Well, this was awkward.

"Is something the matter?" Esais glanced behind him.

She walked to our table and smiled at us. "Hello again, Ms. Lucco."

I returned her smile. "Hello, Officer. Are you just getting off duty?"

She nodded and glanced at Esais. He stood and held out his hand to her, his boyish smile back in place.

"Esais Arcos," he said. "A pleasure, Officer?"

"Parkins, Nancy Parkins." She took his hand. "So what brings you to Hampton?"

"My brothers and I just moved here. My cousin Gabby–he waved his hand to me— "came to help."

"That's an interesting accent."

"From Romania."

"And you moved all the way to this tiny town?" She chuckled and looked at me. "Have you remembered anything else?"

I shook my head. "Like I said, the sound woke me, but I didn't go outside,"

"We also had a fight down at the Grindstone. Someone mentioned a girl looking like you."

I blinked at her slowly, hoping she would take it for confusion. "Grindstone?"

"It's the bar near the motel."

"Oh, well, I did stop by, but I left when it looked like things were going to get rough."

"But you saw the beginning of the fight?"

"I saw a man go flying into a table. I left after that."

"Mmm hmm." She stared at me with her eyes narrowed

and her lips pursed. "Well, Ms. Lucco, you seem to be at the only two places where we had action last night."

"I'm lucky, I guess."

"I hope your luck doesn't hold up."

"Did I show up at the wrong time?" a man asked from behind her.

I grinned at the sound of his voice. Both Officer Parkins and Esais turned to look at the intruder. His hair had grown since the last time I saw him. It now hung over his ears with the ends bleached and the roots dark. He rested his hands in the pockets of his sports coat. His cobalt blue eyes sparkled as his easy smile spread across his tanned face.

"John." I slid out of the booth and moved to greet him, kissing him on both cheeks. He pulled me into a hug, and my skin tingled at the touch of his hands on my back.

"More family?" Nancy turned her head at Esais. "How many people do you need to help you move?"

"Actually, I'm doing an article about festivals in small towns in Texas. Gabby mentioned she'd be here, so I decided to stop by." He held his hand out to her. "John Roda."

She shook his hand. "You're a journalist?"

"Yes," he said. "I was hoping to look in on the Autumn Festival."

"We've decided to do it a little differently this year. We have the carnival running throughout the month of October."

"Interesting. I'll have to check it out."

She nodded to the three of us. "Welcome to Hampton. Let's hope you're the most exciting thing that happens."

"Most likely we won't be," I said after she walked off.

Esais stood up. "Esais Van Helsing. It is a pleasure to meet you, Mr. Roda."

John's arm around me tightened as he took Esais's hand. I looked up at him with a raised eyebrow, but he focused on Esais. His smile grew to match the other man's.

"A pleasure," John said.

The waitress cleared her throat. She held our plates and raised one to indicate we were in her way. We settled back in the booth. My fork scraped against the plate as I scooped up a pile of scrambled eggs. I wrinkled my nose as the taste burned and grabbed my glass of water. The cook had tried to compensate for the blandness with too much salt.

"You want anything, hun?" the waitress asked John.

"Pancakes and coffee," he said.

He ran his fingers across the back of my hand, leaving a trail of heat behind. I leaned closer, letting our shoulders brush. His warmth relieved the tension in my back and made the ache in my chest fade. Esais watched me over the rim of his coffee cup. I coughed and crunched into a piece of bacon.

"So how did you meet Gabby?" Esais asked.

"She saved my life, actually," John said. "I've been trying to pay her back ever since."

I could still remember the look of pain and loss on his face as I stood over the body of the fallen demon that had been his wife. Here would be another person to hate me. Instead, he had been grateful, offering whatever help he could. I had caused him to lose something precious, and I don't know how he ever forgave me. His friendship was a rare gem with so few people I could depend on.

I scanned the diner with my aura sight and nodded at the sight of only humans. "John has a lot of contacts that keep track of the movements of demons. What do you have for us?"

"There's a reason the festival here is running so long. The devil's daughter is running the main event, the carnival," John said.

Malantha. It figured she would be running such an event. After ten years of chasing her down, I had her within my grasp. The game would end here for both her and her father.

"He's not the same as when you fought him."

"What do you mean?" I asked.

"Wait, you fought Ose before?" Esais asked.

"A long time ago. He's one of the few who escaped." I pushed away the images of the mentor I had lost with that fiasco. "So, what's different?"

I leaned back and cleared my throat as the waitress came back with John's food. He winked at her. She gave him a parting smile and walked off with more of a sway in her hips than she'd shown all morning.

John cut into his pancakes with his fork. "You know he's one of the Goetia, right?"

I nodded. "I'd found a copy of one and came across that little gem."

"You mean the first part of the Key of Solomon?" Esais asked. "It lists the demons that King Solomon supposedly bound."

John cut his eyes at Esais, and his smile faltered. He kept forgetting Esais was part of the conversation. I elbowed him, and he jumped.

"The Key, including the Goetia, was one of the books created by devils to trick humans into summoning them," I said. "They claim King Solomon himself wrote it. They wanted to make sure no one else could bind them like he did. What you want is the Testament of Solomon. It's harder to find, but also has the names of the Goetia.

"Interesting. Our library at home had both the Key and the Testament," Esais said.

"Don't do any of the rituals in the Key. You'll end up summoning a Goetia." I looked back to John. "So, is that it?"

"He's not following any of the Thrones."

My fork fell from my still hand and bounced across the table. "That's not possible."

At the same time, Esais said. "You must be mistaken."

John glared at him. "I'm not. He's no longer a part of the Throne of Greed, he hasn't been for a while. I think they're still a little upset about it."

Dante and Virgil didn't have the infernal world quite right. Hell was divided into seven Thrones, each with its very own devil to rule. They played off of the Seven Deadly Sins. Pride, of course, sat at the top. The names had changed, but the concepts had remained the same since well before I was born. The Thrones held on to what they had with iron grips. What had Ose done to break away?

"Well, it seems like someone's caught up to him." I explained my ordeal last night with the biker demons.

John scratched his cheek, contemplatively. "Hmm, I'll see if I can find anything about these D-boyz or the new demon hunter."

Esais cleared his throat. "I have some books. I can look into this demon with darkness abilities."

"I'll assist," I said. "But back to the original question. What is Ose doing?"

John shrugged. "You should probably start at the Carnival."

I tapped my fork against my plate. "He has a hellhound. I'm going to need a little something special to take care of it."

"Name it, and I'll see what I can do," John said.

I leaned under the table to my bag and pulled out a piece of paper. I winced as my shoulder throbbed. John watched me scribble a list before I handed it to him. He whistled, looking over the list.

"This may take some work," he said.

"Can you get them?" I asked.

"Probably. Give me a few days."

I nodded and returned to playing with my food. "Is Ose truly mad?"

He hesitated before nodding. I sighed. This complicated

things. I had enough of the stone jet in my bag to make charms. I hoped they would hold strong.

"Well." I put my fork down. "I think we all have work to do."

"I should get to work on this list." John waved a hand to the remains of our breakfast. "Should I?"

"Please, let me," Esais said with a ghost of his smile. "You've done enough."

John smiled at him and leaned over to kiss my cheek. "I'll be in touch."

As I watched him go, the realization hit me that I hadn't asked to stay with him. Damn, it looked like I was still homeless.

7

Esais held the door open for me as I adjusted the large bag on my shoulder and stepped out onto the sparsely crowded sidewalk. A few cars were parked at the meters, and a mother and her teenage daughter stared into the window of a boutique across the street. I put my hand in front of my face as the sun reflected off of one of the windows of the boutique and right into my eyes. The world wanted to remind me what a wonderful morning this was while I just wanted to crawl into a bed somewhere and slip into oblivion.

"So you and John are lovers?" he asked.

I dropped the bag on the sidewalk. "What? No, just friends."

"Hmm, he wasn't acting that way."

"I'm sorry for that. I don't know what it was about."

"He seemed to play the jealous boyfriend."

"He's not."

Not that I hadn't thought about it. John tried to lightly push for more every time we met, but I'd always rebuffed him. He made me smile in the direst of circumstances. I didn't want to lose my confidant, and if we became intimate, this could take a tragic direction. My love life was cursed. Truly.

"If you say so." Esais watched me lift the bag up again. "Where are you going?"

"I need to find a new hotel. Though we need to make plans for the carnival." I chewed my lip.

"Stay with us."

"Won't he have something to say about that?"

I nodded to where a white car sat parked several buildings down. Adrian watched me from the driver's seat with a narrowed eye. He probably had a gun ready to shoot me if I made any untoward moves at his brother.

"Probably," Esais said. "Tres and I will outvote him, though."

"Where is the little brother?"

"He's not in danger, so probably chasing after a girl."

"Your range is that good?"

He shook his head. "I have a special connection with Tres."

I took a deep breath and straightened my shoulders. "Let's get this over with."

Adrian stepped out of the car as we approached him. He placed his hands behind his back and gave me a glare before turning to his brother. "Well, did you find out anything useful?"

"You couldn't wait at home?" Esais asked.

"He was concerned about you." I couldn't keep the small bit of smugness from my voice.

Adrian cut his eye at me. "We don't all believe your little story."

"We can discuss this at the house," Esais said. "Gabby will be staying with us while we are here."

"What is wrong with her hotel?"

The roar of a motor prevented me from answering. A midnight blue truck towered over the rest of the cars as it sped towards us. Marguerite's face flashed by as she passed us. The truck swerved, almost riding up on the curb, and parked with the squeal of tires. She hopped out of the car and marched over to us.

"That would be what's wrong," I said.

She said, "I lost the D-boyz trail, and I need to hurt somethin' Where's this devil?"

"This is your partner?" Adrian asked, his voice cold. "Funny, you didn't mention her."

I licked my lips as my heart sped. Fencing came in a variety of forms, and I excelled at several. I missed having a good opponent, but perhaps I'd found one in Adrian. His words sometimes proved to be as sharp as mine.

"I just met her early this morning, fighting a new demon," I said.

Adrian's gaze bore into me. "New as in you didn't bother to see if it had a hand in this?"

"If I could keep up with every demon on Earth, well, let's just say we wouldn't be here today."

Esais sighed, rubbing the bridge of his nose. "Adrian, not now."

Marguerite crossed her arms. "Who the hell are you two?"

"Marguerite, this is Esais and Adrian Van Helsing," I said, waving a hand at the brothers. "Boys, this is Marguerite Devereux."

"And what does Marguerite do?" Adrian asked.

"Would you like me to show you?" She brought her hand up with her fists clenched and stepped back with her left foot.

"By all means, try it."

I stifled a yawn and blinked my eyes. "As amusing as this is, we all have things to do."

"Wait, you crossed the salt, but these two could be demons," Marguerite said, looking at me.

Esais's eyebrows drew together. "I see trust is going to be an issue on all sides."

The corner of Marguerite's mouth lifted up.

"I have some of your holy water," Adrian said. "Maybe *she'll* turn out to be a demon, and we can kill her."

"I'd like to see you try," she said with a snort.

"I believe I already offered you that challenge," he shot back.

"Marguerite has demon taint. I'm not sure how much we can trust her." I pushed my thought out, hoping Esais's telepathy would pick it up.

He blinked with his eyes widening in surprise, and he glanced at me. *"You want me to check?"*

So, he could pick up thoughts sent to him—good. I nodded, crossing my arms and pretending to watch the other two continue to bicker. He sighed and kept his gaze steady on Marguerite. He needed to concentrate to scan the thoughts of others.

"You know, I could just find this devil on my own," she said.

"How are you planning to do that? You don't know anything about him," I said.

"Fine," she said, and she pulled out her flask.

She stepped up to Adrian and flung some of the liquid in his face. She jumped back, readying her stance with a look of anticipation. When he took his handkerchief out and wiped his face, her shoulders slumped. She moved to Esais and did the same.

"She's not working for any demons. The opposite, actually." Esais's voice echoed through my mind.

"So what's her story?"

"That's for her to tell."

I kept my face neutral. "Now it is your turn."

The woman held her arms out, looking at the brothers. Adrian pulled a flask of his own out and splashed the woman. Water dripped from her hair onto her face, running down her cheek like teardrops. She brushed them away with a scowl.

"Happy?" she asked.

"No," he said. "But you aren't a demon."

I moved to the rear door of the car. "Can we go now? Marguerite can follow us to the house."

"I didn't agree to let you stay." Adrian remained standing by the hood of the car.

"Let's talk about it off the street, eh, Ader?" Esais said. "I'll ride with Ms. Devereux."

Marguerite shrugged and walked with him to her truck, leaving Adrian and I to our silent battle. Her tires flung up dirt and gravel which rained down on the surrounding cars and the sidewalk as she squealed away. Cars flew by, and people stared as they passed us in the street. Yet we remained, each of us not willing to give any ground.

"You have lost this one," I said. "By now your brothers are at home with Marguerite."

He unlocked the car and slid in. The engine started as I threw my bag in, and he sped off as I slammed the door. I stared out the window as we passed buildings. This time I wasn't looking at the souls of the people but the soul of the town. Humans had a deeper influence on places than they thought. Their emotions bled into the land around them, leaving an impression that faded slowly. Instead of colors, I saw the time of the strongest impression.

A saloon stood where the diner was. A dirt road replaced the paved streets and sidewalks. Men and women dressed in regalia of past times walked the streets, chatting among themselves. These spirits were bound to this place and a time long gone, unaware of the humans that now inhabited the world. Sometimes, I envied them. They were completely unaware they were trapped. The town itself appeared to be normal. The sky, however, was a different matter. A sickly, brown-yellow cloud mixed with red-black lines swirled like a funnel to the north of the town, and a smaller funnel gathered to the west. I rubbed my eyes and leaned back. I was betting one of those places was the carnival. So, what about the other one?

We turned onto one of the back roads. Brick houses lined each side of the street, each almost identical to the next with their manicured lawns. Adrian parked in the driveway of one home that stood one story and was several shades of brown, from the bricks to the siding. He walked to the trunk and pulled out a large crate as I strolled by the bushes that hugged the house just under the windows.

"What sort of protections do you have?" I asked.

"We haven't placed any yet."

A chill down my spine. The hellhound could have come in and killed them in the night, and I wouldn't have known. I marched to the door and yanked it open, letting it bounce against the outer wall with a bang. Esais was in the living room with his brother and Marguerite. Tres sat on the couch, leaning forward with his thighs pressed together and his eyes squeezed shut as tears rolled down his blotchy skin. Marguerite stood by the window with her arms crossed and a smirk on her face. Esais looked up from the book he held in his hands.

"So, it turns out I brought the Key with me," he said.

I glanced from Tres to Marge. "What happened?"

"I'm just teaching little boys to keep their hands to themselves," Marge said.

I glanced at Esais. "I'm surprised you don't have a problem with that."

"He's a grown man." Esais pinned Marge down with a stare. "However, you only get one."

That was something I had no business stepping in the middle of. Back to the important things. "Why do you have no protections? Any demon could waltz right in here!" I snapped.

He pushed his glasses up. "I'm not sure I have any."

"You didn't happen to bring the Testament of Solomon as well, did you?"

He cleared his throat and looked away. "It's a little more delicate and I didn't want it damaged in the travel."

I rubbed the bridge of my nose. To come here without anything to protect themselves was just inviting Ose to take them. I thought at least Jonah or Lucy would have shown them something, but it looked like they had expected me to do so. Esais continued to stare at me with his eyebrows knit and his lips pursed.

Lucy had taken care of everything after Ose's initial attack on their family, so Esais probably never knew what was needed. I sighed, rubbing my temples in a circular motion with my thumbs and forefingers. Adrian brushed past me and set his crate in the living room. They all turned their gazes to me expectantly.

"Can you tell them about the carnival and whatever it is that Marge chased here?" I asked Esais. "I need to make sure we are safe."

He nodded. I grabbed my bag from the car. No rest for the wicked, so I couldn't get any, either.

8

I examined each room. The house lay open with doorways connecting the halls and the five bedrooms, a kitchen, and a living room. A stack of worn, leather-bound books sat on the dining room table with one open in front of a high-backed chair. The air conditioner rumbled to life, blowing cold air into the already chilled house, and I shivered, rubbing my arms. I carried my bag into the first of the bedrooms. They could blame me for breaching privacy when we were safe behind protections.

I pulled out a small vial of ink and shook the bottle. Almost full, but it wouldn't be after I finished tonight. I had to pick up more of the alchemical mixture when I had the chance. I scooted the furniture away from the eastern corner and pulled up the carpet. I bent over the concrete and started scribing the symbol. The spiral pattern of the tiny markings would pull in and dissipate demonic energies and the iron and mercury in the ink would strengthen that power. I moved to each corner, until I had finished all four in an hour's time. The whole house would take all day. I stood and massaged my shoulder as I craned my neck to stretch the muscles. Work like that had aggravated it after last night.

"That looks like it hurts. I could help you with it."

Tres smiled at me from the doorway. I nodded, and he motioned to the bed. His hands ran along my shoulder blade. Warmth flowed from his hands into my arm, and the soreness faded like it had never been.

"Do your brothers know you can heal people with your touch?" I asked.

"Esais knows, but I don't think Adrian ever paid attention."

His fingertips trailed down my back to my waist. I caught his wrist and turned to face him. His cinnamon skin radiated heat under my hand and contrasted with my own olive color. It was a shade lighter than Esais but a few shades darker than Adrian's. His white teeth flashed at me in a grin, and a lock of his hair fell in front of his face.

"Didn't you learn from whatever it was you tried with Marguerite?"

"Worth a try," he said.

"This is your bedside manner?" I asked. "I should file for harassment or something."

He chuckled. "Good thing I'm not your doctor. Besides, you're pretty irresistible."

"Dig deep for that inner resolve. You're too young for me."

"Well, if you knew my great-grandfather, then anyone alive is too young for you," he said with a smile still on his face.

I returned his smile, thinking of Dimitri's laughing eyes. Tres's grin lifted a little higher on the left side, like his. I released a small bit of sadness welling up in me with a long breath.

"I was too old for him, too," I said. "So how powerful is your healing?"

He raised his left hand. "I can heal any wound I've come across, but there are consequences. If I do too much, I start to feel pain. It only subsides when I hurt someone with this hand." He lifted his right hand.

"The ability to harm and heal. Interesting."

"I suppose. I try to stick to regular medicine for most injuries."

"You're a doctor? Aren't you twenty?"

He chuckled. "Twenty-two, thank you. I received my degree in Romania. I think most of my practice will be from my family. Hunting and all."

"Such an achievement."

"With my family, being mediocre gets you killed." He stood and walked to the corner of the room. "What are these?"

"Babylonian devil traps. They work on demons too. I'm surprised none of you know this. What has Lucy and Jonah been teaching you?"

He gave a nonchalant shrug. "I haven't seen either of them in years. It's mostly just been Esais and I."

Strange. Maybe Lucy wanted to keep the demons away from them. "Where is everyone else?"

"Marge and Esais are out investigating, and Adrian is in his lab, working on god knows what."

"Marge?"

He scratched his cheek and snickered. "Yeah, Esais started calling her that, and it stuck."

My shoulders shook with the laughter I tried to hold in. I could imagine Marge's face turning red and her lips thinning every time someone used the nickname. I wondered how long it would last.

"So, I hear you're staying with us," he said.

I nodded.

Adrian leaned against the frame of the door with his arms crossed. "For the record, I'm against it."

His good eye narrowed at me, blazing with heat. If he could burn me with a look, I would have been on fire. He wore a black tank top that showed a hint of muscle. He wasn't a body-builder, but he definitely worked out. He kept his beard groomed, allowing it to grow along his jawline. The dark contrast to his pale skin pronounced his cheekbones.

"I'm sure your protest was noted," I said.

Tres stepped between us. "Come on, Adrian, both women have information we need."

"Then they can provide information and live someplace else," Adrian said.

"Esais thinks we need to be protected, and we can't do that separated."

The younger one stared at his brother with earnest eyes. He laid on the charm, but his brother wasn't swayed. He shook his head, his face a mask of cold disdain.

"She isn't one of us," Adrian said.

"Like you have room to talk." Tres clenched his fists, his smile slipping from his face.

"First of all," I said, "stop arguing about me like I'm not here. Second, Esais has a point; we have too many enemies to live separate. Third, you may not see it, but I actually care about your family."

"Why?" he asked, letting his gaze bore into me.

"Because I made a promise," I said, my voice softening.

"Supposedly to my great-grandfather, yes. I don't know how you fooled him, but I'm not falling for your tricks, and I won't let you sway my brothers," he said icily.

"I'm not trying to trick you," I said.

"Most monsters would say that," Adrian said.

"I'm not a monster," I said.

"Well, you're certainly not human."

I stared at my hands with my face on fire. I should have felt angry—and a part of me did—but it didn't account for the nausea that rose in my stomach nor the tightness that restricted my chest. I grabbed my bag and the ink.

"Excuse me, I have the rest of the house to finish." I pushed past him and into the hallway.

Tres followed me into the next room. "I'm sorry Adrian is such an ass. He always has been."

I looked into the hall. If Adrian heard, the argument would just be moved into here, and I was finished listening to any more insults for the day. I jangled the knob and waited for him to show his face so I could slam the door in it.

"Don't worry. He's gone to the garage. Most likely working on a new weapon and brooding."

"He's entitled to his opinion." If only he could keep that opinion to himself. "I'll leave once I've finished protecting your house."

"No, we want you here. He'll come around."

"You don't seem to get along with him," I said.

Tres shook his head, throwing his hand up. "He's always been this way. He complained about having to take the Oath, though he ended up doing it. Then he and Papa had a big fight about going to America for college."

"College?"

"He was offered a full scholarship to the Massachusetts Institute of Technology when he was sixteen. Something for robotics, I think."

"He's two years older than you, right?"

"Four. Not that it really matters. He's never acted like my brother." He gritted his teeth and gave a derisive snort. "He hasn't been back since he ran off to college in America, not for Mother's and Father's funeral. Not even when Adam died."

I crossed my arms. "You seem a little bitter."

Tres's hands clenched around his pants, bunching them up at his knees. "I don't see why he's here now. He's never cared before."

"People change."

"I doubt it. Besides, what's he going to do? Get arrested again?"

"What happened?"

He smirked. "He made some naughty weapons. Pissed some people off."

I chuckled. "Well, maybe he can make us some. We need all the help we can get."

He took a deep breath and looked at my vial of ink. "So can you explain these traps to me?"

"Sure," I said. He didn't want to take this any deeper. I would have to be patient. "What do you want to know?"

"What's the ink?"

"It's an alchemical compound with crushed agate. Good for repelling hostile spirits."

"Did you make it?"

I chuckled. "No, alchemy is too involved for me. I tend to dabble in the other areas of magic."

"Other areas?"

"The magic that we humans can do comes in five forms: alchemy, talismans or charms, incantations, symbols, and rituals. Anyone can do them, but the magic is precise. One incorrect word or symbol and..." The banishing of Ose flashed through my mind.

I'd been unused to doing such rites then. Now, however, he wasn't leaving this town alive, and there would be no exorcism for him to come back from. He would meet the sharp side of my sword.

"So what are we doing now?" Tres asked.

"It's a symbol—the counter-clockwise spiral of the words blocks demons and their energies from entering this space."

"How long does it last?"

"Until the symbol is destroyed."

"I'll watch you do it for a while, then. We want to make sure they're perfect right?"

I smiled at him and moved to the left corner of the room. He came to stand over my shoulder as I painted. We spent the afternoon working on the traps. Adrian came in and watched from a distance. Tres managed to grasp the concept quickly, and he finished a room with the help of a journal I kept.

I flopped on the bed of my new room with a sigh. My eyelids drooped at the sight of the pillow and blanket. They beckoned to me to crawl in and let sleep take me, but I still had work to do. I wasn't going near the carnival without protection against madness. That yellow cloud meant the area was ripe with it. I emptied out a small bag into my hand. I had five pieces of jet, one for each of us. Carving the Hebrew symbols would take my complete concentration, so I plugged my ears and prepared for a long night.

$\mathscr{H}$ 9 $\mathscr{H}$

The small ticket booth and metal gate of the carnival entrance remained a good twenty people away. The smell of exhaust wafted on the air from the street behind us. I stepped back under the shade of a nearby tree and fanned myself with my hand. A girl of four or five clenched her fists and stomped her feet, her red face upturned to her offender, her mother. I rubbed my ear at the wail that emitted from such a tiny person.

Adrian stared at the family in front of us with his nostrils flared and his mouth pressed in a thin line. The mother put a hand in front of her, rubbing her temple with the tips of her fingers. When the line progressed, she yanked the screaming child forward by her arm. I smiled. My own child hadn't been old enough to throw a tantrum, but he'd had some lungs on him.

"Why have you decided we need to waste a day standing in lines?" Adrian asked.

"What, you don't like children?" I asked.

Tres snickered. "Adrian has never been a family man."

The middle brother turned his one-eyed scrutiny to the

younger one. Tres's grin faltered, and he cleared his throat, shifting closer to Marge, who stood with her arms crossed and one foot tapping a steady rhythm on the sidewalk.

She growled under her breath. "I wanna know why I was dragged here, too."

"Didn't Esais explain this?" I asked.

Esais nodded. "Though I think they were too busy arguing to pay attention."

"I get it," she said. "Devil's hiding place, blah, blah, blah. But why do we have to do this with them?" Marge waved her hand at the crowd surrounding us.

"It is easier for us to move unnoticed," I said.

"And we have to wear these ugly necklaces because?"

"So you don't go mad. But if you hate it that much, by all means." I held out my hand. "I can always use the spare."

"Tres," a woman's voice called behind us.

Adrian stole a glance over his shoulder, then sneered at his brother. "What was that about not attracting attention?"

The woman crossed the street from the parking lot and jogged up to us. She pushed the tiny red braids out of her face and nodded to us before turning her attention back to Tres. She smiled at him, her amber eyes gleaming under her sooty lashes. Her espresso-colored skin glistened in the sun and pulled at the collar of her button up shirt. She leaned her head to one side as she panted a little.

"You didn't mention coming here," she said.

"I didn't know when we met." Tres turned to the rest of us. "Everyone, this is Charlotte Dixon."

Esais held his hand out to her. "It's a pleasure, Ms. Dixon. I'm Tres's brother, Esais."

I moved up once he finished and introduced myself. Adrian gave her a nod, and Marge looked her up and down before going back to her foot tapping.

Charlotte waved her hand to them. "Is this your first time here?"

Officer Parkins crossed the street and walked to us. "Don't run off like that," she said to Charlotte. Her gaze moved to me. "We meet again, I see."

"Officer," I said.

"Oh, she's off duty now. Call her Nancy." Charlotte tilted her head in Nancy's direction with her eyebrows raised. "And she promised me she would leave work behind."

"Right, a day filled with fun." Nancy put on an exaggerated smile, eliciting a laugh from Charlotte. She gave the group a once-over. "So, this is the rest of your family?"

Marge scowled. "This is boring. I'm off." She stalked off into the entrance of the fair.

"She's not. Just met her." I nodded between Charlotte and Nancy. "What about the two of you?"

"Cousins," Nancy said.

"How about we show you around?" Charlotte asked the rest of us.

"Well, I believe Adrian and Gabby wanted to have some time to themselves," Esais said. "But Tres and I would be delighted."

"You have to be joking." I pushed my thought to him.

Tres held out his arm to Charlotte. "Now I can get to know two beautiful ladies."

"I don't want my brother anywhere near the police, and she's already suspicious of you. Go scout the carnival."

"We'll meet up later." Esais nodded to both of us before turning to Nancy. "So, what can you tell me about the carnival?"

Nancy gave me one last look before turning back to Esais. The group walked through the gates, leaving me alone with Adrian. I could think of worse ways to spend time, like torture or the forced guest of a demon, but this came close. I closed my eyes and inhaled, letting the warmth of the sun bathe my face. I could do this. I wouldn't lose to the arrogant prick. I had already overcome many in my lifetime.

I shifted my mind to the pleasant thoughts of Shakespeare's sonnets, exhaled, and imagined my anxiety and annoyance floating away in small puffs of smoke. Adrian watched me with an unreadable expression, his hands clasped behind his back. I showed him my pearly whites.

"Ready?" I asked.

"Your sudden lightheartedness is suspicious," he said with a raised brow.

"I've decided I'm not going to let you affect me. We have a job to do."

Before he could get another word in, I headed into the crowd. I spun to the side, avoiding two children as they ran by laughing and covered in ice cream. The scent of roasted corn and fried foods wafted past me on a breeze. My stomach growled, reminding me I should have eaten breakfast before we left the house. I bought a sausage-on-a-stick and leaned against the stand, waiting for Adrian to catch up to me. I took my first bite. The hot grease burnt the roof of my mouth, and I sucked in air to cool it. I savored the spiced meat as I chewed.

"This is work?" Adrian asked as he approached.

"No, this is breakfast that can be eaten while we work," I said.

He studied me as if I was some small reptile he wanted to dissect. "You eat, you sleep, and you get hurt. You certainly play well at being human."

"Because I am human. How many times do I have to say it?"

"Just because you say it, doesn't make it true."

I rubbed my eyes with my thumb and forefinger and sighed. This man would never believe my words without proof. If I didn't gain even a small amount of this man's trust, our animosity could get us killed. I needed to be the bigger woman.

"What will it take for you to believe me? Do you want Tres to perform a full physical?" I asked.

He opened his mouth as if to make another comment, but when he met my gaze, he stopped. He must have read the earnestness in my face. He tilted his head and furrowed his brow as though he couldn't quite figure me out. I kept my face straight. I still had a few surprises in me.

"Why?" he asked.

"Because one of us needs to call a truce. Hell, if you want, I'll tell you my life's story, but not here and not now."

The muscles in his jaw moved. My breath caught in my throat, and my heart pounded. I wanted him to accept me. I would never admit it aloud, but the opinions of Dimitri's descendants meant more to me than anyone else. The other two would be easier, I hoped. This one, however, remained the exception to everything I knew about the Van Helsings. He always wanted to go on his own path.

"I suppose that is acceptable," he said.

I clapped my hands. "He can be reasoned with! All right, let's get to work."

"And how do you propose we do this search?" he asked.

I finished my sausage and tossed the stick in the trash. I moved close enough to murmur to him without being over-heard, touching his shoulder. He stiffened. Though we made a semi-truce, trust would be a long time coming. Still, we couldn't act as strangers.

"First, we need to pretend we're friends. Otherwise, they'll see us coming," I said.

He nodded and relaxed. "How are we going to find them?"

"Leave that to me."

I tucked my arm in the crook of his elbow and pulled him

forward. As we walked, I inhaled and let my senses expand, once again activating my astral sight. A rainbow of colors greeted me. Bright reds and light yellows emanated from happy fair goers and mixed with the grays and muddy browns of others of a more downhearted nature. All human as far as my eye could see. The yellow cloud funneled in several directions. I followed it to its closest source.

"What are you doing?" Adrian asked.

"Searching auras for demons," I said.

"What you're doing now disproves your claim."

Funny he should say that, considering his brothers' and his own situation.

"We are called emissaries and we are still born as a human," I said.

"So are vampires."

"Vampires are undead," I said, holding a finger up.

"Demons, then."

"Possess a body. If it is still alive, the person they ride is human."

"Interesting. There is still a human in there."

I nodded. "Most aren't willing."

"What about what you did yesterday?"

"Ritual magic? Anyone can do it as long as they have the formula."

He refrained from replying and stared into the distance with his eye narrowed. It hadn't won him over, but he'd gained information. I continued to scan the carnival. Between the glow of pink and green, I saw the red black. The boy wore a leather jacket with the head of a demon on its back. He turned his head, flashing his pocked face.

"We need to move," I said, darting in the direction before I lost my mark.

"What?" Adrian asked as he was yanked behind me.

"I found someone."

I pushed aside a tall man, standing in the middle of the walkway. I didn't stop to apologize. I quickened my steps, my eyes never leaving the black tendrils as they floated past the roller coaster. Adrian caught my arm. I couldn't hear what he said over the roaring whoosh of the cars as they passed us on the ride. I shook my head and pulled away. Had to keep moving.

The yellow I'd been looking for filled my vision as I passed a building. I closed my eyes against the moment of vertigo. The second man I ran into pushed back and I stumbled but regained my balance before I fell. The man looked down at the remains of the chili pie dripping down his Metallica T-shirt then back to me. His face twisted in a scowl.

"Watch where you're going, bitch!" he yelled.

I peered past him, but my quarry had vanished. Damn. I let out a huff and turned my attention to the mullet head in front of me.

"Sorry," I said, not meaning it.

"You're just gonna say sorry? You owe me a new pie!" He towered over me, his belly peeking out from under his shirt.

"I believe we can compensate you," Adrian said from behind me.

He pulled a twenty out of his wallet and held it out. The other man stared at it with a look of confusion.

"I'm sure this is more than enough to help widen your girth," Adrian said, keeping his voice cordial.

The man walked off after shooting me one last glare, unaware of the insult. He didn't matter. I turned my attention to the building that had surprised me and covered my mouth, fighting to keep the bile down. The outside of the building looked like a wooden caravan, but the putrid yellow infected everyone who passed it. Traces of black mixed in with the yellow and spiraled up into the air. My funnel. The gypsy woman painted on the wall leered at me; her grin seemed to divide her face.

"What is wrong with you?" Adrian asked, his voice filled with cold annoyance.

Before I could reply, the door swung open, and a group of teenagers flooded out. They chattered with each other, passing us by without a glance, unaware their happy auras were marred by tiny mustard spots. The dots spread to people they passed like a virus.

"This place," I said.

"I'm not going to rely on cards and tea leaves to find a demon," he said with a snort.

"No," I said.

I knelt down, putting my head between my legs. I sucked in several breaths of air and let my vision return to normal. It was too much. I could feel the slimy yellow tendrils reaching out to me. They wanted to touch me in a place I could not heal. My mind.

"This place; it's demon touched," I said once I could speak again.

He studied the building, as if memorizing every inch of the place. His lip turned with disgust as his gaze reached the gypsy woman.

"Then perhaps a reading would be useful," he said.

I grabbed his arm before he moved too far. "We need the others."

"I believe we can deal with one fortune teller." His voice was filled with confidence.

A flash of leather disappeared behind the roller coaster. Marge followed, hot on his trail, with a wild grin on her face.

"That will have to wait," I said. "Marge has found something to entertain her, which means trouble."

10

I pulled Adrian through the crowd as I kept sight of Marge's back. She slipped behind one of the wooden fences at the edge of the carnival and into a copse of trees so thick it made the inside look like twilight instead of late morning. The carnival workers were busy dealing with customers, so they didn't notice as I slid halfway through the fence.

"Coming?" I asked Adrian.

He waved me along and pushed himself through the fence. I scanned the trees and saw a flash of blonde heading farther into the woods. I grabbed Adrian's arm, pulling him along. A man's yell echoed through the tree line, and I broke into a run. The twigs cracked under my feet, and my heart pounded in my ears.

Maybe she'd found the demon. I didn't have my sword, but I had my knives and a vial of holy water in my pocket. If Marge could keep him busy, I could exorcise him. I preferred Solomon's words to the standard Catholic practice, mostly because the latter required a priest. As a woman, I could never be a priest. Besides, the Church and I hadn't parted on the best of terms.

I stopped short as I came upon Marge holding the biker hostage against a tree. She pressed her foot into the throat of the biker as he lay on the ground with his head propped against the trunk. He struggled to knock her off balance, but she just pushed harder.

"You're pretty weak without your gun," she said. "Now where's your boss?"

He coughed and gagged, wrapping his fingers around her boot.

"I don't think he can answer your questions like that," I said.

Marge spun around, her hair ruffled in the slight breeze. The snarl on her lips lessened as she saw who spoke.

"What do you suggest?" she asked.

"Tie him up and question him. Or hold him at gunpoint," I said.

She patted her jeans. "Damn, I seem to be all out of guns and handcuffs."

I pulled a handful of cable ties from my purse. John had shown them to me a few years back, and the nylon strips had proven useful for a lot of things. I held them out to her, and she smirked.

"I like the way you think," she said.

She snagged them from my hand and turned back to the cowering man. The biker struggled to stand as she moved her boot. She kicked him in the face, causing his head to slam back against the tree and fall forward again. He winced with a groan as blood gushed from his swelling nose. She made quick work of him, putting him in a sitting position with his arms tied between his legs. He blinked up at her, the side of his face already puffing up.

"You can scream and yell, but with the carnival, no one will hear you," she told him.

He glared up at her. "Fuck off, you crazy bitch."

"You have no idea. Now, answer my question."

"What question?"

She bent down and grabbed one of his fingers. She jerked it back. The snap echoed through the woods, followed by his cry of pain. Adrian sighed and walked away.

"I will check to see if he has any friends nearby," he said.

"Where is your boss?" she repeated.

"Around. Fuck, I don't know."

This would take forever. Time for me to step in. "Why were you at the fair?"

"Do you crazy bitches tie people up often? You can't get a real fuck?"

Crack. Scream. Crack. Scream.

"Answer the damn question," Marge said.

"Looking for Ose," he said.

He leaned against the tree and panted. The reddish purple bruise contrasted with the growing pallor of his face. I swallowed and turned my head away. It was only a few broken fingers. He'd be fine with a bit of tape if things ended here. We still had more questions to ask. I rubbed my tongue against the roof of my mouth, trying to kill the bitter taste that had risen.

"Why are you looking for him?" I asked.

His mouth clamped into a thin line, and he stared at the ground with a furrowed brow and narrowed eyes.

Marge raised her foot up and brought it down on his stomach. The boy managed to choke back his yell this time. I turned my head and shifted from one leg to another. The boy had willingly sided with demons. He served them for power and deserved no sympathy from me. He would get none from the demons when he filled his purpose. They would do much worse.

"Ow, ow. Okay," Pock-face said. "There's some sort of contract out on him. He's making something big."

I raised an eyebrow. "And what would that be?"

He hesitated, and Marge raised her foot again. He cringed, bunching his shoulders up. "Some sort of drug, OK?! It's supposed to be with him, wherever he is."

"So, where are you meeting up with your friends?" she asked.

Pock-face stared at a tree behind us. He feared the demon in Tattoo more than our capacity to cause pain. Marge chuckled a dark, gravelly kind of laugh. The fact he didn't talk seemed to please her. I crossed my arms and rubbed my biceps. Marge took out a switchblade and flipped it open, a look of anticipation on her face.

"Tell me," she said.

I closed my eyes and took a deep breath. It was as if the blade was traveling across my flesh like others did centuries ago. The boy's screams intermingled with my own. I hadn't resisted the clergy when they'd taken me from my home after my family's death. They'd dumped me in a cell with nothing but a blanket. For days I'd lain there in a daze, wishing for death.

The inquisitor came not long after with his questions and devices. He restrained me in a special chair. It reeked of old blood and other body fluids from previous occupants. He hadn't liked my response when he asked who I served. Every time I responded with the name of God, the restraints tightened and the blades on the armrests dug deeper. That had just been the beginning. I could still feel the cuts in my arms, the tightening on my wrists, and the burning of my flesh.

"Stop." I stumbled forward and pushed Marge away from her victim. She glared and shoved back.

"What the hell?" she said.

"This is not working." I straightened and put as much calm into my voice as I could muster.

"It's working great. He'll keep talking."

"We can find out what he knows in different ways," I said.

"And what do you suggest?" Adrian asked from behind me.

I spun around and bit my lip. When had he returned? Hell, he didn't know about Esais's abilities yet, and I shouldn't have to be the one to tell him. Both he and Marge stared at me, waiting for my answer.

"What we were doing before was working," I said.

"Seems like a waste of time," Marge said. "Besides, this is fun."

"Why bother with a human lackey when we can question a demon?" I kept my gaze on Adrian. Surely, he would see the best option.

The skin around Marge's eyes tightened. "This seer isn't the demon I want."

"He's not your demon, either. Just a human." I raised my voice to meet hers, moving until we were inches apart.

"He's sided with him. Just as bad."

"He still has a chance to change that."

Pock-face groaned and stared up at me with one good eye. Blood ran over the other from a cut on his forehead.

"I'll take the demons over you any day," he said.

I sighed. He'd made his choice. Marge moved forward and slammed her knee into his face. His nose crunched beneath the force, and he slumped, unconscious. She kicked him in the gut several more times.

"At least give him a swift death." I moved forward and pulled out my knife.

"He could be useful. If he's still alive." Adrian pushed both of us aside. He knelt beside Pock-face and put three fingers on his throat. He stood and dusted himself off. "Let's head back. I don't want to be caught at the scene of an assault."

"We're just going to let him go?" Marge asked.

"For now. Besides, we have to get our fortunes read."

"How is he going to be useful?"

"Wait and see," he said.

Marge threw her hands in the air. She muttered and cursed the entire way back. We'd spoiled her fun, but the violence turned my stomach. I was no stranger to anger, and I enjoyed seeing a demon die, but her anger ran deeper and darker than mine. I would have to make sure it wasn't turned on me or the brothers.

The carnival crowd paid no attention to us as we slipped back in through the fence. The metal of the roller coaster we stood behind rattled as the car sped its screaming passengers along the tracks.

Marge crossed her arms. "So, where is this fortune-teller?"

I nodded in the direction where the crowd thickened to a sea of bodies. Families stood in the food lines, staring up at the menus with almost glazed expressions. Children yanked at their parents' arms and pointed to cotton candy and treats on display at the small, metal stands. This would be a nightmare to get through.

"Through the food court," I said.

"Let's get on with it. Maybe one demon will die today," Marge said.

Adrian scoffed. "I doubt that."

I sighed and pushed forward into the crowd. I didn't want to hear more of Marge's bitching or Adrian's criticism. Neither of them had the experience to contend with a demon like Malantha on their own. He'd spent his time in prison instead of hunting. Marge's tactic was to rush in and beat whatever opposition lay in front of her. Malantha liked games, and both could fall easily into her traps like I'd fallen for a few over the years.

"Wait up," Marge called as I pushed farther in.

I glanced back. A small girl ran full tilt into her legs and stumbled back. She blinked up at Marge and gave her an angelic smile.

"Sorry," the girl said.

"Watch where you're going, kid," Marge said, the scowl on her face softening.

A balding man hustled to them from one of the food lines. His beefy hand reached out and yanked the girl away from Marge. His jowls wiggled as he spun the girl to face him. The man's face glowed red and his eyes protruded from his face.

"I told you not to run off." He punctuated each word with a shake.

The girl's eyes filled with tears. "Sorry, Daddy."

"Get off of her." Marge shoved him in the shoulder.

"Mind your own damn business," the man snarled.

"I'll mind what the fuck I want to. Don't treat your daughter like that."

The man loomed over Marge, his face turning a deeper red, almost purple. She didn't seem impressed with his size. She tilted her chin up, waiting for him to make a move.

I looked to Adrian and raised an eyebrow. He waved his hand at me as if to say "all yours." Great. Once again, I would have to get between Marge and a fight.

"Why don't you take your nosy ass on," the man said. "What I do with my family is my right."

"The hell it is. Maybe you should feel what you dish out."

Marge stepped back, going into her stance. Her eyes were narrowed, and the smile I'd seen earlier came to her face. The man raised his fist. I moved up next to her and put a hand on her shoulder. Behind the man, Nancy was approaching fast.

"Is there a problem here?" she asked.

The man turned to her, dropping his fist. His shoulders hunched, and he dug his hands into his pockets. The redness drained from his face.

"No problem, Officer," he said.

"It looks like a problem. It looks like the two of you are disturbing these people who are trying to enjoy the carnival."

He pointed a finger at Marge. "It's her—"

"Lloyd, am I going to have to call Deb to pick up your daughter so I can take you to the station?"

The man grabbed his daughter's hand and dragged her behind him towards the Ferris wheel. Marge took a step in that direction, but I grabbed her arm and shook my head. I met her glare with one of my own. Didn't she understand we had bigger problems to worry about? She was spoiling for a fight.

Charlotte came up to Nancy with Tres and Esais trailing behind her. Her lips pursed together, and her eyes narrowed. "I thought we agreed no policing on your day off."

Nancy waved her hand at Marge and me. "I wouldn't, but they were disturbing the peace."

"That ass was hurting his daughter," Marge said. "And you just let him go."

Nancy rubbed the back of her neck. "Unfortunately, we don't have any evidence that he's actually hurt her, so there's not much we can do. And that doesn't excuse you from trying to start a fight."

"Everyone here saw what he did to her. Whatever, this town is just fucked."

She stalked off in the opposite direction of the man towards the exit of the carnival. She'd probably double back after the biker.

"Your friend's got a real problem," Nancy said.

"She's not the only one," I said. "You didn't even question that man."

"I know him. I don't know you."

"And you know there are rumors," Charlotte said. "He used to be the nicest guy, except for the last month."

"Perhaps you should look into it, Officer," Esais said. "If the rumors are true, you will have prevented that girl from being hurt further."

Nancy gritted her teeth. "How about you strangers stop talking about things you know nothing about?"

"My, you seem to be a bigger attraction than anything I have to offer here," a woman's voice rang from behind us. "Perhaps I should hire you."

The owner of the voice stood with her arms crossed. Her mahogany hair flowed down her back in waves with golden rings braided into it. Multi-colored scarves made up her skirt, and she wore an off-the-shoulder blouse. Malantha looked every bit the part of a fake gypsy fortune-teller.

Her demon form was altogether different. Black smoke swirled inside a crystal ball. In the center, a pair of eyes with crimson irises gazed out at me. My chest tightened as they stared into my soul.

My hand twitched, but I kept it at my side. I'd left my sundang in Adrian's car anyway. She tossed her hair over her shoulder and smiled at me before moving her gaze over the others. She paused on each of the brothers and flashed me a look with a raised eyebrow. Esais stiffened beside me.

"And you are?" I asked.

Nancy waved her arm toward Malantha. "Briana is in charge of the carnival."

"Interesting place you have here," I said.

Esais took a step forward to introduce himself.

"*Don't touch her,*" I thought to him.

He stepped back, moving in front of Tres. "*This is her?*"

She looked at Esais's protective position. "What lovely men. Are they yours?"

"Yes," I said.

Adrian snorted behind me. Charlotte looked at Tres in confusion. He took her hand.

"Oh, but you two are together?" Malantha asked Tres and Charlotte.

I dug my fingernails into my palm, resisting every urge to go after her. There would be no explaining it to Nancy and Charlotte. "Do you ask personal questions of all your customers?"

"I am a fortune-teller. You have an interesting accent. European?"

I nodded. She knew that already. This was just another game for her.

"Where are you from?"

"I have traveled all over," I said.

"Have you visited Prague?"

My last stop before coming to America. I'd been searching for another hunter she'd targeted last year. I remember slipping through the broken window of the safe house. The stench of blood and decay had wafted through from the back rooms. The body of another hunter had been rotting in the house for days. I'd been too late again. That seemed to be my story with Malantha. She seemed to make it her mission to wipe out the hunters from around the world and used her powers to take many by surprise. Thanks to her, we were a dying profession.

"It stinks there," I said.

"I hear it's lovely in the spring," Malantha said.

"Plenty of danger."

Her smile widened. "There is danger everywhere."

Tres cleared his throat. "A fact we all know too well."

Malantha chuckled and pulled out a deck of cards from

the sash at her waist. She shuffled them with both hands as she peered at each one of us. A wave of dizziness shot through me. The yellow sickness drifted off the cards.

"I hope you enjoy yourselves. And if you ever want to run away, just let me know." She held a card out to Charlotte. "A small fortune for you. Perhaps it's a bit of romance."

I reached up to knock Charlotte's hand away, but Nancy moved faster. She snatched the card from Malantha and stared at it. It shook in her grip before she dropped it with a gasp. It fluttered to the ground, landing face up. The Devil. She shook her head and walked off, her aura turning from the pumpkin color of distrust to a deep charcoal. Small spots of yellow clung to the outer edges and began to eat their way in.

"Where are you going?" Charlotte called after her.

"Well, I suppose she didn't like what she saw," Malantha said to Charlotte. To me, she said, "I look forward to our future meeting."

"I'm sure it will be more entertaining than this one," I said.

She winked at me and spun on her heel, slipping through the crowd with ease. I balled my hands into fists. Was I so little a threat to her she could turn her back on me?

Charlotte looked to Tres, biting her lip. "I should go after Nancy."

"I can come with you," he said.

"No, I need to handle this." She kissed him on the cheek and left.

"I believe we are finished here," Adrian said. "Unless you would like to chase her down now."

"Too many people," I said. "Besides, we lost the element of surprise. She knows who you are now."

I glanced back to the ground and blinked with a chill running down my spine. Feet kicked up old wrappers and plastic cups, but the card had disappeared.

❧ 12 ❧

I leaned against the wall of the brick church across the street from the carnival grounds with a small duffle bag resting by my feet. The sun had set hours ago, and the lights of the Ferris wheel and a few other rides lit the dark sky. The families had exited through the gates, laughing and holding their prizes as they headed home for the night. The crickets were the only things that remained to keep me company.

I sighed and crossed my arms. This was going to be a long night. I doubted Malantha would even leave her fake little wagon, much less leave through the front gate, especially since she knew I was out here. With less people around, I could take a look at the outside, though. John stepped out of the gloom of the night and under the streetlamp with a smile lighting his face. I stood and gave him a smile of my own.

"You don't plan on staying out here all night, do you?" he asked. "She probably knows you are here."

I shrugged. "Most likely, but I need to scout around."

"So you called me because you wanted some company?"

I chuckled and jabbed him with my shoulder, playfully.

"Yes, and I wanted to know if you'd gotten any information on that gang."

He shoved his hand in his pockets. "Walk with me?"

He held out the crook of his arm. I gave one last glance to the gates of the carnival before grabbing my bag and slipping my arm through his. As we strolled down the empty sidewalk, I let the world fade to the gray of the Eclipse.

Once again, the buildings were replaced by much older ones. The yellow cloud of madness swirled above the carnival, its murk obscuring what lay inside. I peered up into the sky, in search of its twin. A small pinprick of pain formed in the inner corners of my eyes. I could only keep this up for so long, but I wanted to find where the other funnel led. If I found it, I would find Ose.

"So, have you learned anything?" I asked as I studied the sky.

"A little," he said. "The D-boyz are big in New Orleans. They apparently sell themselves out as supernatural muscle."

"I think Marge mentioned chasing them from there. How many are actually demons?"

"I think it's just their big wigs," he said. "From what I hear, it's pretty cutthroat. They're trying to stab each other in the back so they can get some recognition."

I shook my head. "Of course. I'm sure the demons perpetuate that. It gets them souls faster."

"Yeah, well, they get plenty of extra strength. They are better than normal humans." He took my hand in his and gave it a small squeeze.

I stopped and smiled. "Are you worried about me?"

He brushed my cheek with his thumb, and I shivered at the warmth it gave. "Maybe a little. There are a lot of demons here."

"This place was probably dead before Ose showed up." I

started walking again, pulling him along with me. "You don't need to worry. I've handled people like the D-boyz before."

He sighed. "Yeah, but I always worry about you. Especially now, with Ose. Maybe one day, one of them will get lucky and find a way to permanently get rid of you."

My laugh echoed through the night. "I doubt that can happen. Allegra may have cursed me, but it's powered by the Throne of Lust. The only two that can break that would be those higher on the totem pole. Pride or Greed."

"Ose was once from Greed," John said in a quiet voice. "What if he has the power? Or what if someone actually killed Allegra? It's her that holds the connection, right?"

I shook my head. "Yeah, she's the conduit. If she dies, the curse ends, but I think I would know if that happened."

"Just be careful, all right?" John stopped again and pulled me close. "I mean, Ose can drive people crazy. I don't want to lose you, any part of you."

His heat radiated all around me, making this hot night steamy. I stepped back and took a deep breath to calm my swiftly beating heart. "You won't lose me. Though, I'm not sure where some of this is coming from."

He shrugged. "I don't know. I've been feeling lately that you mean more to me than just a good friend."

I sighed. "John, you know that can't happen. It never turns out well."

He gave a sad half-smile. "Does that mean you've just given up, because you've had a few bad incidents?"

"Yeah, I have. Anyone I get emotionally involved with ends up dead. That tends to turn a girl off of relationships."

"They just needed to know what came with it."

"Dimitri was a hunter."

"And he didn't die because of you."

"No, but he almost did." I shook my head. "Let's talk about something else."

He sighed. "Fine. What else do you want to talk about?"

"Did you learn anything else about Marge?"

The yellow funnel drew closer as the buildings began to fall away to trees and a few sparse houses. We were nearing the woods that surrounded the town. The crossing between the street and the two lane highway was mostly empty and only illuminated by the street lamps. The cone floated up the right like a great mustard beacon in the night.

"Well, she had a good bit of money. Family was rich," he said.

"OK, so?"

"Her dad died under mysterious circumstances a few years ago. The family covered it up, but there were a lot of rumors going around about it in our little circles."

"Any word on the demon that did it?"

John shook his head. "No one's coming up and claiming it. Though they say it was someone in Wrath."

"And I take it the D-boyz work for Wrath?"

"You got it, sweetheart. " He grinned. "So, I guess this Marge chick is out to renege on her deal."

I shook my head. "I'm not so sure. She seemed pretty pissed. Then again, that may just be her standard personality."

"Maybe they screwed her over somehow. It's not like they're known for being completely on the up and up with their deals."

"True. Too bad Marge won't talk about it."

"You just need to gain her trust. You know, use that winning personality of yours."

"It's not that winning. The Van Helsings don't really trust me. At least not all of them."

"How many is not all of them?'

I smirked at him. "OK, one. Adrian."

"The criminal?" He snorted. "You got the better two. Why does it make a difference if he doesn't?"

I shrugged. "I guess I just want Dimitri's descendants to like me."

"I think you invest entirely too much emotion into that family. Give him time. If he doesn't come around, he's just an ass."

I chuckled and shook my head and pointed in the air. "What's over there?"

He looked over with narrowed eyes. "I think that's the mental institution."

I blinked. "There's an asylum in this town? I didn't think it was that big."

He shrugged. "It's been around since the turn of the century. It's one of those creepy ones, though I think the current head tried to modernize it a bit."

"Makes sense." I turned to head in that direction.

He chuckled. "You take me to all the great places."

The street lights were our only guide as we walked along the deserted sidewalk. To our left, the darkness of the woods loomed, filled with the cricking of insects and the croaks of the frogs. I shivered and quickened my steps. It felt as if something was watching us from inside the forest, yet my sight didn't pick anything up but more shadows. I came upon the edge of a brick wall that loomed over us by at least ten feet. A metal rail lined the top of it.

"May I present the Hampton Mental Institute," John said. "It's a medium security kind of place. No criminally insane."

"You really know a lot about this town."

He stuck his hands in his pockets, a small smile coming to his face. "A good reporter always does his homework."

I peered up into the sky. Beyond the gate, the yellow conduit hovered in the air, like a great whirlwind, sucking away the sanity in the area. "Looks like this is the place."

"You think Ose's here?"

"Something's here. And this would make sense. Let's go take a look."

I walked along the wall, looking for some sort of way up and over. The gate and driveway was a few meters away. Beyond that, the wall extended towards the woods. Maybe there was a tree close enough to let me cross over.

John caught up to me with a small huff. "You're not actually thinking of going in there now, are you?"

"Why not? We need to scout around."

"But are you equipped?"

I pointed to the bag I carried. "I have my sword. Maybe I'll get lucky and take care of Ose tonight."

Two figures loomed up ahead of us. I put an arm out in front of John and stepped in front of him. Ose hadn't left his place unguarded.

❧ 13 ❧

I slid my bag off of my shoulder and reached behind me to unzip it. One of the shadows advanced on us, and I could see the reddish lines in the corona of their aura. My hand wrapped around the hilt of my sundang.

"If you're looking for a beat down, I'll be happy to give it to you," a woman's voice rang with a familiar Cajun lilt.

The tension in my shoulders relaxed. "What are you doing here, Marge?"

Her shadow deflated and stepped closer into the light. "Oh, it's just you."

I tilted my head and nodded to the figure behind her. "Who's with you?"

"The least useless one," she said. "If what he says he can do is true."

"It was more than you were able to do." Adrian stepped up beside Marge. He studied me for a long moment before letting his gaze rest on John behind me. "Out for a romantic stroll?"

"Hardly." I glanced behind me. "John, this is Marge and Adrian."

John cleared his throat and stepped forward to hold his hand out with his easy going smile.

"No point," I said. "They apparently have an aversion to touching people."

He glanced at their faces—Marge's bored and angry and Adrian's impassive—and his chuckle died before it could really start. "Well, it's great to meet some of Gabby's...would I call you co-workers?"

"Yeah, whatever, Blondie." Marge looked over to me. "So what are *you* doing here?"

"Following our devil's trail," I said.

"Interesting," Adrian said. "We were following the boy."

"How'd you know he was here?"

Adrian's mouth pressed into a thin line, and his eyes narrowed at John.

"He's trustworthy," I said.

Adrian snorted. "Because you are an excellent judge of character."

John squeezed my elbow lightly. "Hey, I should probably head back, anyway."

I bristled, the hair rising on my arms. "He has no right to chase you off."

"We were here first." Marge smirked. "Don't worry, I'll send some pics of me kicking this Ozzo's ass."

"Ose." I let out a sigh. "And you're really going to resort to laying claim?"

"It's no big deal." John raised his hand up to point to the light sports jacket. "Besides, I didn't exactly come dressed for B and E."

He gave me a light kiss on my cheek and headed back. I watched him go, biting my lip. He was capable enough, but this night was full of demons and madness. I turned back to Adrian with a glare.

"Tu sei veramente e stronzo," I said in Italian. Yes, he really was an asshole.

"It's kept me alive this long," he responded in my native language.

"It won't last forever."

"No one has forever," he said.

"Some of us do." I walked past them, scanning the wall for an easy way up.

At the end of the wall near the woods, one of the trees from the woods grew close to the corner. With a few swift huffs, I climbed it, perched on the limb, and gazed over the brick wall at an asylum. The building looked like an estate built around the turn of the twentieth century. Barred windows lined the three stories, and search-lights rested on top of the roof, their beams trailing across the large yard. A gravel driveway extended from the metal gate I had passed earlier.

"Are you going to tell us how you know, or are we suspect as well?" I asked.

"You'll always be suspect, but since I know where you sleep." Adrian shrugged. "I attached nanomachines to him in order to track him."

"You attached what?" Marge asked.

"They're machines measured in nanometers, built from molecular components. Most of the published research is still in its infancy compared to what I have been able to accomplish. I have set up an interface between them and my brain."

His explanation swirled around in my head, and I tried to make sense of it. He spoke English, yet the words were foreign to me. I chewed the inside of my cheek. Marge looked as lost as I was.

"So, nanomachines are?" I asked.

He sighed. "Tiny robots."

"I didn't see any robots," Marge said.

"They are microscopic."

"So, invisible tiny robots you control with your mind?"

"In very simple terms, yes," Adrian said.

"So, what else can these magic machines do?" I asked.

A vein throbbed on Adrian's temple. "Not magic, science."

It sounded like magic to me, but most science did, so I would take his word for it. If these tiny robots led us to the biker, they were useful. That's all we needed at the moment. A light flared in one of the corner widows on the first floor, one with no bars. It flickered off, and a shadowy figure climbed out. It stuck close to the building until it arrived at the corner, then darted across the yard, ducking to avoid the lights when they passed.

"Unless someone lost their keys, I'd say the boy is on the move," I said.

"Round two should be fun," Marge said. "You're not going to get in the way this time, are you?"

"Wait until he gets closer to the edge."

The figure climbed the wall at the corner closest to the wood line of the forest that encroached on the northwest side of the asylum. A howl split the night. I waved to the corner not forty feet away from us.

The biker spun in a circle, his head turning back and forth. The hellhound leapt from the trees and dashed toward him. Even hunched, its wolf-man form stood over eight feet of muscle and fur. Its snout peeled back into a snarl. The boy broke into a full run, but the hellhound caught him in moments.

Merda. I had my sundang, but I still didn't have anything to deal with the werewolf part of the problem. It would heal most of the wounds before I could kill it. John had yet to come through with what I needed. We would have to wing it.

"What the fuck is that?" Marge asked.

"Hellhound," I said. "Adrian, get the boy out of here while Marge and I distract it."

"We gonna kill it?" Marge asked.

"No, this is a hit and run."

The hellhound clamped its jaws around the biker's arm and tossed him into the air. He flew a few feet closer to us. I pulled out my sword and hopped out of the tree. I hit the ground and came up in a roll. I ran behind the beast and cut a deep gash in his side. He snarled at me and swung his arm for a backhand. I rolled out of the way.

"Hey, Furry," Marge called.

Her foot slammed down on its knee, and a crack echoed through the yard. He yowled and snapped his jaw down at her face. She hopped out of the way. The hellhound hobbled after her. Her eyes widened as his bones reknitted.

"What the fuck?" she yelled.

"Yeah, that's why we're sticking to the plan," I said.

"What plan? You didn't say shit."

"Then just follow my lead."

"Fine. Whatever."

Adrian groaned behind me. It had to be from the weight of the biker. The hellhound's ears perked, and it rumbled at him. I moved to stand between them and pulled out a glass vial of holy water. My last one—the Van Helsings had better have more.

I moved in and slashed its leg. The hellhound couldn't give chase if we kept working on its leg. Its attention shifted from Adrian's retreating back to me. It growled, saliva dripping from its yellowed fangs.

"You are a beast of few words," I said. "Did Ose take your tongue with your freedom?"

"Shut up, Food," he said with a rumbling voice.

"Sorry, I'm a little tough."

"And I'm bitter," Marge said.

She brought her leg up for a kick, but he grabbed it. His claws sank into her calf as he dangled her in the air. I slammed the holy water into his snout. He snorted and reared, slapping at the glass shards. He swung Marge at me, and I had to leap to the side to avoid getting hit. That didn't help. He threw her into me. The force of his throw sent us flying into the nearby tree. We bounced and tumbled to the ground. I rolled back toward my sword and sprang to my feet in front of the hellhound.

"Run," I told Marge. "I'll catch up."

Blood matted the fur where I had slashed him, but the wound was closed. I spun to the left until I came up behind him to sever his hamstring. His leg buckled under his mass. He turned, balancing himself on his arms and good leg.

He lunged at me, roaring. I sidestepped and raised my sword to catch him in the side as he went by. He lumbered on the ground, struggling to get up. Time for me to run. I dashed through the trees until I reached the road where Adrian's car waited with its motor rumbling. Marge hopped into the passenger seat. My feet pounded on concrete. I flung open the back door and threw myself in. Adrian sped off.

"Where's the boy?" I asked.

"He didn't make it," Adrian said.

I hunched my shoulders, crossing my arms. "So that was all for nothing."

"Not entirely. This was on him."

Adrian tossed an orange bottle of pills with a white cap. The label listed the address and phone number of the hospital. It had no patient name but listed the doctor as Charles Navotny. The name of the drug was typed in bold letters "Menrazine."

❄ 14 ❄

Tres held open the door to the house as Marge limped inside with her arm flung over my shoulder. He stared down at her blood-soaked pants with the side of his lip twitching.

"Looks like I missed all the fun," he said.

Adrian shut the door. "We didn't want to disturb your date."

Tres scowled at him. "So, you're just going to leave me out?"

"No, you do that all yourself."

"You're one to talk," Tres snapped.

I set Marge on the couch and dragged the foot stool over to prop up her leg. She glared at the brothers as they entered the room. They only had eyes for each other as they continued to trade veiled insults.

"How about helping now," I said.

Tres stopped and blinked at Marge's leg as if he'd just seen it for the first time. "Oh, let me get my first aid kit."

I slid to the floor and leaned against the foot-rest. The bottom of Marge's boot blurred and came into focus. The treads were lined with some sort of white material. It looked like bone, but what person would put bones in their boots?

"What's in your boot?" I asked.

"The bones of a Saint," she said.

I snorted and coughed. "That's…"

"What's more useful, idolizing the bones in some vault or using them to kill demons?"

"Where did you get them, and have you actually killed any demons with it?"

She leaned back in the chair with a smirk that defied the pain she must have felt. "I met a few people who deal in questionable artifacts. And yeah, they've worked out well for me."

She proved a resourceful girl. Most of me cheered her on, but a small portion was horrified. To have such a revered person used in such a base purpose poked at part of me that believed in the sacred.

Tres came back with his kit, and I stood. I backed up to the doorway. He pulled out a roll of bandages, antibiotic spray, and scissors. "I'm going to have to cut the pants' leg off."

"Sure," Marge said.

"Where's Esais?" I asked.

"Asleep, I think," Tres said.

"I'm going to wake him. We have a lot to discuss."

I handed the prescription bottle back to Adrian and walked to Esais's bedroom. He lay in the middle of his bed, with one arm flung to the side and another above his head. The blanket lay in a pile on the floor. A red leather book sat on the nightstand. His forehead creased, and his eyelids twitched while his hand jerked at his side. His skin had taken on a grayish tint, and sweat reflected from his forehead in the light of the lamp. I sat on the edge of the bed and shook his shoulder gently. He jumped, his eyes flying open.

"Sorry to wake you. We found something, though," I said.

He groaned, rubbing his face with both hands. "It's fine. I wasn't sleeping well anyway."

"Bad dreams?"

"Mmm, more like a pressure from all around. A sickness."

I moved the collar of his T-shirt, sliding the cord around his neck until the piece of jet lay in my hand. Hairline cracks formed along the outer edges and strained to meet in the center. The structure of the gem remained whole, and the symbols were still intact. The necklace did a good job of protecting him. We just needed to finish this before it crumbled under the strain of too much power.

"Make sure you keep this on you," I said.

He nodded. "What did you find?"

"The biker decided to break into the asylum. Get dressed."

Tres's yelling traveled down the hall to us. Marge leaned against the doorframe with her arms crossed and a smirk on her face. Not a mark remained on her leg. Adrian and Tres glared at each other from across the room. I glanced at Marge, and she just shrugged.

"What seems to be the problem?" Esais asked.

Tres stiffened and forced a smile on his face. "It's nothing. So, I guess it's time for the meeting."

"It's not nothing." Adrian spun on Esais. "Were you aware our brother has the miraculous ability to heal wounds?"

Esais cleared his throat. "Yes."

"How long has this been going on?"

"I've always had it. You were just too busy being brilliant to notice," Tres said.

"He's not the only one." Esais took a deep breath. "*I have power, too.*"

His voice reverberated through my mind. Marge jumped and snapped her head in his direction. The color drained from Adrian's face, and he stared hard at his brother. His lips pressed into a thin white line.

"Well," Marge said. "I didn't know freak shows came in Euro-trash."

"I can't believe both my brothers have been corrupted," Adrian said.

"They aren't. They have been gifted by spirits. His"—I pointed to Esais—"is most likely an angel. I'm not sure about Tres."

He glared at me. "Not more of this emissary nonsense."

"You're one to talk," I said.

"Meaning?"

"Let's just say you weren't left out when the gifts were given to the Van Helsing family."

"And you know this how?"

"I can see it."

He smirked. "Of course, your special vision. Well, I guess you're wrong, because I don't have any power."

I rubbed my temples. I knew he wouldn't believe me. He'd wrapped himself in his cocoon of being human so thoroughly that he probably locked his own abilities. He probably couldn't even hear the woman whispering in his ears. The three of them needed to work this out among themselves. Anything I could add would just be fuel to Adrian's engine.

"Fine, let's just deal with what happened tonight. This won't take long," I said. "Then you can get back to your family issues."

I described what happened at the asylum, with Marge dropping in an occasional comment. Tres ran his hands through his hair, tapped his foot, and sighed the entire time as if he didn't find my story interesting. Esais, on the other hand, never took his eyes off me.

"So, what's the connection to Ose?" he asked.

"I saw something, same as what I saw at the carnival. I think Ose has his fingers in that asylum."

"The mental institution?" Tres asked.

"The one we've been discussing for the past half hour," Adrian said.

Tres shot him a dirty look before turning back to us. "Charlotte works there."

"Great. Help from the girlfriend." Adrian set the bag on the coffee table and walked to the door. "Have at it, then."

Esais looked to me. "We can go to Charlotte's tomorrow and talk to her."

"I'm coming, too," Tres said.

"We're done, then?" Marge stood. "Let me know how tea time goes."

15

Charlotte opened the door wide to let us in. "Good to see you."

She led us into the living room and motioned to a brown couch with patches of strings on the seat cushions. It sat between two tables with the finish worn off around the edges. Pictures of Charlotte and Nancy along with other members of their family covered the wall. Someone had recently vacuumed the carpet, and the smell of lemon permeated the room.

She disappeared into the kitchen and came back carrying a pitcher of iced sweet tea and some glasses. "Please have a seat. Tres said you had some questions?"

"Charlotte, do you know of a Dr. Navotny?" I asked.

She blinked. "He's the head of the mental hospital I work at. I'm surprised you know of him. He really doesn't deal with patients."

"I saw a prescription bottle with his name on it. I found it weird since I'd never heard of the drug," Tres said.

"You know a lot about drugs?" she asked with a stammer. "Where did you find this prescription?"

"We found them with someone we don't think they belonged to," I said. "However, shouldn't there be some sort of approval before a drug is distributed to patients?"

"I really can't say. I'm just a nurse." She cleared her throat, her voice becoming stronger. "But, you know it's illegal to possess a prescription that isn't yours, don't you?"

I straightened up and met her gaze. If she wanted to try and intimidate, so could I. "What would the authorities have to say about your hospital testing unapproved drugs on patients?"

"I don't know what you are talking about. We aren't testing any new medications."

Tres leaned forward and put his hand over hers. "Charlotte, you've noticed that people in the town have been acting odd?"

She stiffened, her eyes going wide as she swung her gaze at him. "I..."

"We think Dr. Navotny is responsible, somehow," I said.

"Are you police?"

I chuckled. "No, the police wouldn't understand this."

Esais leaned forward, his eyes filled with concern. "We want to help your patients. Protect them. You want to help them as well, right?"

Her head tilted as though weighing his words. I tried my best to look concerned by crossing my arms and biting my lip. Her eyes shifted to the side, and she clutched the couch pillow tighter. She looked scared and not just afraid of losing her job. She had genuine fear. She acted as if she couldn't talk about the head of a department without some sort of secret police coming after her. What went on at this hospital?

The door slammed open in the hall with a bang, and Nancy marched into the living room. She froze when she saw us. Her head jerked in Charlotte's direction, and her lips pressed in a thin line.

"You didn't say anything about people coming over," she said.

"I thought you were going to be working until tonight," Charlotte said.

"You know I don't like people snooping around our house."

"They aren't snooping. And you've never had a problem with visitors."

Nancy whirled on me, her eyes wide and red rimmed. "What are you here for? Why are you causing our town so much hell?"

"That's enough." Charlotte stood up and walked to her. "They haven't done anything."

"You're going to take their side over mine?"

"You're acting irrational."

"I think I'll take my irrational self on." She turned on her heel and slammed the door on her way out.

Charlotte sat down and punched the pillow, muttering to herself. She blinked, looking up at us, and sat back. Her forehead rested on the tips of her fingers, and she just shook her head.

"I'm really sorry. I don't know what has gotten into her."

"How long?" Esais asked.

"Ever since the carnival. She's been driving me crazy, claiming there is a conspiracy going on and Hell has come to visit."

Charlotte looked at him, biting her lip. She struggled with something more she wanted to say. Now might be the only time I had to snoop around.

"Where's your restroom?" I asked, trying to look a little desperate.

"Oh," she said, pointing behind me. "Down the hall on the left."

I paused at the first door I came to. The room was neat

and clean, like the living room. A lingering scent of cinnamon drifted in the air. The walls held pictures of family. A picture of Charlotte laughing with a small child stood on the nightstand.

I passed the first door on the left, the bathroom, and stopped at the last door on the right. The room was in shambles. Clothes were pitched around the floor and piled on the bed. I wrinkled my nose at the stench of perfume and old food.

I glanced at the shattered bottles on the floor, then to the stain on the wall. Had she thrown the perfume? Posters had been ripped from their places so only ragged corners remained. This had to be Nancy's room, and it looked as though she'd had a fit of rage.

I closed my eyes, taking a deep breath before opening them again. I scanned the room, trying to find any demonic energy. Yellow light flickered in and out of my vision. The afterimage flashed in my mind of a horned devil tarot card. A hard knot formed in my stomach. Damn Malantha.

The front door opened again with its slam against the wall echoing down the hall. I hopped out of Nancy's room and met her coming down the hall. She froze, her eyes narrowing as she saw where I had come from. Her aura was almost subsumed by the yellow sickness. It undulated and fed into the anger and suspicion that had already been there. She had reached a state of full paranoia.

"What the hell are you doing?"

I pointed behind me. "Bathroom."

"No." Nancy waved her hand to the side. "You were in there. That's my room. Find anything interesting?"

I straightened. "I thought it was a little odd, since the rest of the house is so neat. Did you get into a fight?"

"And that gives you the right to snoop?" She glared at me. "I should take you in for trespassing."

I took a deep breath and calmed my voice. "Nancy, have you been experiencing strange sights, or moments of violence?"

"That's none of your business." Her scream echoed down the hall.

She came at me, her arms wide in an attempt to shove me against the wall. I stepped back to avoid her grip. She gave a frustrated growl and took a step toward me. I raised my hands to indicate I didn't mean to fight. The bathroom was only a few feet behind me. I didn't have much more room to move. Sweat beaded on my forehead, and my heart thumped in my chest. The light from the other end of the hall disappeared as Charlotte, Esais, and Tres crowded the entrance.

"Nancy, stop," Charlotte yelled.

Nancy snarled. "She's spying on me."

"Please think about this. Who would I be a spy for, and why you?" I asked.

"Them."

"*That's not going to work. She'll just rationalize it.*" Esais turned and spoke aloud in a soothing manner. "Nancy, listen to the sound of my voice."

She turned in his direction, her body shaking so hard I could see it in the gloom.

"It's been a rough day, and I apologize for invading your privacy," Esais said. "We will leave, and maybe you should lie down and get some rest."

She nodded almost placidly, and her body relaxed. "Right. A nap will probably help."

She shuffled into her room with her head down and shut the door behind her with a soft click. I let out a deep breath and tried to calm my pounding heart. That was too close by half. She almost had me trapped. I hurried down the hall to the others as they stepped out into the foyer.

"I think we should take our leave," Tres said to Charlotte in an apologetic voice. "I think we've done enough here."

She nodded in almost a daze and looked to Esais. "How... did you calm her down like that?"

Esais gave her a kind smile. "I have a way with words."

"Please don't say anything to anyone. She could lose her job." Charlotte held the front door open for us. "I can handle whatever she is going through."

Tres moved closer and patted her on the arm. "We're here to help, even if it's just a shoulder to cry on."

"That's right," I said. "So, is there anything else you can tell us that will help?"

She looked at all of us again and shook her head. "Please, just go."

Esais stepped outside. "Let's go."

"But," Tres said.

"Charlotte needs some time to think." Esais nodded to her. "Thank you for seeing us. Please let us know if you need our help."

"What did you find?" Tres asked as we walked home.

"Nothing we didn't already know," I said. "Malantha."

"I could feel it in her mind." Esais shuddered. "All slithering and slippery. It tried to invade me."

"Nancy's going mad, and Charlotte's too afraid of her job to talk." I sighed. "That's not going to end well."

"And it doesn't get us closer to Ose," Tres said. "So, what now?"

"I'll call John," I said. "He still needs to bring my supplies. Maybe he can get some information on this drug."

❧ 16 ☙

I shifted from one heel to another as I peered down the street, waiting for John to pick me up. The streetlights glowed in the encroaching darkness. I straightened the straps of the black lace dress and rubbed my arms. This was a business meeting, but I took every opportunity to dress up when I could. When you lived a life of blood and death, looking pretty was a rare treat.

John pulled his silver car up to the curb and stepped out. He held the door open and let his gaze travel down my body as I approached him.

"Nice dress," he said.

Warmth rushed through me and up to my face. "Thanks."

"I was thinking about this Italian restaurant." He grinned at me.

I rolled my eyes. He knew how I felt about Italian food in this country. We played this game often. "This town wouldn't know real Italian if Giada De Laurentiis came and slapped them in the face with fettuccini."

He laughed. "What would you like, then?"

"Somewhere that matches the dress."

"A steakhouse."

He drove fast, taking the curves and turns with practiced ease. The scent of leather surrounded me as I leaned back against the seat, letting the city pass by me through the window with its streetlights blurring into bright lines. The town yawned and blinked its heavy-lidded eyes, still railing against laying its head on the pillow to sleep.

There were several cars in the parking lot for a weeknight. The steakhouse sat near a small pond, and music drifted on the air from the back patio that sounded like a live band instead of canned music. I walked in step with John over the loose gravel to the double doors of the entrance. The hostess led us to a small table for two, lit by a small candle.

"I don't have your stuff yet," he said.

I met his gaze over the edge of the menu and then turned my attention back to the list. I blew a tuft of my hair from my eyes and slumped my shoulders.

"You used to be so efficient," I said.

His eyebrows lifted, and he flashed his white teeth at me. "Hey, some of what you wanted is hard to get."

"That's not why I asked to meet you."

He put a hand over his heart. "You couldn't live without me. I know, I'm pretty irresistible."

I tapped my chin trying to hold back my smile. "You are tempting, but I think I've done a good job so far."

"There you go breaking my heart again." He gave a loud sigh, but his smile remained, letting me know he was jesting. "I guess I'll just have to wait patiently for the day you do come around."

"That may be forever."

He chuckled. "Then I'll have to learn how to be immortal."

"You don't want that," I said softly.

He coughed, and his smile vanished. "I'm sorry. That was thoughtless of me."

I dropped the menu on the table and leaned back, crossing my arms. My throat had tightened; I couldn't speak if I wanted to. John, like so many others, didn't see that immortality wasn't a gift. Not only had I outlived my loved ones, but any new bonds I made would be dust before I knew it. Perhaps others who only had room in their hearts for themselves and sought only power would enjoy it, but I would never be one of them. That felt too close to a demon to me.

My fingers tapped against my upper arm as I studied him for several moments while the waiter brought our drinks and took our orders. I lifted my glass to my lips and swallowed several gulps of water. I smoothed the napkin on my lap as John placed his order. I watched the waiter leave and took a deep breath.

I pulled out the bottle of pills and slid it across the table. "I need to find out about this drug and the doctor prescribing it."

He examined the label. "You think it might be Ose?"

"You missed the action the other night." I smiled. "That bottle came from the asylum."

"Sounds adventurous. How are the Van Helsing boys working out? Are they everything you expected?"

I shrugged.

"Not Dimitri?"

"They have their family issues."

"And you need to remember that."

"What?"

"It's their family."

I gritted my teeth. "What are you implying?"

"I just don't want to see you get hurt."

Our food arrived. I picked at my potato. Was it so odd to have concern for Dimitri's bloodline? The man had shown me love and life at the point when I had just been existing. The least I could do was help avenge his grandson and look after his progeny, especially since Ose was unfinished business for me. I didn't expect to be a part of their lives after this. I couldn't be a part of anyone's life.

"I know that look." John reached over and squeezed my hand. "Stop thinking that. I've told you before."

"John, I..."

"I know, but it's still the truth. After Maureen, there's no one else but you."

I stared at my plate and bit my lip. John and Maureen had been happily married for years until a demon had possessed her. I'd come across them on a beach in Florida one day. It'd been one of those private places with palm trees surrounding it. I'd thought I'd been tracking Allegra. Instead, I found a demon using Maureen to drown her husband. I saved him, but she hadn't been so lucky.

"It's just hero worship," I said.

He shook his head. "I'm not sure what I can do to prove it's not."

"Find someone else."

He sighed. "We're going in circles. How about we forget this and dance?"

He pulled me to the dance floor and wrapped an arm around my waist. The band played Patsy Cline's "Crazy." He swayed with the music, pulling me with him. I chuckled and let the stiffness in my back fade away. Soon my rhythm matched his.

He grinned. "That's better."

He pulled me closer, and I let my head rest on his shoulder. The scent of his aftershave, so much like the sea, filled my head, making my heart beat faster and my cheeks flame. I tried to pull away, but he shook his head and swung me into a dip. My head swam and laughter escaped my lips.

"I think I've been privileged to witness something no one has seen in years," he said.

"Hmm, you seem rather smug."

"Maybe I am. Your laugh is truly beautiful."

He drew me closer, our gazes locked together. Our breaths mingled as our lips brushed. A shiver ran through me, except instead of being cold, my whole body was on fire. As my eyes closed, I saw Dimitri's face. His dark eyes pierced my heart, and I pulled away. My feet wanted to stay while my mind said go. I stumbled back to my seat. John followed.

"What is it?" he asked.

"I can't," I said. "Too much of the past—"

He held a finger to my lips. "Just think of now."

"But this can't go anywhere. You know about my curse."

"Now has nothing to do with that."

"You're talking about a one night stand?"

"Maybe more than one, but we can keep it casual." He winked again.

I bit my lip and looked to the ground.

"Let me guess, you don't do casual. Have you had anyone since that Van Helsing boy all those years ago?"

I crossed my arms and avoided his gaze. "Of course there have been others."

Few others, to be honest. After Dimitri, I concentrated on hunting. Funnily enough, violence is a great relief for sexual tension. However, it is only temporary, so there had been a few men, but none who had ever truly known me. That was too dangerous. John was too dangerous.

I shook my head and grabbed my purse. "I think it's time I headed back."

I stared out the window of the car on the way back. He didn't ask any more questions. Instead, he switched on the radio and let the blaring rock music fill the silence. I marveled at how much had changed over the years.

Cacophony of sound replaced the harmony of horns, strings, and wind instruments. Electricity had replaced fire, such as the street-lights. The world had grown smaller thanks to technology. Yet, here I remained the same.

"Drop me off here," I said as we passed a familiar figure with reddish brown hair.

He pulled the car over and waited for me to get out, with his shoulders stiff and his jaw set. He kept his eyes averted, and his knuckles whitened on the steering wheel.

"Call me when you get the supplies," I said.

He nodded.

I sighed and stepped out of the car. Relief came with a soft breeze that ruffled my hair.

$$\text{❧ 17 ❧}$$

"**S**hould you really be patrolling in your condition?" I asked Esais as he caught up to me.

"Aren't you supposed to be on a date?"

"I'd call it more of a business dinner."

He raised an eyebrow. "In that dress?"

"What, I can't look pretty?" I chuckled. "Nothing happened."

"Not for lack of trying on his part?"

I fell into step beside him. The stiffness between my shoulder blades eased, and I found myself smiling. Esais was easy to talk to, like John, just without all the sexual tension.

"You noticed? It's not that I don't find him attractive, just..."

"Then perhaps he's not right for you."

"I sense you don't like him."

"Something's not right. I'm not sure what."

"He's been through a lot. He had to deal with his wife's demonic possession." I paused. "Have you?" I tapped my finger to my head.

"No, not really. It's just a feeling I have."

I narrowed my eyes at him. "Define not really."

Esais shook his head and kept walking with his shoulders stiff. The bushes along the side of a nearby house shook and the shadows moved, casting a doglike image along the side of a house. I stiffened and unlatched my purse. Esais nodded to me, slowing his pace.

"It's been following me for the past ten minutes. I can't get a grip on its mind, but it feels like the one in the bar." The choir from his contact was an undercurrent to his words.

"Why didn't you tell me sooner?"

"It faded back when you arrived. It keeps slipping."

The hellhound was stalking us. It was probably waiting for us to lead it to the others. I didn't want to play into its paws, but I'd left my sundang at the house again. I longed for the days when swords were common-place.

"How is your head?" I asked, trying to keep the conversation casual.

"Better," he said. "Less cluttered."

Sweat beaded down his forehead, and his eyes glassed over. How much of that statement was true and how much bravado? Judging by the small lump under his shirt, he still wore the amulet, for all the protection it was providing him. I was starting to think that it wasn't enough.

"Do you think you can attack its mind?" I asked.

"I don't know. Maybe."

"I can try to play distraction until you can. Try for a kill. If you can, knock it unconscious, and we run."

"We really need to take care of this thing."

"I will when John comes through for me."

"We need to find another way in case he doesn't."

I stiffened. *"He hasn't let me down yet."*

My steps quickened, and Esais matched my pace. I reached in my purse and grabbed the handle of the knife I'd put in there. I tried to keep very few items inside so I didn't have to dig around for anything. You know, everything a woman needed: knives, pills, lipstick. Too much would make it take forever to find my knife, and in this situation, that could get someone killed, possibly me.

The street was empty. Parents had called their children in from the growing darkness hours ago. Street-lamps stood sentinel through the night while a few lights dotted windows through the neighborhood.

"We need to get somewhere private," I said.

A growl echoed from the side of the next house we passed. Yellow eyes reflected from the glow of the street lights, and a shadow separated itself from the rest. The hellhound leaped at us. I shoved Esais to the side. The beast's weight took me to the ground, and the concrete scraped against my bare legs as its teeth buried in my forearm. I swallowed the pain as I flicked the knife open and buried the blade in its side only to have the wound heal almost immediately.

This time it attacked in wolf form. I think now it had come at me in all of its forms. Thank god it wasn't as strong in this form as in the wolf-man hybrid. Otherwise, I would've lost the arm with the snap of its mighty jaws. It was the size of a mastiff with shaggy fur. It looked almost the same as the demon I'd seen in the bar. The hellhound had taken the werewolf's body long enough for its true form to take physical shape. Was it too far gone to be banished? When a demon remained in a host this long, it was almost impossible to remove them by the sacred words alone. When that happened, only death could release the soul of the body it possessed.

I stabbed the hellhound several more times, not caring that the wounds sealed in seconds. The world faded around the edges, giving off a blurred view. Damnit, I wanted this beast's blood to run down my hands, and this just wasn't working. Esais grabbed the beast around its middle and yanked it back. It released me to snap at him and caught him in his shoulder. I rose to my feet as he tossed the hellhound to the side.

"Focus on its mind," I said.

It jumped at us again. I tackled it in midair, and we tumbled into the grass with me on top this time. I drew my fist back and punched it in the nose. The beast gave something between a snarl and a yelp. It snapped its jaws inches from my face with a resounding click. I leaned back, brought my knife under its muzzle, and buried the blade in its neck. The damned creature could heal around three inches of steel.

"I exorcise ye, and powerfully banish ye, commanding ye with strength and violence by him who spake and it was done; and by all these names," I murmured.

The beast shuddered and shoved me back with its front paws. I landed on my back a few feet away with the air knocked out of me. Even in wolf form, the beast was damned strong. It stood and shook its head, as if trying to clear its nose of a noisome smell.

Esais kept his gaze on the beast with his fist clenched and sweat dripping down his forehead. The beast snorted, tossing its head to and fro one last time before focusing its gaze on me. I crouched on the ground, scanning the grass for the glimmer of my knife. A blur of red and blue flashed in my peripheral, and a siren gave a short wail.

"Freeze," a man's voice yelled.

"What in God's name is that?" Nancy said.

The hellhound turned it gaze to the two police officers and gave me a toothy grin. A sound rumbled from its chest that sounded suspiciously like a laugh. Esais stood to the side, his eyes narrowed in concentration mixed with frustration.

In one smooth motion, the beast launched itself at the police car. Hellhounds were never the most intelligent of demons, but when you have the power to heal almost instantly, I guess you didn't worry about things like cops with guns. Nancy pulled her pistol out and fired. The shot echoed through the air followed by several others.

I flattened myself against the ground as the bullets passed over me. The hellhound yelped as it was caught in midair. It slammed into the hood of the car with a resounding crash. We would definitely be the news of the neighborhood now. It stood and shook its head as it stumbled to the ground. Its body moved from the impact of the bullets, but it paid them little attention. Its shoulders bunched, and its lips pulled back in a snarl. Nancy kept firing with her eyes wide and her face colorless. Esais pressed his back to the house and kept his gaze on the hellhound. Nancy's partner backed away from his position around the car to her side. He kept his gun trained on the beast.

"Nancy," his voice was almost drowned by the gunfire.

The hellhound whined and growled, shaking its head again. It swung its head at me, and its eyes bored into mine. It winced again and dashed into the narrow opening between the two fences, disappearing into the alley.

Esais and I stayed in place, trapped by the flying bullets Nancy continued to fire. Her finger kept pressing the trigger after she'd emptied her magazine. Her partner grabbed her arm. She slammed her other fist in his face, and he tackled her to the ground. I stood cautiously, holding my arm to my chest.

"Nancy, get a hold of yourself," he yelled.

She tossed her head from side to side. "It's the end. Monsters, demons, we're all going to burn."

"What the hell are you talking about?"

"The world is twisting." Her gaze settled on me and didn't waver. "And you're to blame."

18

I hated hospitals. Yes, over the centuries, medicine has improved. Medication replaced herbal concoctions and leeching. Cleanliness prevented wound infection, and diagnostics actually became something more than just guessing, but underneath the sterility lay the scent of disease and death. Not the swift death gained by combat. Those deaths are pure and simple. This one lingered, hung on gasping breaths filled with suffering and fear.

Once, in the sixteenth century, I contracted malaria in Italy while tracking a demon. I had been new to hunting then, still filled with the rage of losing my family and being cursed. I didn't stop to pay attention to the sickness that had spread through the town. I was a week away when the fever hit me.

For days, I lay under a tree, sweating and frozen at the same time. I fought for every breath and my chest ached at the labor. My arms and legs felt like boulders when I tried to lift them. What little food and water I consumed did not stay down. Eventually, I'd been found and taken to a local convent. The nuns cared for me, but could not cure me. After weeks of agony, I died. Every time I entered a hospital, I still smelled that room in the convent.

I tapped my foot and crossed my arms as I sat in the waiting room, trying to figure how anyone found taupe a comforting color. Esais was still with the doctors in the emergency room. A white bandage covered the twenty-three stitches that ran the length of my forearm. Grass stains along with my blood covered my dress, the lace ripped in several places. One strap dangled, broken. This was why I could never wear anything nice. I was doomed to an eternity of T-shirts and blue jeans.

The doors slid open, and Tres rushed over to me followed by Adrian at a more leisurely pace. Tres looked at my arm and scanned the rest of the waiting room while Adrian tossed clothes at me.

"Where's Esais?" he asked.

I nodded to the double doors in the back. "Still getting stitches."

"What did you do?" Adrian asked.

"We were attacked by the hellhound."

"I see. Once again you let it get away, and Esais was hurt."

I flung my arms out wide. "I would love to deal with it. Do you have any alchemical silver? Silver bullets blessed by a priest? I didn't think so."

"Stop," Tres broke in. "Why didn't you come get me?"

"The police called the ambulance."

His right hand twitched. "I'm going to find this thing."

"Once again, no silver."

"I could make it hurt." He clenched his right fist.

"Really?" I raised an eyebrow.

"Really what?" Esais asked from the doors of the emergency room.

Charlotte stood beside him. Her arms were wrapped

around her shoulders as though she was trying to hold herself up. Deep shadows indented her red-rimmed eyes.

"How is Nancy?" I asked.

"They took her to the institution," Charlotte said.

Esais cleared his throat. "I feel like coffee."

"Let me change," I said.

We rode in two cars to the diner Esais and I had met John at. Country music blared from a small radio on the counter. The ceiling fan spread the smell of grease and meat throughout the room. The waitress eyed my tangled hair and the smudges on my face that only a large amount of scalding water, soap, and scrubbing would remove. I met her gaze, daring her to say something. She cleared her throat and hurried away after taking our orders. I sat up straighter and crossed my arms with a small smile.

Charlotte played with her silverware as we waited for our drinks. She straightened the knife until it was perfect, then moved on to the fork. She barely met our gazes, instead focusing her attention on the table. The color faded around me as I scanned the diner, from the waitress and cook to the couple sitting in the back and laughing softly together. All human.

"It should be safe enough to talk," I said.

Her shoulders stiffened as she lifted her head. Her eyes shifted to the left and the right before she took a deep breath and nodded. Adrian sat with his hands resting on his knees, studying her as if she was an interesting specimen. Did he actually see anyone as human?

"All right," she said. "I've been thinking about our conversation a lot in the past couple of days. I know y'all know things aren't right. Nancy thinks you're responsible, but she didn't see what happened before y'all got here. She doesn't work at the institution."

"When did the trouble start?" I asked.

Charlotte pushed the salt shaker against the wall so it was even with the pepper. "He used to be a good guy, until his son was diagnosed with some neurological disease six months ago. I really felt bad for him."

"Who?" Tres asked.

"Dr. Navotny. He became obsessed with his new experimental drug."

"So, the drug is his baby," Adrian said.

Esais sighed. "All to save his son."

Charlotte shook her head. "I don't know. Patients are selected for an experimental run. I haven't seen anyone return from the third floor."

"Tell us more about this drug," Adrian said. "Has it been approved by the government?"

"He's restricted information on it and access to the third floor." She took a deep breath and her gaze met Esais's. "I'm scared Nancy is going to be used."

"Won't you have a say in that?" Tres asked.

"Because we're related, they won't let me treat her."

"I'll go in," Esais said.

"What?" Tres said.

"Why?" Adrian asked. "She's not really our concern."

I looked between the three of them to Charlotte's look of relief and hope. I knew where this was going, but why did it have to be Esais? He'd be behind barred windows surrounded by madness and open to any traps Ose laid. The amulet was already having difficulty fighting against the ambient madness that his gift had compounded.

"We need someone to see what is happening there," Esais said.

"And how are you the best to do that?" Adrian asked.

"I'm the oldest." Esais met his gaze. "*And because I can read minds.*"

Adrian stiffened, his eyes narrowing.

"*I can go instead,*" I thought to them.

"*No, you're the best we have for handling the demons we've seen.*"

"*And if you run into Ose?*" Tres asked.

"*I'm only a thought away.*"

Charlotte moved her head between the stare down. "I can keep an eye on him."

"Do you have a better idea?" Esais asked.

"Even if I did, I doubt it would be followed." Adrian stood and walked out of the diner.

Esais watched him go and shook his head. He turned back to Charlotte. "I guess I will check myself in tomorrow."

"Are the two of you riding with Charlotte?" I asked, and they nodded. "Good, then I will catch a ride with your brother. Excuse me."

Adrian had made it halfway down the block by the time I stepped out of the diner. I slipped off my broken heels and ran to catch up to him. He paused, watching me approach.

"I can push the issue," I said. "Make sure I go instead."

"Why do you care?" he asked.

"I don't want to see anything happen to him, either."

"He's the best option we have with his—." Adrian set his jaw. "—ability."

"They still make you uncomfortable."

"They're unnatural."

I bit my tongue. He barely tolerated the fact of his brothers' emissary status and was still in denial of being one himself. "They're still your brothers."

"Are they?"

"You really need to reconnect with them."

"What would you know?"

"I know someone blessed enough to have a family shouldn't squander it."

He stopped at the car and stared up at the moon. "Too many years have gone by. I doubt it will ever be the same."

"How did you end up in prison?" I asked.

"You don't know? I thought you knew everything about us."

I bit my lip. "I seem like a stalker?"

"Suspicious. No one ever spoke of you."

"Like I'm the dirty little secret." I chuckled. "Well, your grandmother hated me. I'm not surprised she buried my name."

"You have competition now." He offered a bemused smile. The first bit of emotion I had seen in a while. "Arms dealing."

I tried to imagine Adrian selling guns to street thugs. The images didn't match. "Really?"

"I made the weapons."

"Is that what you have shut yourself up in the garage doing?"

"Holy water grenades, actually," he said. "You and I need to deal with these demons soon. I don't want Esais staying longer than a few days."

"What about Tres?"

"We can't really rely on Tres." Adrian shrugged. "I don't think he even knows what he wants. He jumps from one extreme to another."

"I'll get to work on tracking down the hellhound." I opened the passenger door and tapped my fingers on the roof. "It seems to be guarding the asylum. I think it spends most of the time in the forest between that and the carnival."

"That's a lot of ground to cover."

"It should leave trace energies I'll be able to see."

We rode in silence as he came to terms with what needed to be done.

❦ 19 ❦

Tres slammed the trunk of the car as I stepped out of the house. He ran a hand through his hair, mumbling to himself.

"Esais is all packed?" I asked.

"Ready to go to the funny farm." Raw emotions rumbled beneath the control of his voice.

"You two seem close. Closer than Adrian," I said.

"Yeah, after our parents died, Adam went off to hunt their killer, and Adrian was in America for school. Esais raised me."

I didn't say anything, just letting him continue.

"Of course, Adrian ended up in prison for arms dealing, and well, Adam..." He took a deep breath. "Adam is the reason we're here."

"We won't lose Esais, like Adam," I told him.

He turned to me with his lip quivering. His gaze bored into mine. "Can you promise that?"

My heart raced as I remembered making a promise to protect the Van Helsing line to the best of my ability when Dimitri died. This proved difficult since Dracula had cursed the bloodline. I tried protecting Dimitri's son, Alexander, but

I found no way to break the curse, and he'd died at the hand of the vampire his grandfather defeated. After his death, I'd been told by his widow to stay out of her son Andrei's life. She blamed me for her husband's death, which I could understand. They'd only been married for two years. So I stayed away, though in my heart, I felt I'd betrayed my promise. In the end, Andrei and his oldest son Adam died not to the curse but to demons. Something I could have prevented. I wouldn't fail again.

I stood up and took his hands in mine, rubbing my thumbs across his knuckles. "I promise to try my damndest to make sure all of you leave this town sound of mind and body."

He laid his forehead on my shoulder and trembled. We stood in that position for some time. If this was the comfort he wanted, then I would give it to him. I couldn't see Adrian as the type to give comfort to another. Poor child. He was born into a family that couldn't allow for a normal life. For now, a promise to save his brother and a shoulder to lean on would have to be enough. He pulled away and straightened his shoulders with a deep breath.

"Thanks," he said.

Esais and Adrian stepped out of the house. I stepped away from Tres and walked around to the passenger side. Esais walked to his youngest brother and squeezed his shoulder.

"I'll be fine," he said.

I twisted the hem of my shirt in my hands. The jet necklace remained intact despite the tiny cracks. So far, Esais's mental fortitude had held up. We had to trust it would continue. The radio filled in for the words we didn't have during the drive. We passed streets, nearly empty after the morning work rush. The carnival was closed, resting in preparation for the final weekend. The forest separated the carnival and the asylum. It was the perfect place for the hell-hound to roam.

The yellow funnel had shrunk over the carnival, but the one over the asylum had grown. In the light, the building still looked like something from a gothic novel, but maybe I was biased. A new coat of paint had been applied to the bricks. Artful bushes lined the well-manicured lawn along the drive-way. We passed an unmanned guard station and traveled up the driveway to visitor parking. One of the nurses at the greeting station took us on a tour of the facility, at least for the first and second floor.

"The third floor is for our more critical patients," she said.

"That's where Charlotte said the experiments are," I thought to Esais.

He nodded to the door marked "fire escape" as the nurse led us outside. He already had a plan forming. Several patients were enjoying the morning sun with orderlies watching over them. I paused as we passed the fat man Marge had argued with at the fair. He sat on the bench, rocking back and forth and staring at nothing. His daughter clutched the hand of a tired looking woman a few feet away. The little girl's lip trembled as she stared at her father. The yellow on the man's aura blocked out other colors. I winced and moved on.

My phone buzzed in my pocket. I waved the rest forward and stopped near the place we fought the hellhound. Its trail had faded to almost nothing. What little I could pick up led to the woods.

"Ciao," I answered.

"You love me," John said. "I have your stuff."

"Good. Meet me outside the asylum in half an hour."

Tres opened the car for me so I could get my backpack carrying my sundang as well as a few other items. I walked down to the gate to wait for John. It didn't take long. He handed me a large paper sack as I slid into the car. I sorted through the items before putting them in my bag. The only thing I needed today was the small canister of silvered salve to put on my sword.

"You look worried," John said.

"Esais is checking into the asylum."

"And?"

I frowned, staring out the window as we passed the yard. "He might get caught by Ose."

"He's a hunter, part of the great Van Helsing lineage. He can take care of himself."

"But..."

"I wish you'd show this much concern for me." He kept his eyes on the road and his voice neutral.

"You don't put yourself in danger like that."

"You barely know them and you moved into their house."

"I didn't have a place to stay."

"You could have stayed with me."

"Stop the car."

He pulled to the curb and killed the engine. We were back to the point I'd been trying to avoid since he came to town. Before Hampton, I could laugh these comments off, but something about the Van Helsings caused him to push our relationship beyond the friendship wall.

"I don't want to have sex with you," I said.

"Liar."

"It will lead to something more. I can't deal with another Dimitri."

"But you're willing to risk that with his family."

I threw my hands in the air. "Where are you getting that?"

"I can see the signs. You've only known them for a few days, but you're worried."

"They're his family."

"But not yours. Don't expect Christmas cards."

I nudged him with my elbow. "You don't send me Christmas cards."

He laughed. "That's because you don't have a permanent address."

I opened the door. "Thanks for the order."

"I'll let you know when I get any information on the drug."

He grabbed my arm and pulled me closer. His lips brushed against mine. I pressed my thighs together as heat spread from them to my entire body. My legs trembled, and I was grateful I was sitting down. His tongue trailed across my cheek to my jawline and down my neck. What was one night?

No, it would never be enough for John.

I pushed him away.

"Liar," he said.

I gripped the handle of the car door, not looking at him. "Just because I want you, doesn't mean I will go through with it."

I headed into the woods. I hoped I would be fortunate enough to find a hellhound. I needed to relieve some stress.

❧ 20 ❧

I drained the bottle of water and crushed the plastic, savoring the crinkling sound it made. The last rays of the sun turned the sky a pinkish orange. I swatted the mosquito buzzing around my face. Sweat ran down my chest, soaking my tank top even further. The hellhound had been all through these trees. Fading trails crisscrossed newer ones. I had to come to terms with the fact I was lost. Now I had to trudge back and face Adrian. He would probably take his bad day with committing his brother out on me.

"*Don't worry about that,*" Esais said. "*Marge has found her demon.*"

"*Has she? Good for her. Shouldn't you be settling in?*"

"*No reason I can't do both at the same time. I'm going to give you a hand with this.*"

"*Where is she?*" I asked.

"*About half a mile from you. I'm sending Adrian and Tres as well. They need the experience.*"

"*How are things since you told Adrian?*"

His thoughts filled my head with a mixture of annoyance and amusement. "*This doesn't seem like the time.*"

"When is it ever?" I asked. *"I doubt we're going to get another chance for coffee anytime soon. We need to take what we can get."*

He laughed. *"It's strained, but that's normal. Actually, I feel relieved. I've been hoarding that load for about ten years."*

"That was around the time your parents..."

"When they died, yes," he said.

He blocked any images, but I could still feel the sadness that permeated his mind. Losing someone always left a void in you. I wanted to tell him the pain faded with time, but it would be a lie.

"And it would be demeaning to lie to a telepath while he is mentally connected to you," Esais added.

"I'm hoping finding the bastard that killed them will help."

Esais guided me to Marge. She and the brothers were already among the trees at the edge of a clearing. A one-story cabin stood in the middle. Rounded wooden logs made up the outside and the roof. Steps led up to a porch where three rocking chairs sat in front of a window. A row of motorcycles was parked in front, on the gravel driveway that disappeared into the woods.

"Glad you could join us," Tres said.

"What do we have?" I asked.

Marge nodded to the wooden house in front of us. "The demon and his friends decided to squat in the cabin."

"Do you have a plan?"

Marge lit a match. In the flare of the light, her grin split across her face, and she resembled the demons she preyed upon. "We lock them in and burn it down."

"That could spread across the forest. And people may come. Then your demon won't be killed."

"I don't expect him to get killed."

"What about the humans with him?" Esais's voice reverberated through our minds.

She sneered. "They chose to follow the demons."

"I'm sensing frightened minds in there. Did you check to see if they had hostages?"

I waited for Marge to answer. Her open mouth skewed, the upper lip moved to the left while the lower went right. She threw her hands up.

"No," she said.

"Then we're not burning the place down until we can get the bystanders out." Esais's words drifted.

"Can you see them?" I asked.

"There's a family of three, mother, father, daughter. They're unconscious."

We looked at each other, silently drawing lots to see who would go. Soon I found all gazes turned in my direction. I had won. Damn, ganging up on me. I think I liked it better when they weren't united, at least against me. But, they had a point. Out of the four of us, I would be best suited to get a closer look. I had my vision, while the others didn't really have anything to detect demons. We needed to work on that when danger wasn't so imminent.

"Fine," I said, trying to sound more annoyed than I was. "I'll make a sweep of the place. Stay out of sight if anyone comes out."

The gravel crunched beneath me as I moved in a half-crouch to the building. As I drew closer, the bass from the music pounded in the ground below, sending little shivers up my legs. I pressed against the wall just below the window closest to the door. A cloud of cigarette smoke hung in the air, permeated with the stench of booze. I slid up and peeked in, gazing with my second sight at those inside.

A sea of leather and ugly cracked faces filled the living room. They sat on the couches, laughing as they slurped down liquor from their bottles. Tattoo sat at a table with three others playing a card game. This was ridiculous. They'd come all this way to play cards?

Slow, quiet steps took me around the side. I paused to glance around the back, to ensure no one waited outside. All clear. I moved to a window near the back door and peered through the crack in the curtain. A full-sized bed sat in the dark. Shadowed figures stood together in the middle of the room. They were all tall, with their arms stretched above them.

Wait, they weren't standing; they were hanging from the ceiling.

"*I think I found them. Three, right?*" I asked.

"*Correct. How do you plan to get them out?*"

"*Working on it.*" I snuck back around the house to the others.

"So, can we burn the damn thing down?" Marge asked.

I shook my head. "Esais is right."

Her shoulders slumped, and the perpetual scowl deepened. She crossed her arms in a huff. This woman only seemed to be pleased when she was hurting someone. Her home life must have been twisted.

"Don't look so sad. You'll still have your chance to fight," I told her. "We need a distraction to get most of the bikers out of the house. Then we can sneak the people out the back."

"Okay," Tres said in a doubtful voice. "How do we go about doing this?"

"What have we got?" I asked.

"Kicks," Marge said. "But this would still be easier if we burned the house down."

"Besides Marge. I know what she can do."

Tres held his right hand out. "I can hurt like I heal."

Adrian shifted his eyes to his brother with a frown. I shook my head at him, and the ice mask slipped over his face. I let out a breath of relief. We didn't need an argument now.

"I have developed a grenade that disperses holy water," Adrian said.

"How does that work?" I asked.

"The water is converted into mist."

"There's only one demon. Do you have anything else?"

"A few other gadgets," he said.

My gaze traveled to the bikes and I grinned, glancing at Marge. "We may not be able to burn the house down, but there are other toys of theirs to break."

I laid out the plan I'd been forming. Adrian rose from his sulk and helped tweak the plan so it became workable. I could fight and argue with him all I wanted, but I couldn't deny his logic. Despite his attitude problem, the man was a genius.

"We in position?" I asked everyone through our link with Esais.

"Let's do this." Tres's voice drifted in my mind.

Time to begin the show. I covered my ears and counted to ten, waiting for Adrian to make the first move. With a roar, a fiery ball consumed the first bike, turning the black sky orange. Tongues of flame devoured the next cycle with mere licks. Its hot breath blew against my face, fluttering my hair even from this distance.

It took less than a minute before five bikers busted out of the house. They ran toward the blazing wreckage with panic and alarm painted on their faces. Tres pulled the pin on the gas canister Adrian had given him. He threw it in the window, shattering the glass. There were shouts, and three more piled out the door. Tattoo broke them with his shoulder as he held his face in his hands which were red, covered in blisters, and still sizzling.

Marge charged out from behind a tree and ducked behind the motorcycles as the bikers opened fire on her. Adrian returned fire from his hiding spot in the trees. He'd positioned himself at an angle to the house so he would have a clear shot at anyone coming out. Tattoo removed his hands from his face, which was the color of a boiled lobster.

Marge moved straight for him, cracking her knuckles with a grin. Three of the bikers impeded her, so she played with them first. She was poetry in motion. She spun out of the first two attackers' reach and let her leg fly up to kick the third in his stomach and send him stumbling backward.

The bikers were well distracted. Time for me to get the people out. I dashed to the back and busted the lock on the door with a kick. I slipped through the hall and came face to face with one of Tattoo's cronies. Damn.

He blinked at me as his mouth fell open. I slammed my fist up to meet his chin. The shock reverberated through my knuckles and down my arm as his head jerked back. He straightened and glared down at me.

I drew my sword and backed into the doorway. The hall provided little room to fight, but I might be able to keep him cramped and still give myself room, if he was as smart as the rest of his friends.

He sneered. "Running away, girlie?"

I looked from my sword to him. "Yes, I pulled out the sharp weapon because it makes me run faster. You obviously didn't sell your soul for brains. Pity. You might have made it out alive."

He scowled and punched a hole the size of my head into the nearby wall to show me just what he'd traded his immortal soul for. I smirked at him and held my sword ready. I didn't have to wait long. Patience wasn't one of his virtues.

With a roar, he rushed me. I stepped to the side and let him cross the threshold past me. My blade flashed in the light and slashed through the tendons of both his legs. His momentum kept him moving, but he had no support, so he ended up tumbling into the gravel and grass. Small black stones glittered around him in the dim light of the cabin.

"You seemed to have collected several years," I said. "They don't hold account for me."

I finished him with a swift strike and turned back to the cabin and my main goal. No one else was there to impede me, and I walked into the bedroom, flipping the light switch. The family of three hung from ropes attached to the beams of the ceiling.

I pulled my knife out and cut the girl down first. I caught her before she fell to the floor. She groaned and stiffened at my touch. Her T-shirt was ripped at the collar and her shorts so shredded they looked more like a loin cloth. I gritted my teeth at the bruises covering her arms and legs. Part of me wanted to run outside and make those men feel what they had done to this girl.

I counted to ten, taking a deep breath. I needed to get these people out first. Then, I'd take out their pain in the bikers' flesh. I removed the man's gag. He was thick with muscle, not fat, and his nose hung at an odd angle with blood dripping from it. His left eye was swollen and purple, barely opening when I touched his shoulder. He blinked several times, trying to focus on me.

"It's all right," I said. "I'm going to get you and your family out. Can you stand?"

He nodded. His gaze moved to his daughter, and he began to cry. "What have I done?"

"Don't think about it now. Let's worry about getting out of here."

I cut the ropes. He landed on his feet and rubbed his wrists. I moved to his wife and touched her shoulder. Like the daughter, her clothes were ripped. A purple bruise covered the left side of her face. Her head lolled to one side.

"Can you help me with her?" I asked.

His hands shook as he lifted her up. I cut her ropes, and he cradled her in his arms, kissing her on her forehead as tears poured down his cheeks. She stirred, moaning, and her eyes fluttered open.

"Bob?" Her voice came out in a whimper.

"Shh, it's okay, baby," he said.

"Can you walk?" I asked her, and she nodded. "Good. Bob, carry your daughter and follow me."

I led them outside and along the side of the house. An old blue truck sat parked close to the house. Bob lay his daughter in the passenger seat as I held open the door. The yells and gunshots could be heard from the front, but the cabin blocked my view. Tres backpedalled into sight followed by two of the bikers. A shot rang out from the trees, and one of the bikers dropped to the ground.

I yelled to Bob over the cacophony of battle. "Take the truck, and get out of here. Call the police."

I drew my sword and knife as I sprinted to the fight. Tattoo and two of his minions stood against Marge on the porch. The bikers swung their knives at Marge. She dodged the man to her left, but the one on the right caught her in her arm while Tattoo slammed his fist in her stomach. She doubled over, coughing before she looked up at him with a grin. The first biker had his back to me. I brought my knife low and jabbed it into his calf as my sundang sliced across the back of his upper leg. The man tried to turn, but the wounds had bitten deep, and he couldn't stay on his feet. His head slammed against the porch as he fell.

"I want the demon alive," Marge said. "Don't go using your pretty sword swings."

"No playing around," I said.

Tattoo smirked at me. "Ah, the little girl with the sword, claiming to be my death. You weren't that last time."

I struck, letting my movements speak for me and my

blade sliced into his upper bicep. This demon was too dangerous to engage in banter. I planned on keeping him on the defensive to prevent him from using his powers. He grabbed for me, but I sidestepped him, hitting him in the soft spot under his ribs. Marge spun to his right, swinging her leg in three blurring kicks. Tattoo flew back and hit the ground. She grinned and took a step back, bouncing defensively as he stood back up. From the side of the house, the truck's engine gave a grinding whine, sputtered, and died.

The other biker came at me with his arm reaching to pull me in. I blocked his arm with my knife and cut open his stomach with my sword. Tres touched one of the bikers and blood burst from the man's skin. Adrian stood beside his brother with a smoking gun in hand. Three bodies lay around them, dark pools spreading out before them.

A howl rode in on the wind, rising over the roar of the fire. The hellhound bounded from the woods in its wolf-man form. Its muscled hind legs propelled it in the air and onto the hood of the pick-up truck. Bob's eyes widened, and he worked at something behind the wheel of the car. The lights blinked and faded, but the engine did not start.

I hopped the railing on the porch and ran towards the truck. The hellhound smashed its hand through the windshield and crushed Bob's head. His wife screamed, her wail filling the night air. The hellhound ripped the top of the truck off and slammed the jagged metal piece into the cab. The screaming stopped. I stopped short at the gory mess inside the truck. The hellhound grinned at me, drool dripping from its pointed teeth before it took off into the woods.

I raced through the forest after the hellhound. The orange glow of the blaze behind me and the moon provided enough light to navigate. My heart pounded in my ears. If anyone could see me now, they would have been disconcerted by the wild look in my eyes and the grin I knew was on my face. I didn't care. This was what I lived for. The hellhound wouldn't escape. Tonight we would meet in battle, and he would die by my sword. Of course, I needed to make sure my sword could kill him.

The beast's bulk crashed through the underbrush, causing branches to snap with resounding cracks. I fumbled in my pocket for the jar of alchemical silver and paused at a tree, panting. The hellhound's form disappeared into the darkness, but I could still hear him. I would catch up, but I needed what little light I had to be able to do this without slitting my fingers open. With the jar braced against one arm, I unscrewed the lid and scooped a glob onto my fingers. I spread the gelled substance on the blade and peered into the forest with narrowed eyes.

A growl rolled from behind me followed by the snapping

of wood. The trunk of pine careened through the air and straight for me. With a muttered curse, I threw myself to the side and tumbled between two trees, dropping my sword in my evasion. The wooden missile collided into its siblings. The hellhound laughed as I landed with a huff of breath, then took off again.

The bastard was playing with me, but I was going to end this game my way. I grabbed my sword and dashed after the beast. No way in the Seven Thrones of Hell was I letting it get away again. I cleared the forest into a graveyard and had to duck as a rock flew at my head.

My laugh bounced off the gravestones and filled the night air. "You missed."

The hellhound glared at me amongst the crumbling monuments with its long snout twisted in a snarl. In its hybrid form, it towered over all of them. I scanned the cemetery, huffing to catch my breath. The civilized world had forgotten this place. Grass grew over the tombs and mausoleums with tattered remains of ribbons blowing in the slight breeze. The moon's reflection shimmered in a lake that encroached on the graveyard. The grinding of stone cut through the night as the hellhound ripped the head from a stone angel and tossed it up and down.

"The seer wants me to bring you. She didn't say how though." Saliva flew from its mouth as it growled that out. " I'm sure she won't mind a missing arm or leg."

"You'll have to fight for this meal." I drew my knife with my other hand.

His fangs flashed white against his black lips. "Just the way I like it."

"I told you. I don't make a good meal. Not that you'll get a taste. You're just going to die here."

It growled and hurled the head at me. I ducked and darted to the right, only to find the hellhound leaping at me.

I threw myself to the side and rolled, coming up into a crouch. It crashed into one of the trees with enough force to push the trunk halfway out of the ground. I rose to my feet as the beast snorted and turned my direction. Its roar echoed through the night as it rushed at me again.

Ose didn't choose the smartest watchdog. I stepped to the side and put a gravestone in between us. It stopped short with a low growl. It could learn from its mistakes. It leaned over and swiped at me with its giant paw, black claws barely visible. I pirouetted around the tombstone and aimed an attack at his lower leg. My blades flashed in the moonlight, and blood gushed from his wounds. It laughed a deep rumble until its flesh began to sizzle.

"Silver compound," I said. "Makes a great hellhound-killing combination with the iron."

The hellhound snarled and swung its arm at me. Its fist caught the top of the monument as it traveled to me and caused the stone to smash to pebbles. I bobbed down and sliced into the side he'd left open. I hopped back several steps, feeling a wild smile still on my lips. My breath came in short pants, and my heart hammered in my chest. The hellhound yanked the remainder of the headstone from its place and chucked it at me. I dived behind another grave, and the stone crashed into the ground several feet behind me.

"That didn't work the first time," I called. "Did you really think you would catch me this time?"

The beast's chest rumbled as it limped in my direction. The blood loss from its wounds was beginning to catch up to it. A few more good shots would wear it down enough to strike a killing blow.

I darted out from behind my cover and ran through rows of graves. The beast gave a howl and loped after me. The sound of dirt and rock shifting echoed from behind me, followed by the whoosh of something flying through the air. I dodged to the side, but didn't quite make it. The boulder-sized missile slammed into my left shoulder and sent me tumbling through the dirt, almost into a tree.

The tendons in my shoulder popped, and numbness traveled down my arm. I was almost grateful considering the multitude of aches that screamed at me. I stood with a wince and grabbed my sword from where it had fallen a few feet away. The hellhound crouched with its muscles bunching up and charged me in a limping gait.

I was lucky this creature only had a handful of attacks. I dived to the side, as it opened its maw and attempted to sever my sword arm in one bite. Its teeth snapped together, and it snarled, turning its head in my direction. I dashed closer and landed two quick slashes into its shoulder. It snapped at me again with a bark, and its teeth caught the edge of my shirt.

I took several steps back, but it continued to advance. It raised its unwounded paw and struck at me in a quick swipe. It dipped around a tree, and the claws tore deep into the bark, leaving jagged gouges almost halfway through. I suppressed a shudder. I had pissed the hellhound off enough that it had moved beyond all thoughts of trying to maim me and was going for outright murder.

The hellhound stepped back and kicked the tree, causing it to topple in my direction. I jumped forward and hit the ground in a tumble. I rolled and came up to slash the beast in the front of its good leg.

It hunched and stumbled, falling to one knee with its sides heaving. I whirled, letting my sword follow the momentum up into a slash across its throat. The blade bit deep into the fur and flesh. The beast raked its paw across my bare flesh and sent me flying back several feet, where I landed hard with an "oomph." It made a gargling growl as it clutched its neck and toppled to the ground while its body was wracked in convulsions.

I stood with a long groan and limped over to my fallen enemy. The snout disappeared as the hellhound's form shrank. The fur shortened, revealing the tanned flesh of the man I'd first seen at the bar.

His eyes stared up at the stars, now blinded in death. As the adrenaline faded, pain returned in a rush. My back and left shoulder throbbed where the stone had hit me earlier, and I had a mass of other small scrapes and bruises. I hissed as I poked at the long cuts in that same shoulder. Luckily, no arteries had been hit.

I wrapped my arm with the remains of my shirt. I would be all right. As I strode to pick up my sword from near the lake it had landed while I was flying through the air, a high-pitch whistling sound filled the air, and I jumped back. A small knife embedded itself in the corpse.

"Oh, no. I can't have you armed with that again."

Malantha stepped out from between the trees.

alantha wore a yellow sundress with two thin straps holding it up and no shoes. Her hair was pulled back from her face but hung loose around her shoulders. Her feminine appearance hid the evil that squatted in her. She held her hands behind her back and rose on her toes to peer at the body behind me.

"You have slain my hound," she said. "Impressive. I'll make you regret that."

"He wanted me to regret things as well. You see how that turned out," I said.

She giggled a light, airy sound. "I thought you would be taller."

"I thought you wouldn't be so damn girly. It looks like we failed each other's expectations."

"You are going to die tonight. I've seen it." She smiled gently at me, which was like a shock of ice water over my body. "It will only be a small death, of course. Lust has seen to that."

I narrowed my eyes at her. "What do you know about my curse?"

She swayed from side to side, digging her toes in the dirt as she tilted her head to study me. I needed to get to my sword. I blinked at the blurriness in my eyes and swallowed at the roiling in my stomach. My arm still bled, but I could manage to fight. If only I could read what she planned. Did she have a knife behind her back? If I jumped to the side, I could grab the sundang and avoid anything she threw at me. I took a step closer.

"I always wondered why they went through so much effort for you," she said. "Lust could almost have anyone they wanted."

I glanced at my sword and inched closer. "You can't see why?"

"Now I can," she said. "Your light is so bright."

"So, all your visions don't come true," I said.

"You're referring to London? I learn from my mistakes."

"You never did try to go after the Harkers after that. Imagine, a human fortuneteller could best you. But it still wasn't enough. You're still playing this game with me after ten years. I'm winning."

"Are you?"

"You never found the Van Helsings."

She tittered. "Not until you brought them here, wrapped in a pretty bow. Now we can destroy them and have you for our cause."

"You're insane if you think I'll ever help demons."

The tinkling of her laughter screeched in my ears. "Perhaps. But you will be one of us as well, once I deliver you to my father. Then it will take one touch, and you will be ours."

I darted for the sword, but she was on me in seconds. As she grabbed me, the metal tips of her finger claws dug into my arms and left tiny slits in my skin. With the flick of her wrists, I was flying through the air. I landed hard, and the night turned white as pain shot through my shoulder. She wagged her index finger at me.

My head swam, and I swallowed hard to keep the bile from rising up my esophagus. I pulled myself to my knees and reached for the knife tucked in my boot before I stood. As paltry as it was to fight a demon with, it would have to suffice until I could reach my sword.

She came at me, her fingers aimed for a strike at my throat. I evaded back and aimed a cut to the tendons of her right arm. She caught the blade one handed with the tips of her claws while her other claw slashed at my abdomen.

I pulled away from her, bowing my back and sucking my stomach in. The claws sliced through my shirt, and blood welled up from the shallow gashes she left behind. I hissed at the sting they brought with them. She grinned at me as her tongue flicked out over her red stained blades.

"Bitter with just a hint of sweetness," she said. "How close are you to giving in?"

I growled, a sound reminiscent of the mutt I'd just slain, and spun, kicking my leg out in an attempt to knock her to the ground. She hopped up and forward so that she tackled me in her descent.

My lower back slammed into a low mounted gravestone, and a jolt rose to meet the one that came from my shoulder. I swallowed hard, panting to try and recover the breath that had been knocked from me. My chest ached from the lack of oxygen, and my muscles burned from the intense amount of work I had put them through tonight. In an instant, she was straddling me, her claws brushing against my cheek. My throat closed up, and my chest tightened as the world shrank around me.

"I can see you. Every move you make," she sang.

"I'll just have to take out your eyes," I said.

I jabbed at her face with the point of my knife, aiming for

one of those deep brown orbs in question. Normally, I wouldn't tell my enemy how I planned to attack, but she'd seen what was coming all night. She ducked her head to the side with a click of her tongue. At the same time, I slammed my fist into her solar plexus, and her tsking turned into a choke. It was worth the spasm in my shoulder to see that shocked look on her face.

I shifted my weight to one hip, brought my knee up, and dislodged her hold on me. I scurried out from under her and gave her midsection a kick on the way to my freedom. Sucking in deep breaths, I pulled myself up with the help of a marble angel.

She rose to her feet in a smooth motion, rubbing her abdomen, and waved her fingers at me. Your move, the gesture said. She wore that easy smirk I knew I sometimes wore when I was winning, which wasn't happening now. I needed an upper hand, and this knife wasn't cutting anything.

My sword still rested near the edge of the lake several feet away. I flung the knife at Malantha and rushed for my sword. A clang of metal against metal rang through the cemetery. She slid in front of me, crouching low, and her claws raked the back of my calf. A sharp sting traveled up my leg as my jeans soaked through with my blood.

Her leg tangled with mine, and I tumbled into the lake. I splashed about, trying to right myself as I sputtered. She stepped into the water, her dress floating about her.

Her hand snaked out and clasped my throat. "You know murder is a sin. Let's wash it away."

"She lifted me into the air and slammed me into the water. My back hit the bottom, and all the air rushed from my lungs. The water covered me, filling my ears with that muted flow. I wrapped my hand around her wrist, digging my nails into her flesh, but she held me down.

I was trapped. No way out. The darkness filled the edges

of my mind. My lungs screamed for air. She smiled down at me, her face distorted by the surface of the water. My right hand brushed against the sediment in search of something. Anything.

My fingertips grazed the jagged edge of a stone, and I thought a desperate, silent prayer as I traced the edge to a point. My heart pounded as my body begged me for much needed oxygen. I grabbed a makeshift weapon and jabbed it upward into her throat.

Her eyes flared with yellow light like the funnel I'd seen earlier. Her grip tightened around my throat. Blood flowed down her dress and clouded the water around me. I kicked and slammed my fists against her. She didn't even move.

I couldn't hold back any longer. My mouth opened, and water filled my lungs. The clouded water continued to spread, darkening to match the blackness in the edges.

I saw nothing.

✣ 24 ✣

I kneel before the altar with my head bent. My hands clasp together as my arms rest on the pew in front of me. Where there would be a statue of Cristo instead is a naked woman. She has a slew of other men and women embracing her legs with looks of yearning as her hands rest on two heads. Her marble lips are parted in a smile of licentious satisfaction. Along the walls, stained-glass windows depict men and women in various lewd acts. Incense drifts in the air, filling the room with the spice of cinnamon and ginger.

She walks to me, a red light shining down on her from the windows. The nun's habit clings to her curves with the skirt shifting against her thighs as it moves. Her face is perfection, high cheekbones and a tapered nose on flawless skin. She kneels beside me and places a hand on my thigh. My loins tighten and heat spreads up through my body. I draw in a shuddering breath, and her musky sweet scent invades my senses, causing a wave of dizziness.

"You are lost again, my daughter," she says.

I blink. How did I get here? I gasp, the air freezing in my chest. Somewhere far away, I hear water lapping around me. I start to choke. She places a finger on my lips, shushing me. I sigh at the soft caress and barely manage to stop myself from running my tongue along that perfect digit.

"I know you're tired. You have done much." She holds her arms wide. "You don't have to fight anymore. Come and rest."

My eyes grow heavy, and my head nods. Her bosom invites me like soft pillows. My son's screams fill my ears, and I squeeze my eyes shut, but the tears still fall. For so long, I'd fought and bled, trying to hold my tears back, yet the wound in my heart continues to ache. It can all end if I just say yes.

I look into her reddish purple flaming eyes and stop myself from touching her. The beauty and peace are wrong. I blink, covering my face with my hand to block her out if just for a moment. I'm forgetting something important. The water laps louder.

Her lips pinch together. "Why do you continue to deny me?"

The image of a boy's twisted grin flashes through my mind. The demon inside him eviscerated me with knives. My fists clench. "Do you really need to ask that?"

"It only ends in misery for you. Like your last lover."

Dimitri's face fills my eyes. He lays bleeding and dying at Allegra's feet. My last hunt with him. The world crashes down on me, and my shoulders slump under its weight. My eyes flutter. I long to close them. What was the point of all this? I would never win against Allegra or this woman. The waves crash in my ears.

I stand and move to the water basin near the double doors. The liquid is still and dark. A man's voice calls my name, a tenor filled with sarcasm, but not now. Adrian. I step towards the door.

She stands in the aisle, looking sad. "How many times must we do this, daughter? You should accept you are mine."

"I'm not your daughter." I turn my back and open the doors.

❦ 25 ❦

The moon came into focus first, sitting bloated in the night sky. Adrian knelt beside me with one hand on my wrist. I blinked up at him, and his name escaped my lips in a hoarse whisper. His shoulders stiffened, and the concern in his gaze disappeared into an icy frown. The pale, lunar light shone on the sharp contour of his cheek as he turned away from me and stood up. The waters lapped over my numb legs. He'd pulled me from the water. I sat up with a groan, half-covering my face with my hand. My whole chest ached, as though I'd been coughing too much.

I ran my hands over my abdomen and shoulder. Smooth skin replaced my wounds. My hair clung to my elbows and the small of my back. I would have to get it cut again. Death had reverted me back to the way I was when Allegra had cursed me.

Naamah had visited me again. She came to me at every death, offering peace and an end to my curse if only I would submit to her. If only I would become her daughter. Over the centuries, the scenes had changed, yet she was always there.

I swallowed the lump in my throat, staring down at the

water as it lapped against the shore. The ache in my chest grew and changed to something less physical. I longed to see my son again, but that wouldn't happen by giving in to her. Her words were empty promises and sweet lies whispered in the dark. The only way I would be free would be to break the link. Allegra. Naamah may be the power behind the curse, but Allegra was the conduit. However, neither were here, and I had another devil to deal with. I put them from my mind and scanned the graveyard.

"Did she get away?" I asked.

Adrian pointed to the body still floating in the water. I stood and rested my hands on my knees as I waited for the dizziness to fade. Coming back always took hours to adjust to. I'd never gotten used to it, even after all this time. After I could walk without my vision blurring, I dragged the body to shore and rolled her over.

Her eyes were glass, and her face frozen in a look of shock. The girl, Brianna, must have come back to herself to feel her death. Malantha was petty enough to hold the girl's soul long enough to feel it. Most victims of possession were trapped in their own bodies, able to experience their life but unable to control it.

"Damn." I turned back to Adrian. "You came looking for me?"

"You've been missing for a while. Even Esais couldn't find you. The police are at the cabin. You killed both demons?"

I pointed to the girl's body. "She escaped."

I moved to the shore and picked up my sword. I flicked the blood onto the ground and used the dead girl's dress to clean both blades. Adrian watched me in silence, his face betraying nothing. I turned to him with my shoulders stiff in defense.

"We're not going back to the monster argument, are we?" To my relief, my voice came out calm.

He pressed his lips together in a thin line. "Coming back from the dead isn't natural. I tried to resuscitate you, but too much time had passed."

I shivered as I thought of Adrian's lips on mine. Maybe it was just from being wet in the cool night air. It wasn't like I was attracted to him. Even if I was, it was probably just because of the parts of Dimitri I could see in him. He had his strong jaw underneath that trim beard that traced the edge of it. I cleared my throat and crossed my arms.

"Why?" I asked.

"We still need your expertise." He turned back to the forest. "We should leave before the police make their way here. Neither you nor the hellhound were covering your tracks."

"With all the dead bodies, we're going to have to be more careful." I sighed. "How can we get out of here?"

Adrian pointed to the cemetery entrance. The gate hung halfway off the post. "We're going to have to take the long way around. You think your path through the woods can get us back to town?"

I stared down the dirt road leading from the graveyard. I'd passed this way in my search for the hellhound, but everything looked different in the dark. The road traveled opposite from the way I'd come in my chase.

I nodded west of the road. "That should lead us back to the carnival. I hope you're up for a hike."

As we walked, the woods remained silent except for the crunching of our boots and our heavy breathing. We'd disturbed the natural peace enough that all of the creatures had hidden. The shadows played across Adrian's face. He kept his jaw set and his mouth set in a straight line.

"Where is your car?" I asked.

"One of the churches across from the carnival."

"I guess you didn't expect to get this much exercise when you came here."

He let the flashlight he brought with him shine in front of us. "I didn't expect a lot of things."

"He quickened his steps and moved ahead of me a little. I was the one supposed to lead us out. I doubled my pace, giving up on any conversation at all. The lights of the town showed through the trees, and I walked to the edge of the forest. A few cars passed along the road. I waved him in front of me. He moved with quick steps across the street and onto the sidewalk.

I slid into the passenger side. "So, where are we headed?"

"Marge took Tattoo back to her hotel."

"I guess she plans on moving out after this."

"Not with us."

Marge's hotel was across town from the one I'd stayed at. Her truck sat parked outside one of the rooms, with the bed closest to the door. Tres stood outside with his hands stuffed in his pockets and his forehead puckered as he stared down at the sidewalk.

When the car's headlights flashed over him, he popped his head up. A ghost of a smile flickered across his face. It disappeared as I used the roof to pull myself out of the car.

"Are you all right?" he asked.

I waved him off. "I'll be fine with rest, but we have work to finish."

Tres shifted from one foot to another. "Marge said she wanted to have some alone time with the demon."

I swallowed the lump stuck in my throat. It was a demon this time. Marge's tender mercies could get us the information we needed. But my stomach protested at even the thought of stooping to their level.

Adrian opened the door, and I stepped behind him. The tables and chairs were pushed against the walls. Tattoo lay in the center of the room. On the floor, two concentric circles surrounded the Star of David. Astrological and planetary symbols filled the spaces between the points of the star.

My chest swelled upon seeing it. They'd drawn the binding circle exactly like I'd taught them. Marge stood over him with a knife in one hand and a bag of salt in the other. The demon rested his head on the floor. Sweat dripped down his skin, mixing with the blood from the cuts along his arms and face. His leather jacket lay draped over one of the chairs.

"Where's my contract?" Marge demanded. She glanced over to us, her look of anticipation turning to a scowl when she saw me.

"You look like you're getting ready to eat him," I said. Yes, my mind goes to dark places.

"And you look like a drowned swamp rat," she said.

"Close enough. Let's get this over with so I can wash this junk out of my hair. What have you found out?"

"Haven't had enough time with him yet."

He laughed. "This girl can't break me. I'm an alastor."

I whistled. Wrath had sent an alastor after Ose. They were the bounty hunters and assassins of Wrath, available for those willing to pay a high amount of souls. He must have pissed one of the Thrones off thoroughly. And the alastor had just made a telling mistake. He had no idea who I was. I moved to kneel beside him, and he looked up at me with a grin.

"I'm going to break you before I kill you," he said.

He definitely had no idea.

"Who are you working for?" I asked. "What do your employers want with Ose?"

He spat in my face. Tres lunged toward the circle, but I held my hand up. This I could handle. I stood and wiped my face off with a towel from the bathroom. I turned back to him and let a smile hover over my lips. He sneered at me.

"You won't be laughing back at the Throne." I shook my index finger at him in mock thought. "Now, I believe alastors who return unsuccessful have to pay a heavy price. A lot of pain, yes?"

The grin dropped from his face, and Marge's scowl deepened. Once again, I'd taken away her fun. As if she hadn't gotten enough action for the night. I know I had. I took a deep breath as a wave of exhaustion passed through me. I strained to keep the smug look on my face. I only had to keep this game up a little longer.

"You're bluffing," he said.

"El Shaddai, Elohim, Elohi, Tzabaoth, Elim, Asher Eheieh, Yah, Tetragrammaton, Shaddai," I said, "which signify God the high and almighty, the God of Israel."

Red light filled his eyes, and he rolled on his back, his legs and arms jerking hard enough they bounced off the floor. I stopped chanting, and he slumped. The rise and fall of his chest were his only movements.

"Who are you working for?" I asked.

He glared at me, but a look of fear had replaced the look of derision that had been in his eyes before.

"The big man downstairs," he said through several gasps for air.

"Lucifer?" I blinked. "What does Pride want with Ose?"

"That's above my pay grade. All I know is he and his bitch of a daughter have been stealing from the Thrones."

"But the demons that work for Ose still have an affiliation to one of the Thrones. They have to."

He snorted and shook his head. "Check again, Sweetmeat."

I sat on the bed and rested my chin on my hands. Ose had the ability to free demons from their Thrones. John had said Ose had been liberated, but I didn't know he could do that to others. Not only did it take the power from the Thrones, but it threw the hierarchy of Hell into chaos. It would make sense that Pride would be the first to come after him. It was on the top of the food chain. What did the drug Ose was working on have anything to do with separating demons from the Thrones?

"Why is Ose here?" I asked.

The alastor snorted again. "How should I know? Vacation spot?"

I stood and drew my sword. "You're in for a disappointment. Ose is ours. Don't worry, you won't make it back to hell to receive your punishment."

"Hold up," Marge said. "I'm not done with him."

"No, not your way," I said.

"Why the hell not? He's a demon."

The alastor stared at Tres, a slow smile spreading across his face. His eyes shifted to Adrian and back.

"What are you looking at?" Tres asked.

"Don't feed the bears," Adrian said.

"Shut up."

"We don't have to sink to their level," I told Marge.

She gave an ugly laugh. "They're not human. Hell, the human he's in gave up his body."

The alastor laughed, still looking at Tres. "Your daddy would be disappointed in you."

Tres's face twisted in a scowl. "What do you know about my father?"

I glanced over at the alastor. "You shut up. Tres, don't listen to him." I turned back to Marge, holding a finger up. "So, you're willing to dirty your soul. It's already in danger."

"What do you mean by that?" she asked.

I tilted my head down but kept my gaze on her. "I think you know."

"Your daddy was proud of his family's work. But you've fucked it off. You're the least favorite son."

Tres lunged at him. Adrian grabbed his brother's arm. Tres spun and slammed his fist in Adrian's face, causing him to stagger back. His eye patch slid to the side, revealing small raised lines of pink scar tissue that surrounded his eye. He returned a punch of his own. Tres tried to put him in a head-lock. Both wrestled, moving back and forth. The heel of Tres's boot rubbed against the line of the binding circle, smudging it. The alastor laughed.

The room flashed red for a second. It was so fast that, if I'd hadn't been a skilled hunter, I would have mistaken it for a trick of the light. I moved to the circle, my sword ready.

Too late. Tattoo lay on the ground, groaning.

The alastor had fled.

I dabbed the damp rag around the cut on Tres's forehead. The wound ran from under his hairline to the left eyebrow, but looked shallow. He'd received it when his head had met the corner of the nightstand in Marge's hotel room. The punch Adrian had given him had swelled his eye shut. He winced, sucking in his breath at the sting of the alcohol. He glanced at the towers of books stacked on the dining room table with pursed lips. We'd relocated after our debacle with the alastor to what I'd come to refer to as the safe house.

He grinned when his gaze met mine. "Looks like our roles are reversed."

I smiled despite the fact I should be chiding him for his actions. "I only know the basics."

"Well, the basics have gotten you this far."

My smile faded a little. "They've worked at times."

The times when it didn't work, I'd died. I kept from saying that part aloud. My humanity was already in question. Adrian had kept dragging his gaze to me throughout the night while we cleaned up Marge's hotel room. I didn't enjoy these deaths. Each time I had to fight against my own urge to give up, to follow Naamah's words. Then, when I won that battle, I had to worry about where I awoke. I shuddered and shook my head.

"Ugh," Marge said from the doorway. "All right, to avoid seeing more of this, someone tell me what the fuck we are supposed to be doing? Thanks to the two bumbling brothers here, I lost my demon."

"We're all to blame for that," I said. "We need to move forward."

She waved a hand at the brothers. "These three came here without a fucking clue about what they were dealing with."

"Then we will solve that issue now," Adrian said from behind Marge.

He moved around her and sat on the couch. The puffed-up skin rose around his eye patch. He wore his usual emotionless mask as his gaze traveled over the three of us. I kept my focus on wrapping Tres's head in a bandage, glancing at Adrian occasionally.

"We have been here for a week and still are no closer to finding Ose," he began.

"A lot has happened, though," Tres put in.

The choir began their song as Esais joined in. *"Yes, which is why we need to stop and consolidate what we know."*

"Let's start with tonight," Adrian turned in my direction. "What is an alastor?"

"It's an avenging demon that serves the Throne of Wrath. The other Thrones

will hire them against rival demons. When on Earth, they like to visit the sins of the fathers on their sons." I nodded to Tres. "That's what he was doing to you."

Marge snorted. "And you fell for it like any newbie."

"Like you're any better," Tres snapped.

"I am better," she said. "I know what I fight."

"And now we do as well," Adrian cut in.

Marge narrowed her eyes at him. "Look, just because you learn fast doesn't mean you're skilled. I've been killing these bastards for a while now."

"Why?" I asked.

She jumped, and her mouth closed on her tirade. She blinked at me. "What?"

"Why do you hunt them?" I asked. "You seemed to take a lot of pleasure in causing them pain."

She rolled her eyes. "And you don't? Why do you kill them?"

Allegra's catty smile flashed in my head. Once again, I was sucked in, forced to watch her lick my husband's blood off each of her fingertips. My child screamed as the smoke of his burned flesh choked my lungs. Ice filled my veins, rushing to every part of my body and leaving no room for anything other than hatred. I would see that fiend dead by my hand. It would probably be the last thing I did.

Marge smiled, watching my face. "Now, cut and paste different names and dates. You'll have my story."

"Except for the part where you made a deal with a demon," I said.

"What?" Tres stood, pushing me away from him. "You're working with demons?"

She sneered. "I didn't make a damn deal. We can't all be cursed with immortality."

Five steps took me to the Cajun girl. My fist flattened against her cheek, and she remained as firm as the wall she leaned against. I pulled back, shaking my hand. The split skin stung worse than I remembered. The bitch was tough. Her tongue pushed out her cheek as she ran it along her jaw. Her smile twisted into a scowl. Tres looked on, his mouth hanging open, while Adrian smirked. Both did nothing to get between us. They waited to see what happened next.

"*Children, could you stop, please?*" Esais said.

She ignored him and planted her foot in my abdomen. The kick sent me flying into the table, toppling the stacks of books. Tres stumbled out of his chair to avoid a tower falling on top of him. I pulled myself up, rubbing my hip where it had hit the edge. The mess spread across the floor, all bent bindings and wrinkled pages.

The choir's volume doubled, and their pitch rose, echoing through my ears until I couldn't hear anything else. Esais's voice thundered above it. Each syllable was a dagger to my head. Wincing sent more jolts of pain through my head.

"*Enough,*" he said. "*We don't have time for this ridiculous fighting.*"

Marge slid down the wall, holding her forehead. Adrian rested his elbows on the table and rubbed his temples while Tres fell forward on the chair he'd vacated. After what seemed like an eternity, the cacophony receded and sound returned to normal. The pain became a bearable throb.

"*We have already failed to protect people tonight,*" Esais continued at a manageable level. "*Let's try not to lose anyone else due to our negligence.*"

"*Casualties are bound to happen,*" I said.

"*It could have been prevented,*" he said.

We had a bleeding heart as the head of the Van Helsings. It surprised me, especially with his family history, that he hadn't learned not everyone could be saved. Of course, this wasn't a concept that could be explained; it had to be experienced.

"*Perhaps you've forgotten what it's like to care for the wellbeing of others,*" his voice whispered.

The others didn't notice the last one, so I thought back at him. "*Some thoughts are private. Besides, I helped that family.*"

"*But you were more intent on the demon,*" he spoke only to

me. His next words reached everyone. *"I can say Marge is not working with the demons. Now, can we move on?"*

Adrian gave a short nod. "We still need to find Ose, and we still have two demons at large."

I bit my lip and concentrated on Adrian's words, pushing any self-contemplation away until later. "What have you found on the hospital, Esais?"

"I met with Dr. Navotny one on one today."

"And?" Tres asked. "Was this whole thing worth it?"

"If it's not Ose, it's someone close to him. The man exudes a miasma of madness. It was hard to stay in the same room with him."

"How is your charm?" I asked.

"It's fine. Tomorrow I will scan the orderlies, especially the ones that work the third floor."

"That leaves us to deal with the two demons," I said. "I'd say Malantha first. She is the most dangerous as Ose's second."

"How do we blind the seer, though?" Adrian asked.

"Actually, she is blind to you. Lucy performed a ritual for you and your brothers. It's why Malantha never found you for ten years. I had a similar one on me but..."

But she had found me at the graveyard tonight. She'd known I would be there. My ritual hadn't been strong enough. It must have broken when she'd seen me at the carnival. I shivered, remembering the eyes behind that crystal ball.

"I'm going to have to cast the ritual on myself again before we can do anything. Otherwise she will know. It's going to take me three days."

"Three days?" Tres asked. "That's inconvenient."

"Rituals take longer than symbols or charms, but they're a little more powerful."

"We know what we need to do. Now, I'm going to sleep. You should all do the same," Esais said to everyone.

He barely kept the exhaustion in check as the choir faded

away. I sighed and began to pick up the books. He'd had a long day. Not only had he been admitted into the hospital, but he'd stayed in mental contact with us up until the fight. It was just stress. Still, if he continued to push himself, he'd make it easier for this madness to take hold.

"I think I'm going to get some pain pills," Tres said, heading to his room.

Marge walked down the hall with a wink at me. She even took pleasure in the one kick. I didn't show it, but she somehow knew I was still hurting. The woman was twisted. An itch formed in between my shoulder blades from Adrian's gaze. I crouched down and stacked the books in a pile, ignoring him. The air conditioner clicked on.

"Do you think he will last the three days?" he finally asked.

"He's strong. Have faith," I said.

"That's something I've never excelled at."

He shook his head and moved into the kitchen. The door leading from the kitchen to the garage slammed shut. I walked to the hall and paused at Tres's door, still cracked open. I knocked lightly and opened the door. He had his back to me and his shirt off. Wide scars started from each shoulder and ran down his back until they crisscrossed in the middle. He spun around and glared at me.

"I'm sorry," I said. "I just came to check on you."

"Did you get a good look at what Ose left me?" he asked.

"Ose did this to you?"

"During his last visit."

"You were with your parents."

Tres's mouth twisted in a bitter smile. "He thought it would be fun to play with me. I'm lucky Esais showed up." He covered his face with his hands and ran them through his hair. "I still don't know how he did it. He was supposed to be in America with Adam."

The power of an emissary was a strange thing. If an angel gifted Esais, then it made it very possible for him to travel there in time. Tres slipped his shirt back on, avoiding my gaze. I reached out to touch his shoulder, but he pulled away from me.

"You can't heal the scars?" I asked.

He laughed. "Ever since that night, I can't heal myself."

"Oh, Tres."

"I don't want your pity. I've had enough of that for one lifetime. I just want Ose dead."

"Done," I said.

I paused at the door for one last glance, but he kept his back to me. I headed to my room with my shoulders slumped. The weariness I'd held off for hours refused to be ignored any longer. It dragged me into unconsciousness.

❦ 27 ❦

The door swings open, allowing the light to spill on the dirt. The burning oak Dario had cut drifts on the air. Home invites me in from the cold night. Yet, my feet cling to the cobblestone, and my hand remains glued to the handle. My husband and son wait behind the door, but still I hesitate.

The stars blink out above me, until only the Dog Star remains as my guide. Its light fills my vision. Soon all that remains is me and the light, alone in the cold emptiness.

My vision clears, and the door opens wider. I step inside. The basket of veal and grain I carry drops to the ground.

She lounges in my chair with my babe resting in the crook of her arm. Her black hair coils atop her head like a sleeping snake. The red of her gown clashes with the mauve of her skin. Her lips curve up as I enter, giving a flash of pointed teeth. She trails her claws down my husband Dario's cheek while he rests his head on her knee.

"Welcome home, Gabriella." Allegra's lilting voice rings through the room.

I freeze, my breath stuck in my throat. My eyes remain on my son. He lies sleeping, his soft face pale and relaxed.

"Surprised to see me alive?" she asks.

She stands, knocking my husband to the ground. He runs a hand through his shaggy hair and crawls after her with his tongue hanging out. He presses his lips against her feet. I turn my head and clench my fists as Allegra's laugh fills the air. Blood drips from my palms onto the ground.

"Stop her," *a voice, like a roaring fire, whispers.* "Do not abide this evil."

I try to move, but my feet stick to the ground and my hand slows in its reach towards the scene in front of me. Allegra leans down and Dario takes our baby from her. He cradles him, crooning a lullaby, and looks back up at Allegra. She is the only thing he sees as he places our child into the fire.

My screams mix with the baby's wails. I lurch forward, but my feet are lead. Smoke fills the room, gagging me. I cannot look away from the tiny figure writhing in the flames.

"Marco." *His name falls from my lips with a sob.*

Allegra laughs, reaches down, and helps Dario to his feet. He laughs with her, his face still holding that slack look of bliss. In that moment, I hate him for his ignorance. She runs a hand down his cheek. He closes his eyes, leaning into it. They kiss, slow and deep, savoring every moment, and he wraps his arms around her waist. Her claws trace dawn his chest and dig into his abdomen. He gives a small grunt and pulls her closer. With a quick motion, she snatches his heart from his chest. She holds it out to me with a smile, letting his body drop to the ground.

"You tried to stop me, but your husband's heart is still mine," *she says.*

The demon leans over me, still holding my husband's heart. I try to claw at her eyes, but she knocks my hand away. She grips my jaw in her hand and forces me to meet her stare. An amaranthine flame flares from her pupils. I fall into her gaze.

"I will reward you for your ingenuity," *Allegra says.* "I will make you ours."

The purple intensifies, encompassing her eyes. It slips into the cracks in my mind and fills me. Nothing else exists.

28

I woke with my sheets soaked in sweat again and Allegra's voice still ringing in my ears. The afternoon rays shone through my window. Unconsciousness had held me captive to my dreams for most of the day. I wiped my face and pushed down the feeling of sorrow. My cell phone sat on the bedside table, a gift from John, who convinced me it was useful to keep in touch with people. No calls. He must still be upset over what had happened yesterday. In my fear of losing him by starting a relationship, I may have lost him anyway. I sighed and sat up. Lying in bed wouldn't help anything, and I had a ritual to perform.

When I entered the room, Marge sat with her feet propped on the kitchen table. One of Esais's books balanced on her knees, and she flipped through it as she ate a sandwich. I breathed in the scent of real Columbian coffee and walked to the counter to pour a cup.

"Where are the others?" I asked.

"Tres has run off to his girlfriend, and Adrian's locked himself in the garage."

"So, how long do you have on your contract?" I asked.

Her head jerked to me, and she narrowed her eyes. After another minute she nodded. "About five years."

"Why'd you do it?" I asked.

"I didn't," she snapped. "My mother tried to get us out of the hell we were in and made things worse. She traded my soul, not hers, because I was the one suffering."

I frowned. "I didn't know others could sell your soul to demons."

She shrugged. "Something about legal guardians being responsible."

"That's just wrong. There should be a way to fight that."

"I'm trying. If I kill the demon that holds my contract..."

"Do you even know who it is?" I asked.

She shook her head.

"So you're just traveling around, killing whatever demon you come across?"

She shrugged. "I'll find one eventually who knows."

This sounded familiar. My mind flashed back to a young angry widow carving a swath of demon flesh in Italy. I'd had a mentor though. Good Padre Ricci with his balding hair and watery eyes. He also thought every dead demon was a boon to humanity. Because of that, it had taken me centuries to get on the trail of Allegra. Marge didn't have forever. This woman had been through a lot. She'd come out damaged, but she still stood at least, and I had to make sure she remained so.

"Marge, you need to have a plan. Otherwise, you're just wasting what little time you have left."

"So what do you propose I do?"

"We'll research. I'll check with a few of my contacts to see what they know."

"Mine led me here. You see how well that worked out," she said.

"I doubt the alastor has left. He won't risk failing a

mission if he can help it. By killing the hellhound, we may have made things easier for him."

She finished off her sandwich and stood up. "Well, I'm going out to look for it."

I nodded. "Good luck."

The front door slammed, and I moved the curtain, watching her until she was out of sight. Good, she wouldn't be here to stop me for the next part.

In the living room, I found the bloody remainder of Marge's pants still in the trash. Tres had been upset enough from his argument with his brothers to forget about them, and we'd been too busy since then to think about emptying the trash. As much as Marge claimed to be skilled, she was still lax in certain things, such as leaving her blood lying around for people like me to use in ritual magic.

I walked to the den with my bag and closed the wooden door behind me. I moved the furniture to the edges of the room and rolled up the carpet. From the bag John had given me, I pulled out a jar of alchemical paint made from quicksilver, the reason he had taken so long in getting my ingredients. Most people mistook quicksilver for mercury. It took the most skilled alchemist to tell the difference. I wasn't one of them, but I knew a few. Quicksilver remained a mystery in alchemy, but was still one of the most powerful components. Many an alchemist had theorized on the origins of the substance, but nothing had been proven. I never really cared. I preferred using it for its ability to channel magic in ritual work.

I painted a circle on the concrete that took up most of the free space in the room. Inside the circle came a triangle with its points touching the circle. Within the triangle I painted a square and in that I painted a smaller circle. I set a small table into the innermost ring and placed my sword, a bowl of herbs, two wax dolls, and a mirror on it, along with several black candles. The color black repelled or blocked energy. I laid out a small brazier with burning sage to purify the room while I cleansed myself.

I let the water from the shower run down my body. My stomach was doing flips, and the muscles in my back bunched together. I breathed out my anxiety, imagining it to be viridian smoke leaving my mouth. These emotions would taint the energy I intended to channel for this ritual. I envisioned my body surrounded by a Prussian blue aura. I stepped out of the shower in a focused state of tranquility and slipped on a white robe. I was ready.

By the time I came back into the den, the sage had burned itself out. I placed small bowls of angelica incense on the three points of the triangle. The herb was attributed to the archangel, Michael, and the fumes would dispel evil or hostile magic. I picked up my sundang. Many Hermetic ritualists liked to have a special sword for working their magic. My sword was an extension of me and so it allowed me to channel energy easier.

I raised the blade to my face and closed my eyes. I envisioned myself growing larger and larger until I floated in space, with the planets floating around me. A star hung above my head, blazing with white light. I raised my sundang and pierced the star. Its energy flowed through my sword and into me. I opened my eyes and walked to the outer circle. I moved clockwise with the tip of the blade pointed along the edge of the outer circle. A blue light tinged with gold-white trailed from the sword's point.

I stopped at the eastern point and drew a five-pointed star. It hung in the air, its white light playing shadows along the bare walls of the den. I pierced its center and projected my energy through it until the star glowed cerulean.

"Ihvh," I chanted.

I continued my path until I reached the southern point. I

drew another star and pushed my energy through it as I chanted. "Adni."

I walked until I reached the western point and did the same. "Ahih."

The last star was at the northern point. "Acla."

The circle closed around me with an audible hum. A cylinder of blue white light rose to the ceiling. I breathed deeply and moved to the altar, facing east. I held my sword in front of my face with the tip facing up.

"Before me, Michael," I said.

Michael, the Sword of God, led the seven archangels and was the general of Heaven's Host. His element was air, and he was the Guardian of the East.

"Behind me, Gabriel."

Gabriel was the Word of God, another of the seven archangels. He led the trumpet angels. His element was water, and he was the Guardian of the West.

"To my right, Raphael."

Raphael was titled God's Healer. Many miracles were performed in his name. His element was earth, and he was Guardian of the North.

"To my left, Uriel."

Uriel was the Fire of God, the punisher. He took great pleasure in his work, supposedly. He was the Guardian of the South.

"About me flames the Pentagram." I touched the blade to my forehead and the four stars flared. "And in the column shines the six-rayed star."

I set my sword on the altar and let out a breath. The circle had been cast and the divine entities called for protection. Now came the actual ritual. I picked up the mirror and arranged it so it pointed down on the table. I wrapped the scrap of Marge's pants around one of the wax dolls. I cut my hand, bled into a white cloth napkin, and wrapped it around the second doll.

"I name you Malantha, and I constrain you by the most holy names of God, *Eloy*, *Adonay*, by all the sacraments, by him who has forsaken you. No more shall you do us harm. No more shall your eyes spy us," I said.

I let my will and energy flow into the dolls as I spoke the words. On their foreheads, I carved pentacles, five pointed stars surrounded by a circle. I set the dolls into a bowl of herbs consisting of salt, bay laurel, angelica, and garlic. All were used to protect against evil. I placed a black cloth over the dolls, imagining Marge and me being hidden from Malantha's eyes.

The mirror rattled on the table, and tiny cracks appeared along the edges. Smoke obscured the surface except for a pair of eyes that glared at me. Malantha could sense the magic I was working against her and she was fighting me. The devil's traps I put around the house would keep her from entering, but if she broke the mirror, she could cause my own magic to backlash upon me. I steeled myself with a deep breath and pressed my hand harder on the dolls, as I kept the image of blinding those demon eyes.

"I command you, by the power of the Eucharist, which redeemed mankind from sin, no more shall you interfere in my life, nor in the lives of my loved ones. By the power of God and by my will, I command you."

The smoke in the mirror faded, leaving only a black surface with hairline fractures making their way towards the center. I smiled. The black meant I had weakened her enough with this ritual. I stood and walked counter-clockwise, releasing the energies of the circle. I would return the next midnight and the one after to repeat the words enough to completely blind her foresight of us. Then came the real battle.

29

Marge gripped the chain-link fence, looking up at the top several feet above her head. Small wisps poked out from under the black cap she'd worn to cover her strawberry blonde locks. I snickered. Marge would probably kick me if I ever referred to her hair as golden locks. She looked over at me, her brow wrinkling.

"What?" she mouthed.

I shook my head, waving her on. We all looked like sneak thieves in the tight black shirts and pants we were wearing. The rest of us hadn't needed to cover our hair; mine was black and the boys had dark brown. Tres said we looked like a group of teenagers on their way to vandalize property. I'd failed to understand his excitement, but all my trespassing had been done after my marriage. I didn't feel the nostalgia of my youth.

The fence clinked every time Marge put her foot on it. She paused at the top to survey the area below before hopping down. I watched for any guard approach as I waited for my turn, which came last. The impact of the landing jarred my knees, but I kept my balance.

We'd entered into the food court. Streetlights bathed the boarded stands in a yellow light. The ground was cleaner now than it'd been during the day, thanks to the cleaning crew that swept the place after closing. I wrinkled my nose as a breeze brought the smell of stale popcorn. Still, it felt good against my damp face. The air remained humid, even at two in the morning.

We slipped in between the stands, peering around corners before scurrying to the next safe haven. At this moment, security became more dangerous than any monster. We couldn't kill a human if we were caught. We'd have to abandon the plan or end up in jail. I preferred to stay away from the law. Nancy's suspicions and the incident with the dog attack had already put us under enough police scrutiny.

"How much farther?" Tres asked, keeping his voice low.

"Past the Ferris wheel, across from the roller coaster," I said, pointing.

I shivered as we crept past. The wheeled monstrosity loomed above us with its caged seats rocking in the wind. Metal scraped against metal as they moved. A shadow that looked almost human moved in one of the cars, and I stared hard at the car, but it remained motionless. With a long breath, I moved on. We weren't here for a confrontation.

I stopped in front of the wagon, facing off with the gypsy woman. Gloom shrouded the painting, but I felt her smile. Heaviness weighed the air down as if it was water. It closed in on me, pressing on all sides, and I took a deep breath and let it out, counting to ten. I jumped at Tres's hand on my shoulder.

"This is it?" he asked.

I nodded. My tongue felt thick in my mouth. I didn't trust myself to speak without stumbling over the words.

Marge hopped up the steps and jiggled the handle. "Locked."

"I got it," Tres said.

He pulled a silver Swiss army knife out of his pocket and flipped a thin pick out. He bent over the lock with a penlight in his mouth. After studying the lock, he selected another lock pick on the knife and set to work. In a matter of moments, the door swung open.

"I didn't know your brother had such talents," I murmured to Adrian.

He shrugged. "Did you think Esais would learn how to do it?"

I shut the door behind us as we crowded into the tiny room. Tres played the light over the room. A circular table stood in the center of the room, draped in layers of scarves and surrounded by three chairs. A crystal ball sat atop it. Tasseled scarves adorned the walls, their colors muted by the lack of light. With the right illumination, this would have given off a gypsy feel.

Goose pimples rose on my arms as a chill swept over me. This place was wrong. The walls crept closer. I bumped into Adrian in my haste to search a small table near us. The gloom obscured his expression, but from the jerk of his head, he was annoyed.

"Okay, this place is too small for all of us," I said. "Two can do this with no problem."

Marge snorted and pushed past me to the door, leaving the rest of us to stare at each other. I wanted to join her, but that would leave Tres and Adrian. They wouldn't know what to look for and might bumble onto something harmful.

"I should stay," I said, straightening my shoulders.

"I will, too," Adrian said.

I blinked, staring at his semi-obscured form. Was this some sort of torture he wanted to put me through? I could think of no other reason why he would volunteer to be in my company. Great, not only did I have to scan this place again, but now I had alone time with my least favorite Van Helsing.

Tres handed me the flashlight with a shrug. "I'll keep watch with Marge, then."

I turned to the table, putting my back to Adrian. I took a deep breath and looked beyond what normal people saw. A small pressure built up in my head and released. Instead of the usual gray, the cabin was filled with the sickly mustard color. I gulped back the bile rising in my throat, which caused the burning in my stomach to increase. The same yellow from outside swirled around me, filling the wagon. It reminded me of water I'd seen spill from a sewage plant. I swayed, wiping my damp forehead.

"Are you all right?" Adrian asked. He almost sounded concerned.

I nodded, letting air out through my mouth. After a few minutes, my stomach stopped trying to rebel against me, though the burning remained. I focused on trying to find the source of this. I noticed that the tiny black lines created spirals in the yellow. They floated together, forming a picture if I unfocused my gaze.

"About the symbol you used to protect the house," Adrian said.

The swirls formed the face of a catlike creature, a large predator. It looked a lot like those pointillism paintings created by Monet, confusing up close but could make sense if you stepped away from them. The fangs of the cat were bared in a grin. I had seen that face so many years ago.

Ose.

"What about it?" I asked.

"Is it possible to combine the symbol with another to form something that can kill demons?"

I stared at him, taking in the cool emerald and yellow-orange that surrounded him. Even the muddy red of the anger comforted me. I shut my mouth and shook my head, trying to concentrate on his words. Still, I didn't take my eyes off of him.

"A symbol?" I asked.

"Yes, like the ones around the house."

"I've never heard of using them that way. Symbols like that are very specific in their creation."

He raised an eyebrow. "Am I distracting you?"

"No, it's just…"

"You usually seem capable of talking while doing your scan," he said. "What is different?"

I sucked in more air. "This place is intense. I'll be fine. Why do you want the symbol?"

He cleared his throat, placing his hands behind his back. "I have an idea for a weapon that will harm demons."

"Based on a symbol you've never seen before?"

He chuckled. "Which is why I asked if you had a symbol. You, at least, seem to know what you're doing."

"Is that a compliment?" I asked, a smile pulling up the corners of my mouth.

"Maybe." He turned his head away.

I walked to the center table and sat on the single chair. The black began to move once I took my gaze from Adrian. My eyes focused on the scarf. The biggest concentration came from under it. I lifted the tasseled cloth away and revealed a small table. A rectangular object sat wrapped in red silk. Not that I could see the red with all the black and yellow that radiated from it. This had to be the source. My hand paused in midair. I didn't want to touch it, but I had to see inside.

Adrian turned from the table he was inspecting. "Did you find something?"

I laid the object next to the crystal ball. A stack of cards lay in the silk, their edges yellowed. On the topmost card, a goat-headed figure crouched on a pillar, his clawed feet digging into the stone. In his hand, he held a torch, and his wings spread out behind him. A man and a woman stood chained to the pillar, naked with small horns protruding from their heads. The card lay upside down, but I still knew the name printed at the bottom. The Devil.

I'd had my tarot cards read by a fortune teller once. Dimitri had introduced me to Lucy, the daughter of his Uncle Jonathon. After a few months of cajoling, she'd convinced me to let her read my fortune. I still remember the terrified look in her eyes when she'd scanned the cards she'd laid out in what she called a Celtic cross spread. The third card she'd drawn had been the reversed devil. A pure evil in my past. She'd almost kicked me out right then, but I'd begged her to continue for even the possibility of finding Allegra. Now, I stared down at the same card.

Touch me, a voice whispered.

My chair tipped backwards in my haste to get away. Every card held a piece of that black and yellow, and it reached for me. Adrian's face appeared in my view as I lay on the ground. Concern flitted across his face before he covered it with a smirk. I glowered at him and pointed to the cards, where they sat so innocently on the table.

"Those are the cause," I said.

He looked from the cards to me. "You sure?"

I rolled my eyes. "Yes."

"So what do we do with them?"

"You have a match?" I asked.

He felt in his pockets and pulled out a Zippo lighter.

"That works," I said. "Now we need something to burn them in."

I moved to the table near the back door and lifted a small cauldron. Tiny scratches adorned the inside, as if it had been scrubbed by a Brillo pad. This thing had seen some use. The fortune-teller may have been a Wiccan before being possessed. Not that it mattered. Demons didn't care what religion one followed. I'd seen some of the most outwardly pious of priests become vessels for hellspawn. If you weren't strong of will, they had you. Well, I would use it to prevent more damage the demon could do.

I put the cards inside, making sure to touch only the silk covering. Adrian's lighter clicked in the silence and caught the corner of the cloth. The flames raced down and licked the edges of the cards. I watched the blackened edges fleck away as the fire consumed the Devil. A flash of yellow smoke erupted as flames consumed the entire deck. The smoke formed in the face of Ose's cat grin.

"That should get her attention," I said. "We should join the others before she gets here."

Adrian pulled out one of his holy water canisters. "Then we find a good place to ambush them."

Muffled shouts came from outside. I opened the door in time to see Marge and Tres running in two different directions. I sighed. So much for setting up and ambush.

"You get your brother," I said. "I'll go after Marge."

＃ 30 ＃

My feet pounded on the concrete as I passed the Tilt-o-Whirl. I paused long enough to scan the shadowed space in between the game stands. Though Marge was capable of dealing with several demons at once, I didn't think she was a match for Malantha. That wouldn't stop her from trying, though. No plan and no ambush meant we were in for a hard fight. The best idea would be to find the Cajun woman and make a hasty retreat. We could plan a strategy when we were safe and could prepare. If only I reached her first.

The first strains of music passed me on the breeze. It sounded slow, strained like a player on its last leg. I squinted, staring at the flashing lights a few hundred yards away from me. The tension roiling in my chest and the hairs on the back of my neck screamed trap. But if I noticed this, the other did as well. She would probably be there.

I stopped in front of the fun house. It was painted to look like a castle, with two towers, dripping with black vines. At the top were the words *Enchanted Castle*. Out of one of the windows, an animatronic maid waved a cloth down at me.

The bridge leading into the castle was motorized, with one track running in the opposite direction of the other into the small dark doorway. A chill ran down my spine.

I shifted to my other sight and gazed up at the house. I didn't reel as the yellow and black spiraled out from the ride, stronger than the tarot deck. I blinked back to my normal sight and bit my lip. It was in there, waiting.

Marge's head appeared in one of the windows on the second floor as she passed by. *Dio*, I had to go. I couldn't leave her to be surprised by the monster lying in wait. With a huff to catch my breath, I crossed the bridge into the dark of the castle. Red lights lit a jagged stepped walkway. The walk was set on two tracks that moved back and forth in opposite directions. The walls pressed at me from both sides. I gulped and focused on the ground in front of me, keeping my arms tight to my sides.

Light flared on as I stepped onto a platform from the stairs. The walls appeared to be painted in a castle stone pattern. Opposite me, I could see the doorway to the hall. Then the room began to spin. The hallway entrance flew past in a blur. If I timed it wrong, I could break a limb. I walked in the opposite direction that the room spun, keeping my eye on the doorway. I counted in groups of ten. The door passed the hall on every six. At the next seven, I hopped into the hall.

"Ridiculous," I muttered.

Pistons pressed the walls close together and then pulled them apart. I took a deep breath before I moved in. Halfway through, I couldn't go any further. Every time I tried to shift forward, something held me from behind. I looked back to see my jacket caught on the corner of one of the walls. I pulled hard, ripping the fabric. I rushed to the stairs at the end as the last wall came hurtling toward me.

I ascended to the third floor and ran into a stretched

version of myself. She gazed down at me, panting each breath I took. I'd reached the mirror maze. A high pitched giggle filled the room, overtaking the static-filled music. The hairs rose on the back of my neck. That wasn't Malantha's voice.

I pulled my sword out and a knife from my boot and moved down the path the mirrors led me. A squat version of me raised her eyebrows as I passed a mirror. Some sort of mist filled the room, covering the floor and fogging my perception. All around, reflections stared back at me.

I stumbled into one. Warm flesh met my hands instead of cold glass. I jumped back and craned my neck up at the man before me. He wore a lab coat with the name tag of "Navotny" visible. His cheek bones jutted from his face like his skin had been stretched over his skull. Tears streaked from his sunken eyes, leaving a well-worn path down his face. Yet, he bared his teeth at me in a lopsided grin.

"Enjoying my home, Gabriella?" he asked.

"I think you need to move," I said.

"You haven't changed at all."

Ose's leopard face of the demon continued to grin at me. The pupils of its eyes were heavily dilated until they were completely black. The yellow of his mangy fur resembled that same sick color. The last time I'd seen him, it had a more golden tone.

"You look worse."

"You don't see the beauty? I was like you. Before I'd been chained by the blind, but now I serve something greater."

"You lost your chance to serve something higher. You rebelled against God."

His face twisted in a scowl. "My siblings and I should not have accepted punishment from such a pretender. He gave us free will so we could choose to love him. And when we didn't, he punished us. What kind of mercy is that?"

"You tried to make yourselves higher and failed. You knew there would be consequences."

"Thanks to you, I have found something better. I will show you."

"No, thanks," I said. "I like my sight just the way it is."

He shifted, and a bit of yellow caught my attention. Marge lay in a heap behind him. I glanced from her to him. There was no way I would be able to get around him in the narrow hall, unless I could break the mirrors. If they were hollow, I could slip through some to Marge.

I moved to the closest mirror, holding my sundang and knife in a defensive position. He shrieked in laughter and took another step forward. His slow movements were deliberate, like he was trying to draw the whole thing out.

"Sharp objects won't hurt me, they only make me bleed," he said.

"You haven't been the best of hosts," I said, nodding to Marge.

He turned his head back. His voice took a mournful quality. "She didn't like what I had to show her. Some people can't understand my world."

In seconds, he was inches from me. Faster than the hellhound; I didn't even see him move. He dangled the necklace that hung around my neck between his spread fingers and laughed as it shattered. Some of the shards embedded themselves in my chest. His hand covered my face, and he slammed me into one of the mirrors. The glass shattered around me, and my back hit the wall of the funhouse.

"I can smell your fear of this place," he said. "You are now ripe for what I have to show you."

The world spun. I lay in a glass coffin, cradling the burnt husk of my child. Allegra's face filled my head, laughing as she shoveled dirt on top of me. She blew me a kiss before she covered my vision. I cried out, slamming my fists against the walls of my prison. It broke, and I fell into darkness.

Dimitri floated above me, his hand reaching out to me. My fingers brushed against his, tickling my skin with his warmth. A woman's arm wrapped around his shoulders, and he turned from me before I could get a grip. Still, I fell.

My bones ached from the utter chill until I couldn't feel anything. I wouldn't feel anything ever again. Esais's face passed in front of me with blood dripping down his forehead. His eyes, pale with death, stared at me with an icy nothingness. Behind him, an army of the dead knelt. Tres threw his head back, laughing, mad with power. Bone horns protruded from his forehead, leaving jagged pieces of flesh where they had ripped through. Adrian held my own sword, glaring at me.

"This is because of you," he whispered.

He swung the sword at me, slashing me in the chest. The force of the blade made me fall harder. Blood flowed from me, and the darkness filled me. I'd lost all sensation in my body. I no longer knew whether I still fell or if I had hit bottom. The cold emptiness of the dark surrounded me with no end.

Still, something burned inside me, an ember. It lay sleeping deep within me. If I could wake it, I would feel again. I could be something. I reached for the ember, willing it to spark. It shuddered. No, it couldn't go out. I would be lost then.

"Gabby!" a voice called.

Who was Gabby? What was it? It sounded familiar. My cold lips moved, playing over each syllable. The ember brightened at the word. Yes, I knew that word; I'd always known it. It was a part of me. That name was mine.

"Gabby, come on. I can't pull you out of there," the voice said again.

Shapes began to form in the darkness, and dim lights appeared. I could feel the wall against my back. Warmth returned to my body and my cheek stung. I blinked several times at the blur in front of me. It formed into John Roda's face. He frowned at me and slapped my cheek again.

"Ow, stop," I said, smacking his hand away.

"Finally," he sighed. "Now do you think you can get up?"

I had slid into a sitting position with my knees digging into my breasts. My feet were pressed against the frame of the mirror. How long had I been like this?

"What the hell happened?" I asked, wiggling my legs out of their cramped position.

"Ose caught you," he said.

He pulled me up and out from the mirror. My legs shook when I put weight on them, and I had to grab his shoulders to keep my balance. I didn't let go immediately. I rested my chin on his shoulder and closed my eyes, breathing in his scent. He smelled like the fresh scent of men's aftershave with a hint of rain underneath. I loved it. It was nothing like dirt and darkness. He cleared his throat, and I pulled away, feeling heat rise in my cheeks.

I crossed my arms. "What are you doing here?"

"I followed you here," he said, scratching the back of his head.

"So, you came to spy," I said.

His eyes met mine. "I was worried. With good reason."

"Why?" I asked.

"I wanted to apologize for what happened a few days ago."

I looked at Marge, who lay in a fetal position, whimpering. Her eyes were squeezed shut on her wet face, and she trembled. I'd forgotten about her. I knelt next to her and touched her shoulder. She jumped and rolled away from my touch.

"Not again," she cried. "No more, Dad!"

She held her fists in front of her, not nearly as strong as I'd seen her before. Poor girl, Ose had brought her past up as well. She'd said her mother had made a deal to get them out of a bad situation. I guess the person she'd been running from had been her own father.

"Marge, you need to snap out of it," I said. "What happened to the hardcore bitch that likes kicking demon ass?"

She screamed, struggling against me, and her fist connected with my shoulder. It bounced off after jarring my shoulder bone. I grabbed her wrists before her panic could actually hurt me. She struggled even more, now fully screaming. Her necklace of jet lay down the hall several feet away. It must have been torn off in her meeting with Ose. I glanced down at the broken remains of my own jet.

"Grab that necklace, and help me get it on her," I said.

John grabbed the necklace. She thrashed her head from side to side as he tried to slip the necklace on her. Her screams grew louder, changing from fear to fury. She glared up at me, snapping her teeth in my face. The look of rage twisted her face so it barely looked human. I shivered. Was I seeing the true Marge?

"There," he said, finally getting it on.

The effect was immediate. The struggling stopped, her eyes rolled up in her head, and she sagged with a moan. I held onto her wrists, watching to see if this was some sort of trick. I looked up at John, and he shrugged.

"I didn't expect it to knock her out," he said.

"Help me get her outside," I said.

I stood and rubbed my upper arms. This place still made my skin crawl. The sooner I stood in the open air, the better. He lifted her up and headed down the mirrored hall. I followed behind him, wrapping my arms around me for comfort. A metal slide awaited us, glittering in the night. It had a rounded top as a cover.

"You're joking." I looked from it to him.

"You're just a spiral slide away from freedom," he said, grinning for the first time tonight.

I sighed. "I'll go first, then you can push her down."

I gulped and sat on the slide, closing my eyes. In a few seconds, it would be over. Those seconds lasted an eternity as I slid down the thin tube. I reached the bottom and hopped up as fast as I could. The wind on my face never felt so good. He waved, and I gave him two thumbs up. Down came Marge. She slid feet first with her arms hanging above her head. Footsteps pounded on the concrete as I pulled her away, and I looked up as Adrian and Tres approached.

"What happened?" Tres asked, moving to Marge.

"Ose," I said. "You?"

"A dead end," he said with the shake of his head.

Adrian turned as John came sliding out. He held one of his grenades in his hand. I stepped in front of him before he could toss it.

"You remember John from the other night?" I said. "He came to help."

He looked from me to John and straightened up, placing his hands behind his back. "Very well."

I walked to John, smiling at him. "Thanks for your help."

He played with a lock of my hair. "I couldn't let it get you."

"We need to get out of here. Do you need a ride?"

He shook his head. "I need to talk to you, though. Meet me tomorrow?"

I nodded and he pulled me against him. His lips brushed my cheek, causing a tingle to run up my back. I shivered. He pulled away, with his easy grin, and headed into the shadows. I turned to find both Adrian and Tres staring at me.

"What?" I asked defensively.

"Nothing," Tres said with a smirk.

"Let's go home then," I said. "I want a long soak and a bed and to get this glass out of me."

A shadowed figure stood near the gates as we passed. I did a double take at the worn sackcloth robes and frayed white hair. Tres turned back as I stopped and stared. He placed a hand on my arm, and I jumped, turning my wide eyed gaze to him. He peered at the gate with a puzzled frown.

"What is it?" he asked.

I glanced back at the empty space. "Nothing. Let's go."

That's all it could have been. Nothing, just one hellish long night. Because I surely wasn't seeing ghosts of long dead priests without using my aura sight.

❧ 31 ❧

Padre Ricci folded his hands on the table of the diner. The sleeves of his sackcloth robe dangled off the edges. He blinked at me through watery eyes surrounded by wrinkles and gave me a thin-lipped smile. The lunch crowd paid us little attention. The waitress came and dropped off my tea before moving on to more demanding customers.

"This is dangerous territory you stepped into, bambina," the padre said.

A light fluttering filled my stomach. The world blurred around us until all I could focus on was the man in front of me. It had been centuries since anyone had called me child. Of course it had been centuries since I'd spoken to this man before he'd died. Alarm bells rang in my head, but I still wanted to feel his warm hands resting on mine. I gripped my tea cup tighter to prevent myself from reaching out to him.

"Nothing we haven't been through before." I took a sip on my tea and stared down at the table.

"He's different from the last time we fought him. Even then, the exorcism did not work correctly."

"And we know how that ended," I murmured.

I'd been ready to give in to the inquisitors. If they'd found a way to end my existence, I would have gladly accepted it. Father Ricci had found me shaking and rocking on the dirt floor of my cell. He'd taken me under his wing and shown me I'd been given a chance to eradicate evil from the world. I'd learned a lot about demon hunting from him. He'd given me the purpose of tracking demons down for him to exorcise. Ose had been our last hunt together. It had ingrained itself on my mind forever.

We'd spent months searching out Ose to find him in the heart of Rome, hiding in an altar boy and taking pleasure in inciting the cardinals to sin. We'd caught and bound him. However, the exorcism on a devil as powerful as Ose had been too much on Padre Ricci's heart. When he'd dropped to the ground, I'd panicked and pulled out a book of chants from the padre's bag. My mouth fumbled over the words of the banishing incantation. A wind filled the tiny room and yellow light surrounded Ose before he went limp. I rushed to the father, but I couldn't save him. He died in my arms. I'd been left to explain to the church how once again I'd been the only one alive. The words had been wrong, but Ose had been banished. To this day, I never understood how.

"Have you come to give me guidance?" I asked.

He patted me on the hand. "You are the teacher now, bambina."

"I don't feel like it," I said. "After all this time, I still feel lost."

"How could you be lost? You have a family again."

"Not my family. They're dead."

"All die, bambina."

"Except for me," I whispered.

"Your work is not complete. The Lord still has need of you in this world."

The bell above the diner door rang as John walked in. Padre Ricci stood and gave me a warm smile. He passed John with a nod, but John didn't look at him. John's eyes were on me. He slid into the seat the padre had vacated.

"Morning," he said.

I nodded and peered around for Padre Ricci, but he had disappeared. "*Buon giorno.*"

John glanced behind him. "What are you looking at?"

I shook my head. "What did you want to tell me last night?"

"I got information back on Menrazine," he said. "The drug resembles some basic antipsychotics with a few subtle differences."

"Such as?" I asked.

"The sulfur used has been compounded differently than normal. Probably brimstone."

Ah, brimstone, another rare element that was mistaken for a common one, sulfur. I'd come to be quite familiar with the smell since demons reeked of it. It became especially strong after exorcisms. I'd even found trace amounts of sulfur left behind after the demon had vacated its host.

"So, what does this drug do?" I asked.

John shook his head. "Without a blood sample of someone taking it, I couldn't tell you for sure. For all intents and purposes, it's an antipsychotic."

I crossed my arms and leaned on the table. "So this got us nowhere."

"Well, I did find an interesting reaction," he said.

He pulled out a small Petri dish and put one of the pills in it. He held his hands out, as if doing a magic trick. With a flourish, he produced a vial of holy water. He poured a few drops onto the pill. The reaction was immediate. The pill began to sizzle. Soon, it became a white fizzing mess. I jumped back when one of the bubbles popped and flung its contents at me.

The waitress rushed over. "You can't do that in here."

John smiled up at her and covered the dish with a lid. "Sorry, sweetheart. I wanted to show my friend here my science project."

"Well, take that outside."

"I'm done for now."

A chill crept up my spine as he pushed the covered dish to the side of the table. The contents continued to bubble and pop until the entire pill had dissolved, leaving a small residue at the bottom. There had to be a highly concentrated amount of brimstone for that kind of reaction. What was Ose attempting with Menrazine? One thing I knew for certain, I didn't want Esais anywhere near that drug.

"Listen, Gabby, I want to apologize for the way I've been acting." John scratched the back of his head. "I guess I've been a little jealous. I mean, you always go on about Dimitri."

"What?" I tore my eyes away from the dish. "Oh, don't worry about it."

"No, I'm sorry."

I smiled. "Apology accepted."

"You're distracted again."

"Just trying to wrap my mind around the drug."

He sighed and nodded. "It's pretty crazy. I wonder what he's using this for? What's even more interesting is there were no traces of sodium on this at all."

I looked at him blankly. "So?"

He chuckled. "You really should study up on some of this."

I waved my hand at him. "You know I don't keep up with alchemy."

"This would be chemistry."

I pointed to the slightly bubbling goo. "Brimstone? That's alchemy."

"Well, sodium is used in a lot of medications."

"So, sodium would have the same effect as salt itself?"

"If that was the case, there would be a lot less possessions with as much salt as people eat. But it probably has a small effect on the demons."

The hair on the back of my neck rose. Bob and his family walked down the street and stopped at the large window of the diner. Their clothes were slick with blood, but they had no wounds. They stared at me with dead eyes through the windows of the diner. A woman stepped through Bob's daughter and hurried along as if nothing had occurred. I swallowed hard as a chill traveled down the entire length of my spine.

Why was this happening now? I wasn't even using my second sight. They turned and continued down the sidewalk. I craned my neck until they passed the last window. I stood, causing my chair to scrape across the ground with a grinding squeak. I dropped a few bills on the table.

"I need to go," I said. "I'm not feeling well."

He half stood, one leg resting on his chair. "What's wrong?"

I gave John one last glance as I darted past our waitress. "I'll call you later."

I rushed out the door and down the sidewalk. People glared at me as I pushed past them, but I was too late. Bob's family had disappeared.

❧ 32 ❧

The setting sun blazed against my back as I held my sundang out in front of me. Beads of sweat ran between my shoulder blades. Even at twilight, the heat threatened to drown me in its stifling presence. I drew a long breath and focused. The back-yard of the safe house receded. Soon, nothing existed besides me and my weapon. We became one. I let my body go through the motions as my mind traveled elsewhere.

I was starting to see the dead. I'd seen ghosts throughout my long existence. Restless spirits existed all over the world, and their temperaments depended on each individual. However, I'd never seen personal ghosts. Padre Ricci should have received his eternal reward four hundred years ago. Had he returned because I was fighting Ose? This afternoon had been the first time I'd seen him, though. And what about Bob and his family? They had only been dead for a few days, with the police still investigating what had happened in the woods that night. Could Bob have become a ghost that quickly? My knowledge of ghosts was lacking as I could never speak with any of them.

Ose's hand covering my face flashed through my mind along with the sound of shattering stone. He'd crippled my defenses. I had to face the fact that he'd had a deeper effect than I first perceived. So how would I be able to tell reality from delusion? Father Ricci was most likely not real, as was Bob and his family. However, my next vision might be less obvious. Perhaps Esais was skilled enough to aid me in getting rid of this insanity.

Someone cleared their throat. I spun around with my sword raised. Tres leaned against one of the pillars that held up the porch awning. His arms were crossed, and one corner of his mouth lifted in a smirk.

"You're truly a thing of beauty," he said.

I straightened and wiped the sweat from my brow. "I hope you didn't come to flirt, because I'm not in the mood."

He held up his hands. "Easy. I just came to see if you wanted to visit Esais."

I frowned. "At the hospital?"

"Unless he got out and you didn't tell me."

"I don't think that is wise right now. If Ose sees any of us, it could lead him right to Esais."

He scowled. "Well, how will we know if he's all right?"

"You could mentally reach out to him."

"That doesn't work out so well. He hides things from me."

"It's the best we have at the moment." I closed my eyes and sent out my thoughts. "*Esais?*"

The choir blared with a sforzando and gradually lowered until I could hear an almost whisper. "*Yes?*"

"*Are you all right? You sound weak.*"

"*I'm fine. It's just...trying to be in this place.*"

"*Tres is worried. He wants to see you, but I'm afraid that will lead Ose to you.*"

"*Good point. One moment.*" The choir faded, briefly. "*There. I believe I have everyone?*"

"You couldn't use a damn phone?" Marge's voice sounded like she was shouting into a microphone.

"This is currently the most secure option," I said.

"When are you leaving that place?" Tres asked.

"Not yet," Esais said. *"They moved Nancy to the restricted ward two days ago."*

I sat on one of the patio chairs and drank the bottle of water I'd brought out. Tres came to sit beside me, folding his hands together. His brow was furrowed at his brother's response.

"What have you learned?" Adrian asked.

"Whatever is on the third floor has the orderlies frightened. Their thoughts are chaotic and jumbled. I can't make a lot of sense of them."

"What about the drug?" I asked.

"Navotny's keeping it tightly locked away. He prescribes it only to the third floor. The nurses don't even know what it is. Security has been a lot tighter since a bottle was lost last week."

Pock-face had died during his break-in last week. We'd obtained the drug instead, but I could see Ose wanting to take precautions. We needed to find out what he was doing with that drug.

"Do the nurses administer the drug?" I asked.

"No, they think it's odd that only Navotny does," Esais said.

"I checked out the doctor's house. Looks like no one has lived there in months." Marge's voice pounded in my head. How she could be louder than everyone else was beyond me.

"We need to get into the third floor," I said. *"He has to be developing the drug there."*

A chill raced down my spine at the thought of facing Ose alone in those dark hallways. His hand rose to cover my vision again, and I plunged into darkness. My chair tipped over. I landed on my back, gasping as the air in my lungs rushed out. Tres rushed to kneel beside me. I pushed him aside and sat upright. I pulled the walls up on my thoughts so only what I projected would get out.

"I'm fine," I said. *"Does Navotny ever leave?"*

"For the past few days, he's left around midnight. He stays gone until four am."

He was probably at the carnival with his lackeys, like we'd seen the night before. *"That's when we do it. Tonight, then?"*

"So, how do we get in?" Tres asked.

"The less people we have in there the better. I'm going alone, with Esais to help me get in," I said.

"You're not leaving me out of this. You can't even sit in a chair without falling out of it right now."

"I don't want a repeat of what happened at the carnival. Besides we need people on patrol for Ose and the two demons that are unaccounted for."

Tres glared at me for several moments before getting up. He slammed the door behind him as he entered the house. A few minutes later, the front door slammed shut as well. I think he did it just to make more of an impression on how mad he was.

"I'll talk to him," Esais said.

"Babysitting as usual," Adrian said. *"If you can spare me, I have a project I need to finish. Something special I have planned for Ose."*

"Fine," I said. *"Marge, can you handle patrolling?"*

"Yeah, whatever. Now get the fuck out of my head."

"Gladly. Everyone get some rest." I waited until the connection between all of us had been severed and sent my thought out to Esais. *"Are you sure you can handle this?"*

"I'll be fine, Gabby. Besides you're going to be doing most of the work."

"True. I'll see you tonight, then."

I headed inside the house. I needed to center myself for the mission. Despite what he said, Esais sounded strained. I couldn't let him waste energy on me now when he may need it later. My mental issues were small at the moment. I just had to be on guard for any slipping. I would be fine.

Right?

$$\approx \quad 33 \quad \approx$$

At twelve-thirty in the morning, I walked through the front doors of the asylum with my sword strapped to my back. Thanks to Esais, the guards had turned off the security system and cameras. Then they and the order- lies decided to take a nap. I crept down the dark hall to one of them, a slumped man in a white uniform and took his keys. My nose wrinkled at the acrid taste of medicine and pine cleaner that clung to the back of my throat.

"I'm in," I said. *"I'm heading to the third floor now."*

"I'll watch through your eyes," Esais said.

I felt no change, but I knew he would be able to see what I saw. I opened the door to the inside emergency stairs and stared up. The inside of the stairwell was as silent as a tomb and just as tight. I swallowed hard as sweat beaded on my forehead. I gripped the railing as I headed up. The door to the third floor opened with a creak, and I peeked into the hall. The lights were dim, and besides the buzz of electrical equipment, silence filled the hall.

A map of the floor covered the wall of the nurses' station that took up the middle of the floor. All roads led here. If I continued down the hall, I would run into a set of doors. Past the doors was a hall set in a U-shape blocked off by another set of doors. Ose's lab was probably behind the blocked-off section of the floor. The rest appeared to be open.

One of the orderlies lay with his head against the corner, snoring away. I pulled his set of keys off of his belt. They jangled as I sifted through them, testing for the right one. The click of the lock echoed through the hall. The doors swung in, and I stepped through. Names were posted in the middle of the doors I passed. D. Martin, L. Brickman, N. Parkins. I stopped at the last door and opened the small window above the name tag on the door. The room was made up as if no one had stayed there.

"Nancy isn't here," I said.

"They couldn't have released her early. It's only been a few days."

"Maybe they moved her to the lab. We'll keep an eye out."

I stopped at the next door, labeled M. Navotny. The sliding window in the door was bolted closed. I took the clipboard that hung on the wall and scanned the papers. The name read Mark Navotny, age eight. Almost everything else was blacked out except for one line that read: "Patient in sole care of Dr. Navotny. Do not open door." I put the clipboard back and turned to the doors across the hall. Each of them had a bolted window as well. Interesting, but not what I was here for. I'd come back if I had an opportunity.

"I think we've found the son," I said.

"Most likely," Esais said.

I shivered as the choir echoed through my head. *"Do you want to rest? I could slip in and out."*

"I'm not going to leave this all to you. What if something goes wrong?"

"Just don't push yourself too much."

"I won't. Don't think I didn't notice you're hiding something from me."

"We can discuss it later. When this is over and you are rested."

I pushed any worry to the back of my mind and continued down the hall, passing more rooms with names. How many patients was he experimenting on? Surely someone had to notice this in this little town, besides Charlotte.

The hallway turned right and presented one metal door with no handle and small bolts along the edges. On the wall beside it was a plastic device that had a slit running vertically along the middle. I held up the ring of keys. All were metal and too thick to fit that slot. Trying to break in would be like storming a castle. I'd come all this way to be foiled by a door.

"Well, hell," I said. *"What now?"*

"Hold on, I'll contact Adrian." The choir faded.

The sound of squeaking metal, like a rusty hinge, echoed down the hall. I peered around the corner I'd come from, but it remained empty except for the sleeping guard at the end of the hall. I moved to the other end of the hall. That side was empty as well.

"So you're having trouble with a door." Adrian's mental voice sounded amused.

"It's connected to a key card scanner," I said, annoyed he could pick up on my defeats so easily.

"Move closer. Esais is showing me what you see."

I moved back to the machine, taking in every detail with my eyes. *"Is that enough?"*

"It should be simple to break in," he said. *"Do you have a screwdriver? We could try to short the electrical current."*

"No. Would this involve wires?"

His exasperation resonated through my mind. *"Never mind. I don't think you have the time nor do I have the patience to guide you through it this way."*

Heat rushed through my face. *"I could probably figure it out."*

"This is supposed to be quick and quiet, right? Hmm, the nanites could do it."

"The tiny robots."

"Yes."

"So, we can't do anything tonight. This was a waste."

"How long will it take to break into the machine?" Esais asked.

"I can have it finished in a few hours," Adrian said.

"We try again tomorrow," I said.

I spun around at the sound of slithering. My arms fell to my side, and a dull roaring filled my ears. The creature shuffled down the hall, one shoulder hanging lower than the other one. His right arm extended down into a tentacle instead of a hand. His skin was an inky black. The frame and torso remained a boy, but his face had no eyes, no nose, and no mouth.

"What the hell is that?" Esais exclaimed.

A chill ran up my body, and the hairs rose on the back of my neck. My heart pounded in my chest.

"Something that shouldn't be," I said. *"The demon's true form has mutated the boy."*

"What? How?" The choir faded as he faltered.

"It takes more years than the boy has lived."

The demon child shuffled forward. It paused, its body going into a shaking convulsion. A whistling wheeze came out. He hunched over, his limbs twisting in odd directions. I took a few steps back as he reached for me.

"He's in pain," I said.

"We have to do something," Esais said. *"We have to save him."*

"I will try to banish the demon, but I don't know what that will do to the child."

"Oh, God. Is this what Menrazine does?" The choir hit a crescendo that reverberated through my head.

"Esais, I need you to calm down so I can concentrate." I rubbed my temples. "El Shaddai, Elohim, Elohi, Tzabaoth, Elim, Asher Eheieh, Yah, Tetragrammaton, Shaddai, which signify God the high and almighty, the God of Israel."

Nothing happened. My stomach plummeted. Banishment didn't work. I'd heard about this phenomenon from books, but in all my time I'd never come across one. When a demon spent time in a human host, the body started to take its aspects. The longer they squatted, the more the body became their home until the flesh resembled the demon's true form. However, demons rarely stayed for so long, and the ones that did stayed out of public sight. They tended to set up cults around themselves in third world countries, the heavy religious kind of cults, not the sophisticated ones like the Hellfire Club or even gangs like the D-boyz.

I shifted to my aura sight and choked back the small scream that rose in my chest. Instead of colors, I could see the spirit form of the boy. He reached for me with his left hand, his face a mask of agony. His right shoulder melded with the black form of a faceless demon. It writhed, trying to tear away from the child. It was no use because from the waist down, they were one. I tore my gaze away, allowing my vision to return to normal. This couldn't be real.

"Is this a delusion? It has to be one, right?" I asked

He didn't answer immediately. The child moved closer. *"No, it's really there."*

"Dio è misericordia," I whispered.

"Gabby, we need to do something."

"There's only one thing left to do."

I took two steps forward and drew my sword. His tentacle hand elongated and attempted to entangle my legs. I sidestepped and moved close.

"He's just a child. What are you doing?" Esais's voice pounded in my head.

"I have no choice. The child's soul is becoming part of the demon. If we don't stop it, we will never get another chance."

The arm lashed out at me again. I leaned to the side, letting it pass by me. I wrapped my arm around the child's shoulders and drew him to me. This close I could see the tiny slit where his nose should be. This was the source of the wheezing. I fought to keep the lump down in my throat.

"Shh," I said. "It will all be over soon. No more pain."

"I can't watch this." The choir disappeared along with Esais.

The sword slid into the demon child's chest with little resistance. He sagged, and the wheezing stopped. I lifted him in my arms, biting my lip. I couldn't leave him alone in the hall. I carried the body back to his room. The door hung open. I lay him on the bed and pulled the cover over him before heading to the first floor.

Esais wouldn't look at me when I entered his room. His skin had taken an almost gray color, and his cheek-bones protruded from his skin. Bags drooped from his reddened eyes. I swallowed, blinking back the tears.

"I didn't have any other option," I said.

"I know," he said. "You should leave. I can't hold them asleep much longer."

I took the long walk back to the house. Emptiness greeted me. Even my bed was cold as I curled into a ball with the blanket pulled over my head. The tears I had fought to keep back trailed over my nose and onto my pillow as sobs escaped my lips. The boy's tortured face stared at me every time I closed my eyes. The two had been so melded together I wasn't sure if killing the boy had freed him or sent him to oblivion with the demon.

✿ 34 ✿

The tiny figure writhes in the flames as the black smoke fills the room. Its fumes gag me. My nails splinter as I dig them into the wooden floor, screaming.

"Marco." I say his name through a half sob.

Dario turns back to Allegra with the look of a dog waiting for praise. She smiles and holds her arms out to him. He goes to her. They kiss. She makes sure it's slow, so I must witness every moment. She yanks his heart from his chest. Another scream is pulled from my throat. She lets his body drop and holds up his heart, letting the blood run down her arm.

"You tried to stop me, but your husband's heart is still mine," she says.

Allegra leans over me. I raise my hands to claw her face with my broken nails, but she bats my hands away. Her grip on my chin is like steel, and I am forced to meet her gaze.

"I will reward you for your ingenuity," she says. "I will make you mine."

The purple flames in her eyes fill every part of me. They are all that exist.

"Ah, Gabriella, still in this place I see." Her voice penetrates the flames.

I blink and find myself back in the living room of my home. The fire burns without my son in it. My husband is absent. Allegra sits in the same chair with the demon child in her lap. His tentacle is wrapped around her shoulders, and his head rests on her breast. She caresses his cheek.

"This one was different, wasn't it?" she asks. "Did he remind you of your son?"

I say nothing. She rises from the chair, setting the boy down. She walks to the hearth and runs her finger along the mantel. She gazes up at the painting of Dario's father.

"How many times have we returned here?" she asks.

Over the centuries this dream had occurred time and again. This was the first time I'd been cognizant of it being a dream.

"Even that Romanian boy was not enough. You still come back here." She turns to face me. "You're never going to be reunited with your son and husband. I won't let you."

"Haven't you had your fill?" I ask, my throat still aching from the screaming and crying.

"Not nearly. You tried to kill me."

"You seduced my husband and tried to corrupt his soul."

She laughs. "Oh, I succeeded. His sins were not absolved at his death."

I hang my head, letting tears fall down my cheeks. "I failed. You have him, you live. What do you want from me?"

"You're special." She smiles. "It's so wonderful to see my game working. All this anguish you have. Even if your husband was an unfaithful louse, you still cling to his memory. You won't let another man touch your heart."

"I loved Dimitri."

"You let him go so easily."

The demon child moves to the hearth and steps into the fire. The flames darken, taking a purple color. It spreads along the walls of the house, consuming everything. It surrounds Allegra and me, casting shadows on her face.

"Let's face the truth," Allegra says. "You will always remain here with me."

❧ 35 ☙

I gasped awake. I pushed my pillow away from my face and sat up. The clock beside the bed read three-thirty a.m. Less than two hours of sleep. I lay back on my pillow with a moan and closed my eyes. The image of my child burning in the fire flashed in my eyes. My throat constricted, and I sat up with an annoyed sigh. The point in between my eyebrows ached, and the world was unfocused, but I was awake.

I slipped on a pair of jeans and a T-shirt. In the bathroom, I let the water run as I stared at my reflection. The bird's nest at the back of my skull caused the rest of my hair to stand out from my head. The shadows under my eyes could hide a person in them. Another sleepless night lay ahead of me. I hadn't had much rest since I'd arrived in this town. Maybe it was because Ose and I had a past, but something about the demons sparked old memories.

After splashing some water on my face, I attacked the tangled mess on my head with a brush. I glanced in the mirror at the girl behind me. She glared at me, her beautiful form a mangled mess. I tried to save her only to have the hellhound slaughter her with her parents. I spun around and stared into empty air. The mirror held only my reflection. I set the brush down and rubbed my eyes. This lack of sleep had me seeing apparitions.

Classic rock blared from the garage. Adrian must be working hard there. I wandered through the kitchen and opened the refrigerator. My gaze played over the lunch meat, milk, and leftover Chinese food before closing the door. A guitar riff dragged my attention back to the door that led to the garage. My hand paused on the door handle as I looked back on the hallway, cold and empty. The door creaked as I opened it. I couldn't hear it as much as feel the vibration it made.

Adrian hunched over a workbench with his back to me. Styx's "Renegade" played from a radio sitting on the corner of the workbench. I moved closer to see what he was working on. On a cloth lay pieces to several different guns. A handle from what looked to be a flintlock sat beside the cylinder of a revolver. He looked up from examining the metal cylinder when I cleared my throat.

"You should be in bed," he said, turning back to the barrel.

"I couldn't sleep," I said.

"So you decided to come bother me?"

"I didn't see a 'do not disturb' sign."

"What do you want?"

"I came to see what you are working on."

He pointed to the wall where a series of sketches hung. They were circles from my sketch book. I recognized the banishing circle and the demon-binding circle. I rested my hand on my chin as I studied the largest one in the center. The symbols along the outer edge were for the binding circle, but the design was used for the banishing circle. Padre Ricci stepped up beside me and squinted at the symbols.

"This could destroy a demon," he said.

"Where did you get this symbol?" I asked Adrian.

"I created it from the others. I'm surprised no one has tried it."

"It's impossible for humans to do. If the symbol is incorrect, the magic doesn't work or there are disastrous consequences."

Ose's banishment from so many years ago flashed in my mind. He'd said my mistake at the words had changed him, shown him the truth. I'd driven him mad, and now he intended to do the same to me. I shuddered, and Padre Ricci placed a hand on my shoulder. I smiled at him and stiffened as I remembered he wasn't real.

Adrian frowned over at me. "Someone had to create them in the first place."

"They were secrets whispered by spirits. Only they..." I trailed off as I stared hard at Adrian with my aura sight.

The ghostly woman leaned over his shoulder, still whispering in his ear. She touched his hand as he picked up a metal tube. Humans couldn't make a new circle, but spirits could. And emissaries, those touched by spirits, always broke the rules of magic. Spirits were the ones who taught magic to humans. Adrian's inspiration from this spirit allowed him to accomplish something I'd never seen before, the formation of a new Hermetic Circle.

"So, how does this all work?" I asked.

He held the tube in my direction. "This propels gas into the chamber and burns the symbol onto the bullet as it is fired."

"So, no tiny robots?"

"No."

I wandered over to the radio and fiddled with the dial. The music became replaced with static as I searched for another station. He paused and set the tube down, turning his whole body in my direction.

"Is there something else you want?" he asked.

I shrugged. "This is the only part of the house that didn't seem empty."

"So you came here looking for comfort."

"No," I said, defensively. "Why would I need comfort?"

"I don't know, perhaps you're sentimental, like my brother."

"He told you about the boy?"

"I was still connected to the two of you."

"You disapprove?"

He turned back to the table and picked up the barrel again. After examining it in the light, he took a file and began working on the inside. "Esais believes in the good of everyone. That is going to get him killed one day. If you think the same thing, then I'm surprised you've survived as long as you have."

I'd seen plenty of examples throughout my life. One man killing another over money or a woman. The main reason most people obeyed the law was because they were afraid of getting caught. It made tempting humans so easy for demons. What better way to use a soul than to sell it for a wish?

"I have seen it, but maybe there is something to what your brother believes. Why do you do this if not to help people?" I asked.

"You know about the oath."

"You mean that is the only reason you hunt?"

"It is the family business."

I snorted. "One you haven't been involved in for years, from what I've heard."

"Maybe you should stop listening to stories."

"Maybe you should start listening to others."

He rolled his eyes. "And the monster lectures the hunter."

"Back to the insults." I threw my hands up. "I guess I was lucky for a few days' reprieve."

He set the barrel back down and let out a deep sigh. He moved between the radio and me, changing the station back to classic rock.

"I agreed for us to work together. That doesn't mean we need to have any heart to hearts."

I stepped back from him, but he continued to meet my gaze with his glare. I must have been addled in the brain to think I should seek Adrian out for comfort. Strangers would have offered more solace.

"You're right," I said. "I shouldn't have thought there would be anything more."

"That is your mistake."

"I won't make it again."

I pushed the door shut and leaned against it. The air conditioner clicked on, replacing the silence. The dark hallway yawned before me. To hell with it. If I was going to feel sorry for myself, I might as well do it with alcohol and not alone in this house. I called John.

❧ 36 ❧

"Where do you want to go?" John asked when I closed the car door.

"Does your hotel have a minibar?" I asked.

"I have some beer and a bottle of bourbon."

"Your place, then."

I turned on the radio. The Ramones' "I Wanna Be Sedated" blared out at me. I hummed along as the houses passed by. If I ever needed sedation, tonight would be the time. John chuckled.

"Do you like anything modern?" he asked.

I shrugged and started to sing. Music was one of my joys in life. If a song moved me or fit my mood, I treasured it, despite its time period. I stared out the window. The town's bedtime had passed long ago, but Bob and family had forgotten that. They stood outside Rickie's Diner. A chill ran down my spine.

"What's wrong?" John asked.

I started, glancing back at him. "What?"

"You stopped singing."

"Nothing."

I leaned back and closed my eyes. Whatever I saw was in my own head. I concentrated on the blackness and cleared my mind of any thoughts. John's hand on my arm woke me. I blinked the blurriness from my eyes. The white brick of the Hampton Inn stood before our parked car.

"Living the high life?" I asked with a smirk.

"Are you expecting a five star hotel in this Po-dunk town?" he asked.

We took one of the side doors and traveled up to the second floor. A porcelain vase sat on a white marble table. Replicas of classic paintings hung on the walls in gilded frames. I followed the flower design on the thick red carpet to John's door. He unlocked it, and I slipped under his arm as he held it open for me. I sat on the four-poster bed, playing with the pattern on the white bedspread while John opened the small refrigerator. I took the beer bottle from him as he sat down. I twisted off the cap and took a long drink. Little bits of ice clung to my esophagus, making me cough.

"So, you want to tell me what's bothering you?" he asked.

I took another sip of the beer, smacking my lips at the bitterness. This was my reason to come here. So why were the words stuck in my throat? I'd known John for years, and he'd always been supportive. Persistently so. After I'd killed his wife, I told him to pick up the pieces of his life. Instead, he'd followed me everywhere, claiming to want to help, but he'd gotten in the way more than being useful. I'd had to be abusive almost to the point of hurting him. He'd disappeared for months, long enough for me to think I was finally rid of him. When I saw him again, he'd brought me information. Reliable information. He'd used his background in journalism to build contacts. From then on, he'd been a pillar of support. And here I was, having trouble divulging my problems. I opened my mouth and shut it again. I held my index finger up to him and downed my beer.

"I'm seeing things...people," I said. "Ones that have died."

"You see dead people?" he asked with a grin.

I tilted my head to the side and pursed my lips. "Didn't I just say that?"

He shook his head. "Never mind. So, ghosts?"

I held up the remains of my amulet. "That night at the funhouse, he affected me more than I thought."

He stood up and pulled another beer from the refrigerator. Our hands brushed, his warmth contrasting with the frostiness of the beer. I shivered, wanting more. I opened the bottle and took a deep gulp.

"Thanks," I said.

"So, you're having delusions? Of who?"

"People from the past and from here."

"The past like Dimitri?"

I took another drink. Allegra laughed and leaned against the wall near the window. She crossed her arms and blew me a kiss.

"I told you," she said. "Always."

I covered my face with my hand. Tears spilled from my eyes, and my throat closed up. I whimpered, my face contorting into a grimace. John put his hand on my shoulder, but I moved away. The bed shifted as he stood. I heard the hum of the refrigerator and the tinkling of ice. He replaced my beer with a glass.

"It's time for something stronger," he said.

I drained the drink, enjoying the burn as it traveled down. I sniffed and held the glass out to him, waving for another. He brought it to me. By the fourth, the tears had subsided. I stared down at my hands.

"In my time, a woman was supposed to be docile and chaste," I said. "She tended to her family and supported her husband. It was a woman's honor."

He handed me the refilled glass. "Sounds nothing like you."

"Mmm. I was an honorable wife until my husband strayed. Even beyond then. I waited. But he stopped coming home. Our livelihood was in danger, and when I found Allegra, I had to do something."

"You killed her."

"I failed." I traced my finger along the rim of the glass. "I wonder if I should have taken the woman's honor and done nothing. Would that have been better? I would have had my son."

"You tried to do what was right. To stop the demon."

"Then I should have called a priest." I drained the glass and let it fall to the ground. I lay back on the bed.

He lay down beside me, propping his head up with his hand. His brow wrinkled, and he worked his jaw in thought. "What about all you've done over the centuries? All the demons you killed."

I snorted. "I think the Church would have handled it eventually."

"I would have died without you."

I didn't know what to say to that. Were all the people I saved worth my unhappiness? If these delusions continued, I wouldn't be able to save anyone. I covered my eyes with my arm.

"What use am I if I can't tell what's real and what's not?" I asked. "I'm losing the only thing I have of worth."

He pulled my hand from my arm and stared into my eyes. "Do what you came here to do. Kill Ose."

"What?"

"It's his power. Kill him and you get your mind back."

"But what if I fail?"

"You won't. You're the invincible, Gabriella Di Luca."

I smiled and leaned up to kiss his cheek. At the scent of

his aftershave, I shuddered. Allegra's husky laugh filled my ears. I pushed his shoulder until he lay flat on his back and straddled him, my heart pounding in my chest. He smiled up at me.

"I thought you didn't want to have sex with me," he said.

I quieted his voice with my mouth. His lips opened, and our tongues twined together. I played with the edges of his shirt before yanking it up. He moaned as I gently raked my nails down his bare chest. I ground my pelvis into his, savoring the warmth that spread from between my legs every time I pressed into his hard cock.

He pulled the buttons of my blouse until they came undone. I tossed it away with my bra. He leaned up and caught my nipple in his mouth. I gasped, my breath coming out in a hot sigh. My whole body tingled deliciously. It had been too long.

He rolled us until he straddled me. His gaze traveled down my body, his eyes dark with desire. I let my sight change and watched our auras as they began to meld, both iridescent pink with passion. His was tinged yellow with triumph. He'd been waiting for this.

He leaned his head down, trailing kisses along my breasts and to my stomach. His tongue circled my belly button. I shivered. He unbuttoned my pants and slid them off me. My panties came next. He ran his tongue along the side of my lips before pressing it against my clit. I arched against him, burying my hands in his hair. The air was thick and hot with the musk of our passion.

His fingers dug into my hips as his tongue plunged inside of me. I raised a hand to my mouth, biting down on my finger. I writhed beneath his ministrations, building more and more until I could almost burst. He pulled away, and coldness washed over me. Eternity passed in the mere seconds he was gone. He returned, his hard shaft pressed against me.

His eyes were almost black. "You're beautiful."

He rammed his hard cock into me. Our flesh radiated with searing heat. Allegra had disappeared. All that mattered was this man filling me. Our hips met and pulled away in a fast needy rhythm, our moans mixing. The colors of our auras swirled together. I exploded, shattering into a thousand pieces. He stiffened and throbbed inside of me, burying his face in my hair.

He rolled off me, and lay on his back, panting. I rested my head on his shoulder and yawned, my eyes fluttering. John's warmth had filled me and given me a moment's respite from the cold reality and illusion of my life. Everything else faded to the background.

❧ 37 ❧

As the evening sun shone in my eyes, my problems returned with a headache. I groaned and buried my face in the pillow. My arm patted the other side of the bed. Empty.

I threw the pillow aside and looked around the room. John had left me alone. On the table sat a tray with a bagel and orange juice. Allegra sat at the table, dangling a note in front of me.

"He's adorable. So good you found another distraction," she said. "It doesn't make a difference."

I stalked to the bathroom and slammed the door behind me. I let the faucet run, the hot water steaming up the mirror. Every fiber inside me wanted to kill her, but she wasn't really here. I would just end up attacking a chair or the wall. She had disappeared when I walked back into the room.

I picked up the note from the table and scanned it. John had gone to try and find something to stave off my madness. A smile touched my lips. He was starting to remind me of a knight, trying to slay the dragons I couldn't. I had to do my part, too. I was the one with a sword after all.

I called a taxi to take me back to the house. Adrian sat in the kitchen. He watched me enter as he stirred his coffee.

"Where have you been?" he asked.

"Out, nothing to do with business."

He frowned. "Out playing then. While my brother is lying in the hospital."

"Are you trying to guilt trip me?"

"This isn't the time to play around."

He was back to finding reasons to blame me again. I'd had a respite since the night of the carnival. I must have annoyed him very much last night. Or perhaps he was taking his frustrations out on me.

"What is your issue with me now?" I asked. "Is it the fact I came back to life?"

He moved to the sink to wash his cup. "Humans can't do that."

"It's part of my curse."

"Immortality doesn't sound like much of a curse."

"It is if I can't be happy. I'm forced to stay as I am. I can't grow old...I can't have children. I just die over and over again."

He paused, glancing at me over his shoulder. "How does it work?"

"I'm not certain. For all purposes, I've been told I was dead. Over time, my body heals, and I return to life."

A thoughtful look crossed his face. "To what extent?"

I tilted my head. "What do you mean?"

"You can be drowned. What about shooting? Decapitation?"

"I was trapped in a burning building once."

I could still remember the lick of flames on my skin and the smoke that choked my lungs. Allegra stood laughing over me as I lay tied on her floor. I'd found her in a brothel in Sweden. She had once again been seducing men and leading them astray. As a demon of lust, she was adept at this. I'd snuck in there expecting to catch her unaware. She'd caught me instead. The incense she had used knocked me unconscious, along with the rest of the people in the house. When I'd woken, smoke and fire surrounded me. Her parting laugh rang through my ears as the flames consumed me.

"And you are still here," he said.

"I woke up someplace else months later," I said.

It had been my old home, the one my son had been born and died in. Of course, this had been over a century later, and the house had been rebuilt with a new family living there. They'd been shocked when I had shown up in their kitchen. They suspected me of being the very beings I hunted. I'd had to flee the entire town that night, but I'd made sure to own that home eventually.

"So, you recuperate. Is it always in the same place?"

"Yes." My voice warbled at bit.

"Why?"

I glanced up at him, confused. "Why what?"

"Why did it curse you? You said it was a demon, correct?"

"I tried to kill her. I thought I had, but she showed me how wrong I was."

I could see her again, smiling with her hand covered in my husband's blood. My baby's screams still filled my ears. I blinked back the tears, forcing the memory to fade in the background.

"Then, why didn't she just kill you, like Malantha did Adam or Ose and my parents?"

I met his gaze. In the last question, I had actually heard emotion. His eyes held resentment. He wanted to know why I was so special. More deserving. I wasn't. At least I didn't think so, but I never had a say in anything that happened. Not with me, and not with Adam.

"I think it was because I could see what she was. It caught

her attention. And maybe I was the first to hurt her in a long time."

"As usual, the humans get the short end, while the monsters get rewarded." He set the clean cup down with a loud clink.

I bowed my head. "I wish it had been different."

"Wishes don't come true."

He walked down the hall, away from me. I followed, unsure of what else to do. There wasn't much of a distance he could put between us.

"This is no gift to me. I can't change, I can't die, and I can't be happy," I said, my fists clenching.

"But you are still here," he snapped. "We don't get to be happy, either. Do you know what happens when a Van Helsing has a child? We die. Hopefully, we get a few years to spend with that child. My father was lucky. He was able to have four of us. But he still died and my mother with him."

"At least you have the hope of peace. I have a choice of sitting alone somewhere and losing my mind or doing this."

He sighed with his shoulders slumping. "This isn't a game of who has it worse."

"No," I said, lowering my voice. "But I'm tired of you resenting me for something that I don't want."

He looked down at his hands, and for once, I had a glimpse of what he was feeling. I even agreed with him. The world was bad enough with sickness, poverty, and humans killing each other. Add the supernatural on top of that, and it was amazing anyone could find a bit of happiness. Most of humanity did it by disbelieving in anything that didn't fit into their idea of reality. They forgot or found convenient explanations for the otherworldly. Those of us who couldn't, we fought it, but we were never happy. Marge was right. Our stories remained almost identical except for the names and minor details.

Adrian had a right to be angry. It wasn't just this genera-tion that had to deal with the creatures of the dark. His family had a legacy and a curse. And after generations, they were known. Vampires across the world would pay to see the entire bloodline wiped out. Now, the demons were trying to accomplish that goal as well, and the Van Helsings rarely ever hunted them. It was all because Andrei wanted to create an organization for hunters. If we survived this, it was a dream I would make damn sure came true.

"Adrian," I said and stopped, looking around the silent house. Was he the only one here? "Where's Tres?"

He shook his head. "I haven't seen him."

A chill ran down my spine. "All day?"

I ran to Tres's room, throwing the door open. Empty. The bed was made, like it hadn't been slept in. I turned and started when I found Allegra standing directly behind me.

"One down, two more that you will get killed," she whispered.

Adrian watched me oddly as I skirted around her and headed back to him. "What are you doing?"

I held a finger up. *"Esais, have you seen Tres?"*

"No, why?" He still sounded exhausted.

"I think he's missing."

There was a pause. *"I can't sense his thoughts."*

"What does that mean? Is he dead?" It felt as if a hand closed over my heart. Could Allegra's words be true?

"No, I would have felt that. He's unconscious. I can't pinpoint where exactly, though."

I shivered again and looked to Adrian. "I think Ose has Tres."

A mask shifted over his face. "Where?"

I spoke aloud this time so Adrian could be included. "Did anyone at the asylum see him?"

"No," Esais said after a moment. *"Not even the third floor."*

"We'll check the fair, then." I nodded to Adrian. "Call Marge. I'll get my things. Oh, and bring your toys. I want this place taken out permanently."

I headed to my room and closed the door behind me. Tres was still alive. We had to hurry to make sure he stayed that way.

"You're just going to get these boys killed." Allegra sat on my bed, with one leg crossed over the other.

She was taunting me now. As always, she wanted me to doubt myself, to break. That wouldn't happen. For over four hundred years, I hadn't broken. I certainly wouldn't due to a facsimile from my own mind. I changed clothes and sheathed my knives.

"You can keep ignoring me, but I won't leave," she said. "I'll always be with you."

I picked up my sundang, examining the blade. The sharpness hadn't worn down. How I wished to plunge it in her heart and watch the life drain away.

"You're going to fail your Dimitri again," she said.

"Don't talk about him," I snapped, spinning around.

Her smile widened. Now she had elicited a response from me. "Oh, but it's true. Even if you fight Ose, these children will die."

"Stop saying that," I said. "It won't happen."

"Your track record says otherwise."

"They'll all get through this," I said, "even if I have to sacrifice myself."

"How would you do that?" Allegra asked. "You can't die."

I looked down at my sword, unable to answer.

$$\approx \quad 38 \quad \approx$$

A gain I stood before the Enchanted Castle in the dead of night. This time, I carried two gas cans in my hands. Adrian and Marge stood beside me. I stared up at the painted stones and trembled. The drawbridge beckoned us in. Wisps of shadows danced on my peripheral, and it felt as if my mind itched. I didn't want to look at this with my second sight. It would be the same.

"How do you want to do this?" I asked.

"You spread the gas, and I will set the charge," Adrian said.

"Charge?"

He held a small cylinder. "It only took a few moments, while you moped in your room and Marge came back from whatever she was doing."

"I wasn't moping."

"Just like you're human. Not the point now; we need to douse the inside and outside. Once we are a safe distance, I will activate the charge. It will create a spark to start the fire."

"I'm not going back in there," Marge said. "I'll do whatever you need out here, but I sure as hell am not going inside."

My grip tightened on the handle of the gas can as I turned back to the funhouse. If I had a choice, I wouldn't go back in, either. That would leave Adrian alone in there, however. Despite my wanting to ignore them, Allegra's words stuck with me. I would not let this Van Helsing be killed. Nor his brothers. I hadn't been there for Adam, but I would for them.

"I suppose that leaves the two of us," I said. "Do you need to set the charge inside?"

He nodded.

"I'll go with you and pour the gas." I hesitated, looking up to the second floor. A cold sweat broke over my skin, and I smacked my lips at the dryness in my mouth.

"Would you like me to go first?" Adrian asked.

"Since you volunteered." I set one of the gas cans in front of Marge. "We'll meet back here."

Adrian snorted and took a step toward the bridge. Marge grabbed the gas can and headed for the back. I pulled a flashlight out and shone it at the dark hole. The funhouse was powered down this time. I sighed with both disappointment and relief. I'd hoped Ose had been the one to have Tres, but he wasn't here. We would have to deal with him later. For now, we needed to get Tres and remove this as a base of operations. Adrian stopped at the entrance and looked back at me. His finger tapped on the side of the building with a steady rap.

"Are you coming?" he asked.

I gave the building another glance before catching up with him. He shook his head at me and stepped inside. With no power, the first trap remained motionless. I splashed the gasoline on the wall, the stench swirling around me. My chest tightened as we walked. I kept my focus on Adrian and ignored the fact I could touch both walls. I'd conquered this room before; I could walk through it again.

"Why are you staring at me?" Adrian said.

I jumped at the sound of his voice. Even though I had my eyes on him, I hadn't actually seen him. Heat flooded my face, and I shifted my gaze to the ground.

"Nothing," I said. "Are you ready to move on?"

He turned and headed to the stairs. They remained dark. I inhaled, counting to ten before following him up. The walls in the next hall stood frozen, staggered throughout. Some were widened normally while others looked as though you couldn't fit a small child through.

Adrian continued on without a pause. He weaved through several walls, proving my perception was off. I gulped and followed suit. Halfway through, I couldn't go any further. I turned my head again and stared at the wall in front of me. It almost touched my nose while the back of my head rested against the opposite wall.

Had it moved closer? It was so tight.

The fumes of the gasoline lightened my head. It looked as if the walls were angled, making the move forward even tighter. The way back looked the same. I was stuck.

"What is the problem?" Adrian asked from the end of the room.

"I'm stuck," I called.

"Nonsense," he said. "I made it through."

"The walls tightened."

"Oh, for..."

Sounds of his return echoed down the hall, scraping at times as he slid through the tighter spots. I tried to focus on the sound instead of the fact I was being crushed to death. He just shook his head when he caught sight of me. I imagined I looked pretty pathetic with my eyes all wide and sweat pouring down my pale face.

"Give me your hand." He held out his hand for me to take.

"It's too tight, I'll never fit," I said between pants.

"It hasn't gotten any tighter since I went through. Now, do you want to be caught by the police?"

No, I didn't. Once again, it would lead to too many questions and charges for trespassing and arson. That was, if Adrian didn't decide to blow up the funhouse with me inside. He was the type of man to do it. After all, I was just a monster to him.

I took his hand, and he yanked me out. The wall scraped my chest, pulling my breasts in directions they didn't belong, but after a few seconds, I was free. I stood there for several seconds, sucking in a lungful of air before nodding that we could move on. We made it through the rest of the hall without another episode from me. He held my hand the entire way.

I froze when we reached the mirror maze. My reflections stared back at me from under the black, hooded jacket. Adrian merely shrugged and moved on. I rubbed my arms and followed behind him.

"Where is all that confidence?" he asked.

"I had a bad experience here," I said.

"Get over it."

It was like nothing fazed him. He feared nothing and expected the same from those around him. Well, he did distrust and dislike. It was infuriating. I glared at him, blowing a lock of hair from my eyes.

Allegra smiled at me and waved her red-tipped fingers at me as we passed the next mirror. I shook my head and stepped back. A stretched reflection of me stared back. I rubbed my eyes and fought the panic that rose in me. Her laughter filled the room. I jumped, looking around.

"Did you hear that?" I asked.

Adrian looked behind him. "Other than your incessant chatting?"

I turned to glare at him, but stopped when she laughed again. It was warm and sultry and, as always, it roiled my stomach. I spun around and caught sight of her in all the mirrors. She held baby Marco in her arms. She tossed him at me. He slipped through my hands and hit the floor, his tiny body flopping.

I screamed, pulling at my hair, and backed into the corner. My chest tightened again, and my breath came out in short gasps. The room spun as my heart pounded in my ears. I had to sit down. She towered over me, all around me. They drew closer, allowing no escape. I wrapped my arms around my head and whimpered. I snapped my eyes shut. These were just more visions, more evidence of my madness. I counted to ten in hopes they would be gone when I looked again.

I opened my eyes and met my own reflection. I lay my head back against the mirror and panted for several minutes. This was wrong. I was supposed to be the bad-ass demon hunter. They feared me. It wasn't supposed to be the other way around. Yet, here I was, huddling beside a mirror like an adolescent.

"What are you doing?"

And that clinched everything else. My nemesis had witnessed my breakdown. I'd never hear the end of this. His gaze traveled down the hallway then back to me.

"Did you run into something?" he asked.

"I'm not well," I admitted. "Ose got to me."

It was the hardest thing to admit out loud to him. I was supposed to be the skilled one, the actual demon hunter, and I had been compromised by a devil. I expected more ridicule. He stared at me for several moments and closed his eyes with a sigh.

"How long has this been going on?" Esais demanded.

Damn, Adrian had called his big brother. "Since the last time we were here at the carnival."

"Why didn't you say something? I could have helped. Now you are too far away."

"Because you sound exhausted just defending yourself. And the others need their talismans."

"Stop playing martyr." Adrian pulled his talisman from around his neck and held it out to me.

"That works for now. After you find Tres, come see me. I don't care about exhaustion. We need you sane."

I gaped at him holding the necklace out to me. This had to be some sort of trick. With trembling hands, I took it, savoring its warm weight, and slipped it around my neck. My heartbeat slowed, and the lump in my throat dissolved. The world became a little clearer.

Adrian helped me to my feet. I picked up the gas can and began splashing each mirror three times as Adrian set the charge. The fire marshal would probably find multiple hotspots in this room, but it needed to burn. I kept my gaze away from the reflections and Adrian. I just focused on the task at hand.

Adrian stopped at the slide and shook his head. "I am not using that."

"What's the matter?" I asked. "Too fun?"

He pointed to a small stairway in the corner. Oh, I had missed that the last time. Of course, I'd been a little preoccupied then. A shiver ran down my spine. Hell, I was a bit preoccupied now. Good thing I had Adrian to point out the obvious, because I would have missed it. To be thorough, I sprayed the stairs behind me as I followed him. This would be a great blaze. Too bad we couldn't stay to watch it. Since joining up with the Van Helsings, I'd become a firebug.

"How far away do we need to be?" I asked.

"We should probably be outside the park."

"How much is it going to hit?"

"The funhouse will go up and maybe a few of the surrounding rides."

I blinked at him. "That's some device you made."

He kept his hands in his pockets as he walked, like we weren't about to commit a felony. "It's nothing really. The gas main is going to do most of the work."

Right, he probably had a lot in his arsenal as the weapon-maker of the group. I wondered if he had invented anything that wouldn't kill something. Even when he didn't want to do the family business, he'd sold his creations to men who wanted to make war. Violence was in his blood, and he hadn't seemed to escape it.

Marge stood with her arms crossed and her foot tapping in front of the funhouse. "Took you long enough."

I ignored her. "We should head for the fortune-teller's wagon. She might have Tres there."

Our footsteps echoed through the empty carnival. I peered into dark corners between rides and behind stands for hidden attackers, but I found nothing. She had to be holding him in a trap. A large, round figure stood on the steps of the wagon, shrouded in shadows. The light over the wagon flickered on and revealed the fat face of the man Marge had fought with over his daughter.

❦ 39 ❦

Lloyd rocked back and forth on his heels on the steps of the fortune-teller's wagon. He held the limp form of his daughter by one of her arms. A few pieces of trash rolled around the courtyard that divided us.

"Took ya long enough," he said. "Sorry, but your prince is in another castle."

Marge surged forward. "You son of a bitch."

I caught her arm and studied the man in front of me. My vision blurred as I switched to my aura sight. The alastor's eyes bore into mine from below its horns. Goose pimples broke over my flesh. The man's soul was starting to combine with the demon, like the boy's but to a much lesser degree.

I let Marge go. "This is the one you're after."

A malicious grin spread over her face. "Even better."

"So, you decided to join Ose," I asked him. "What happened to your mission?"

He sneered. "Thanks to you, the hellhound is dead. With Ose, I avoid punishment and break the chains that hold me."

"You've forsaken your Throne." I shook my head. "I

always knew demons were deceitful bastards, but at least they could have been counted on to be bound by something."

Marge closed the distance. "Does this really matter?"

The alastor gave a sharp whistle as she moved. He held the girl in front of him like a shield and ticked his head toward Marge. With that, six men stepped out from the game booths surrounding the wagon.

"Wonderful, more lackeys." I put my back to Adrian's. "Can you handle yourself?"

He pulled out the gun he'd been working on. Now assembled, it looked strange, like something out of a science fiction novel, yet ancient at the same time. The handle was curved and connected to a cylinder big enough for six cartridges. The long barrel had a point at the end of it. On the point, two metal tubes traveled back to where the barrel and the chamber met.

"I need to test this out anyway," he said. "I'll help Marge. Keep the rest off of us."

I covered Adrian as he found a good shooting position in one of the empty stands. Six humans and the alastor, not bad odds. I readied my stance with my sundang and knife drawn. Three closed in on me before the others. My blade flashed in the moonlight as I slashed the side of the first man. The other raised his fist to swing at my head. I sidestepped him and delivered a jab to his spine with my knife. I swung to the side and cut the last man in his abdomen. They fell to the ground, groaning and bleeding. I turned to face the three remaining lackeys.

"Is demon power so important that you would die for it?" I asked.

Two looked at me and each other with uncertainty. They backed away a few steps and took off into the darkened park. The last man pulled out a gun.

Merda.

I ducked behind the man with the side wound, who was getting up. I dropped my knife and swung him to block the gunshots coming in. The explosion of the gun echoed through the night, drowning out the moans of the men around me. My human shield jerked with each bullet that hit him.

"Adrian," I called. "Could you handle the man with the gun?"

A shot rang out from behind me followed by a cry from the lackey and a thud. He didn't get back up. I dropped the man I held and turned to the wagon. The alastor raised the girl's body in front of him as Marge aimed a kick to his side. From the look on Marge's face, he'd been using this tactic throughout the fight. Typical of a demon.

I grabbed my knife and stepped over the dead and dying. Marge and the alastor had fought their way down the steps and halfway across the courtyard. I snuck behind him and raised my sword to attack. He spun around, holding the girl between us. Marge planted her boot in his backside. He stumbled and glared at her. The minute he looked away, I sliced through the tendons in his arm. The girl dropped to the ground as his arm curled up. Marge landed a kick to the back of his knee, and he lurched several feet before hitting the ground. She planted her boot on the side of his face, pressing it to the ground.

"Once again," she said. "Where is my contract?"

"I don't know who owns it." He coughed, and the darkness started to pour from his eyes.

I ran forward. "Marge, grab him."

A tendril formed out of the darkness surrounding him and slapped me. I flew back and landed on my ass. I groaned, getting to my feet. Tomorrow, my backside would be covered in purple and green. In the blink of an eye, darkness encompassed me, killing the lights. I could hear Marge's grunts as she struggled with the alastor. I froze as I tried to pinpoint their location. If I attacked now, I may hit Marge. She was smaller than the body the demon wore but it sounded as though they were in a tangle on the ground.

"I have it," Adrian said from close behind me. "Just give me a clear shot when you get light."

A white fire flared up behind me with a small roar. Adrian held a flare in his hand. The darkness receded to the corners, and the tendrils around me disintegrated. I started at how close they were to me without knowing it. I dashed to Marge and grabbed her around her waist. We rolled to the side, my momentum tearing her from the alastor. Adrian's gun roared, and a red light flared in the alastor's chest where the bullet entered. Lloyd fell limp to the ground.

I stood, panting, and helped Marge to her feet. She rushed to the girl and knelt down beside her. Her hand pressed to the side of her neck before she scooped the child up.

"I'm taking her to the hospital," she said. "You two do what you need to do."

She sprinted into the darkness with the girl in her arms. Adrian walked up the stairs of the fortune-teller's wagon and swung the door open. He sighed, pulling out another charge and placing it on the frame of the door.

"Empty," he said.

"He has to be at the asylum. Esais must have missed him."

"No one knows anything of him. Ose must have snuck him in," Esais said.

"Figures you would be listening," I said.

"You said my name, it caught my attention. I will be waiting for you here."

"Let's burn this place first," I said. "One less place for them to go to ground. This ends tonight."

I emptied what gas I had left on the wagon, and we

hurried back to the fence. Adrian was already halfway up the fence when I started my climb. He stopped at the top to help me up. I hopped down the rest of the way, the shock jarring my bruised backside. I rubbed it as Adrian landed. He sprinted for the car with me hot on his heels. He had already started it up as I slid into the passenger seat.

"Ready?" I asked.

He pressed the button. The gunfire from tonight couldn't compare to the boom of the explosion. The car rocked from the shock of it, and the sky bloomed a brilliant orange.

"Which way do we need to go?" he asked.

"The police will be coming from the west. There shouldn't be more than two or three yet. It's a small town with a usually low crime rate."

He peeled out, heading east. The sound of the fire mixed with the sirens. Their response time seemed to be quicker. We'd really caused a disturbance in this little town. After several turns and twists, the blare of the sirens faded, and we both let out the breaths we'd been holding.

"Take this street to the bar. We can act like we're heading home from there," I said.

He nodded and turned left. We didn't see the police car until we were at the next stop sign, mostly because it had lain in wait, dark and silent when we passed it. Its lights flared behind us. Adrian cursed and pulled over.

"We got lost coming from the bar," I said.

"Right, let's hope he doesn't want to search me."

The cop knocked on Adrian's window, and he rolled it down. Nancy poked her head in and smiled at us. She giggled, holding her hand to her mouth. Cold sweat broke over me at that action; it was so familiar. An image of a girl in a sundress and metal claws flashed in my head.

"It looks like I will be able to claim the prize instead," Malantha said with Nancy's voice.

❧ 40 ❧

The car bucked as it ran over a pothole. The force lifted me off my seat and caused me to plunge into Adrian. He glared at me but kept control of the wheel. I gave him an apologetic look and sat upright. Behind us, the siren of the police car wailed and the lights flashed.

"Do you really think we're going to get out of this?" I asked, buckling my seat belt.

"I'm not going to be taken in, by hellspawn or human."

He glanced at the rearview, then accelerated until we were practically flying down the two-lane road with only the trees watching us pass. The demon had had two seconds to laugh before Adrian had taken off. It had been almost funny watching her scramble into her car. I guess she hadn't seen that one coming. Adrian had taken a quick route to one of the farm roads and headed out of town. The dark lay ahead of us and the blazing red and blue behind.

"What if she calls for backup?" I asked.

"They're too busy dealing with the explosion. I doubt all of them have been roused."

"I meant Ose."

The corner of Adrian's mouth lifted in a smirk. "Even better."

"You think we can deal with both of them at once."

He spun the wheel, and the car jerked to the right onto a dirt road. I gripped the armrest on the door and slammed my left hand onto the dashboard to keep from sliding. The trees started about ten feet from the road and created a massive wall that traveled on for miles. In daylight, it was almost impossible to see the roads until you were right on them. How Adrian had seen it in the dead of night baffled me.

Malantha sped past the turnoff, and her tires screeched down the road. She didn't have Adrian's reflexes. Still, she could move the car pretty fast. A few minutes passed before she was on our tail again. A cloud of dirt and dust flew back in both wakes of the cars. Tonight, I was glad Texas had so little rain recently.

"So, what's the plan here?" I asked.

"You have your sword, and I have the gun. Seems simple to me."

"Wait, that's Nancy she's in."

Adrian shrugged. "An acceptable loss. Exorcism didn't work last time. We take this demon out permanently."

"What about the oath?"

"This is not the time to get into morality and ethics. I killed the fat man at the carnival and some of the bikers, yet I'm still fine."

He spoke the truth. The oath his family swore dictated they must protect humans from supernatural evil. Actually, it was a long list stating what they were protecting them from. This meant they couldn't sacrifice a human just to kill a demon. Bad things were said to happen if they consciously broke the oath. Consciously broke it, so they could try and fail to save someone and only feel guilt in the end. Or in Adrian's case, the need to work on his next weapon. Nothing bad had happened to him, so the others had been beyond saving. I would have to ponder later.

"There," he said and swerved the wheel to the left.

I had enough warning this time and leaned so I wouldn't slam against the door. My heart raced, and my right hand twitched. I could feel it through my body, the adrenaline. There was a fight coming. Everything grew a little brighter in my eyes. I could hear the gravel grinding against the tires under the wail of the siren. The tree around us shook in the wind. The branches swayed in the headlights.

The road ended in the cemetery on the lake. Adrian slammed the car into the iron gates without bothering to slow down. The rusted metal screeched as it buckled, and we were in with a new hood ornament. Thank god this cemetery was old or the fence would have given us more trouble.

"Grave to your left," I said as he skidded on the loose gravel. Like I said, old graveyard.

He sped along the main road and fish-tailed the car into a stop by a mausoleum. We both sat there, panting. Our gazes met, and I grinned.

"Nice to know you're a crack driver," I said.

He chuckled and stepped out of the car while I grabbed my sword from the back seat. Its touch sent a tingle through my arm. I shivered in anticipation and joined Adrian in a crouch on his side of the car. He had his gun ready. The police car came to a screeching halt thirty feet away from us. When Malantha opened the door and stepped out, he fired. She ducked behind the door of the car with a muttered curse.

"Drop your weapons, and come peacefully," she yelled at us.

"Do you really expect us to fall for that?" Adrian asked.

"No, but it was fun to say. Why don't you just give up? You're not going to win."

"We have the gun," Adrian called.

"It's not going to do much good. Besides, I have one, too."

She shifted against the door. I strained my neck to see her peering through the crack between the door and the car. I ducked back down and nodded to Adrian. He motioned his head around the car. He wanted me to go around behind and catch her unaware. I crab-walked around our car and paused to peek around the edge.

"I doubt you even know how to shoot," Adrian said. "I am clearly at an advantage."

"If so, why don't you stick your head up?"

She popped up at the same time he did and fired off a shot. It went wide, not even hitting the car. His shot would have hit her, but she ducked, and it shattered the car window. I crept to the opposite side of the car and made my way around.

"As I thought, you can't aim," Adrian said.

"Which brother are you?" Malantha asked. "The book-worm, the baby brother who Daddy maimed, or the one who didn't care enough to return home? I'm betting on the last. You have that arrogance."

She was peeking through the shattered window when I approached her from behind. I switched to my aura sight as I continued to creep upon her. My heart squeezed in my chest, but I kept any noise from escaping my lips. Nancy's soul and Malantha's were joined. I couldn't save Nancy with an exorcism. The best I could do would be to give her a swift death. Just a few more feet and her head would be mine.

Malantha swung the gun around and aimed at my head. "I thought you were being a little too quiet. No quips tonight, Gabriella?"

I started to move, and her hand tightened on the trigger. I froze.

"I may not be a good shot, but even I can hit you at this distance."

"It wouldn't last," I said. "Like the last time."

"But it would leave your dear Van Helsing child alone."

I smirked. "He can handle himself."

A metal can flew through the air and landed a few inches from us. White mist billowed out of it. Malantha winced, covering her face. She screamed as her flesh wrinkled like burning plastic and turned red. She threw herself away from the car and the holy water grenade. I grinned and moved in for the kill.

"Wait," she yelled. "You wouldn't kill this girl you were supposed to protect?"

I held my sword a breath away from her neck. It was still Nancy. "I don't see another way to save her."

Her eyes rolled up in her head, and she convulsed. She coughed again and looked around with a look of frightened confusion. She looked down at her hands, and a hissing wail escaped from her lips. She snapped the gun back up to me.

"What is all this?" Nancy asked.

I didn't have anything to tell her but the truth. "You're possessed by a demon. I think the effect may be permanent, and the only way I know to free you is to kill you."

Her hand began to shake, and her eyes widened. "I...is that where these dreams are coming from? All I see is death... and rot."

"She made you insane first so you would be sent to the asylum. You were part of an experiment."

"I don't want to see this anymore. I can feel her rot eating away. Please make it stop."

I swallowed hard and nodded. I pressed my blade to her chest. "I'll make it quick."

Her eyes filled with gray smoke, widening further. "Wai—"

I pierced the girl's heart before the demon could finish her word. She wouldn't escape me this time. She dropped to the ground, silent and staring. I closed her eyes with a murmured prayer. Adrian's cry pulled me from it. Ose stood on top of the car, holding the Van Helsing's limp form by the neck with one hand.

"You just keep causing trouble," he said.

❧ 41 ❧

My entire body stiffened except for my gaze, which moved between Ose and Adrian, and my heart pounded in my head so hard it echoed through my ears and vibrated my tongue. If I moved, he might snap his neck. If I stayed where I was, he still might snap his neck. Choices, choices.

He tossed Adrian to the ground. "I'll deal with him later. For now, you and I must speak."

"The only thing you will be speaking with is my sword." I held it in front me as I took a defensive stance.

He moved in a blur. Before I thought to swing my weapon, he grabbed me by my throat and slammed me against the trunk of a tree. He stared down at me. My chest constricted with each gasp for air I tried to drag from my lungs. I wouldn't, no couldn't, think about how he had his hands on me. I was trapped with no escape. Like the human whose body he wore. Yes. I grabbed at the train of thought like it was my only life raft. Did Dr. Navotny regret the choice he had made? I wasn't sure if he knew what Ose was doing. With other demons, I could still feel the human inside, but Ose's presence filled the entire body.

"You not only burned my home, but you killed my daughter," he said.

"You won't need a home after I am finished," I said. "You can join your daughter in oblivion."

"A lot of bravado for your position," he said. "I have already touched you once. I will make you completely mine."

I jammed my knee into his groin. Demon or not, he still had a man's anatomy. He grunted and buckled slightly, but did not let me go. I clawed at his hand, digging my nails into the flesh deep enough for blood to well around them. His grip on me tightened. I wheezed tiny breaths through that vise that almost crushed my throat. He would leave bruises if I survived this.

The edges of my vision darkened, and I started to float. I was drowning again, but this time there was no water.

"Get off of me." My struggle for freedom began anew.

I jabbed my fingers at his eye, but he just grabbed my wrist. He squeezed until the bones crumpled with a crunch close to my ear. The burn raced up my arm in a flash.

I choked back a scream. The harder I fought, the more he constricted. Without any leverage or a good weapon, I was no match against a demon's strength. Hell, in this position, I wouldn't have been much against a normal man, though the groin thing would have worked on them. That didn't mean I would give up fighting.

He grabbed my waist and lifted me in the air long enough to slam me into another tree. He pulled me down, raking my skin against the bark. I panted, cradling my wrist close to my chest as my stomach cramped into a hard little ball.

"I can be violent, too. But I prefer you give in. You will replace the lieutenant I lost because of your people," he said. "It's time to show you what I have planned."

His palm covered my face, blocking out the moonlight. The graveyard melted away, and skyscrapers rose from the ground. The streets were filled with demon hybrids like the boy in the asylum. They moved to gather around a circle. It was composed of two concentric rings with script between them. The writing writhed and changed, loops went straight and lines twisted. A violet mist filled the center and rose to join the clouds in the darkened sky. A figure rose up from its slumped position inside the circle and began to spasm. The creatures hissed, falling to their knees and raising their misshapen arms. I tore my gaze away, closing my eyes. When I opened them, the graveyard returned.

Ose's lips twisted in a snarl, and his eyebrows drew together. His finger brushed against the cord around my neck. With a muttered oath, he pulled Adrian's pendant out from under my shirt. He glared down at the tiny piece of stone resting in his palm.

"How many of these do you have?"

I laughed, hoarsely. "Thousands. I'll just keep coming."

"I never said I would kill you."

He ripped the cord from my neck, leaving a stinging lash behind, and tossed it into the grass. The stars whirled above me as he yanked me away from the tree. It was pretty for a moment before I slammed into a tombstone. It crumpled under the force. My breath escaped in a swift whoosh, and stars exploded in my vision again, except this time they were in my head. Bits of stone dug into the scrapes on my back. I swallowed my cry so only a weak moan escaped.

I tried to scramble away from him and gain my footing, but the ground floated above me. Or was that below? I was able to get to my knees a few feet away. Dirt scraped against stone, and he was in front of me, surrounded by a cloud of dust. He grabbed the top my head and lifted me up. I pulled at his fingers and kicked my feet at him, hitting only air. I panted. I had to get away. I couldn't do this.

My teeth gnashed the flesh of his wrist, but his grip remained firm. I wrapped my good arm around his, brought my legs up, and slammed one into his face. His head jerked back, and he staggered, but his grip on me never wavered. With a growl, he lifted me up and slammed me into a headless angel. His breath warmed my face, and I wrinkled my nose at the smell of blood and brimstone.

"Just give in," he said.

The world shifted, and I was back in the ruins of the city. The symbols lit into a violet light, and the group spun like a dial counter-clockwise. The mist in the center swirled in the opposite direction, speeding up until it represented a small tornado. All other lights dimmed and the wind picked up, blowing old newspapers and candy wrappers against windshields of abandoned cars. The demon hybrids raised their heads to the sky. The air became so thick, filled with the stench of brimstone.

The figure in the center of the circle stopped its gyrations and stood straight. He adjusted his tie and stepped toward the edge of the circle. I gasped a rancid breath down and raked my hand in front of me, clawing Ose's face. One of my fingernails caught in one of his eyes and plunged in deep. With a shout, he flung me off of him.

I flew through the air and crashed into one of the mausoleum's gates. The hinges broke with a creaking squeak, and I landed on the lock. The gate and I skidded into the mausoleum several feet. I groaned, struggling to get to my feet while still clutching my broken wrist to my chest. Its throbbing was just one constant reminder of how bad I was losing this battle. The walls flickered out of focus and into the dilapidated buildings and demon hybrid horde. I shook my head. It wasn't real.

Focus, Gabby. Get up.

Ose stepped over me to walk to the raised stone coffin that stood in the center and slid the lid open. Oh, hell no. I jumped up and sprinted for the doorway. I made it to the threshold before he grabbed my hair and yanked me back. I tripped over the bars of the broken gate and my feet sprawled out from under me so I was dragged by my hair. I stabbed my nails into his inner wrist, drawing a few drops of blood. I should have known that was a lost cause.

"I see you need time alone," Ose said.

He slammed my head against the edge of the coffin. White light exploded in front of my eyes, and blood gushed from my nose. He tossed me into the coffin. I rolled onto my back, holding my face. Blood continued to flow from my face, down my cheeks, and drip onto the coffin. I swallowed back the bile that rose up and tried to lift my head. The coffin spun so fast the mosaic looked like a spiral. Just like the violet smoke.

I lay my head back with a groan. The scraping of stone filled my ears. My breath caught in my throat. I had to get out now. I reached for the edge of the coffin, and Ose slammed his fist on my fingers. I yanked them back out of instinct. The gap and my freedom became just a mere sliver.

I pounded my fist against the top. "No."

"You ripen here while I deal with the Van Helsings," he said.

My light disappeared as the stone lid grated into place.

$\maltese$ 42 $\maltese$

I clawed at the lid of the coffin while my shrieks bounced off the walls, filling my ears. The stone scratched my fingers and tore my nails. My head swam, and I lay back panting. This couldn't be happening. Something splattered on my face. Was that dirt? I couldn't be buried again. I was in a mausoleum above ground and not in a coffin, like before. One of my earlier mistakes had left my body to be discovered by locals. I'd awoken in a coffin with six feet and hundreds of pounds of dirt separating me from freedom. For months I had lain trapped, dying from lack of air over and over again. No one had searched for me, and no one would now. I would be here for months, even years.

I choked out another wail and pounded against the lid of the coffin. My voice dissipated into hoarse cries as my hands dropped to my sides. The burning in my arm had faded to a dull throb that matched the one in my head. The air in the coffin thinned. I only had a few breaths left before my lungs would start screaming, and then there would be nothing but Naamah. My last visit had only been days ago. Who knew how many times I would see her during my imprisonment? I could resist her, but that time in the coffin had nearly broken me. Ose's poison in my mind had weakened me. Between the two of them, I would fall, but to whom? The grit and stone underneath me faded away as I began to float. My hands felt twice the size of my head.

Light flickered in my eyelids, soft and yellow. The candles flickered and the curtains of my bed fluttered with the soft breeze coming from the staircase leading up. I lay in my burial chamber. Dimitri had it built for me so I wouldn't have to go through another grave incident. After his death, I'd hadn't returned, but instead made arrangements with Jonathon Harker in case my body was discovered again. I stood and walked to the full-length mirror, shivering at the cold stone under my feet. Rubies and diamonds glittered from the silver and gold inlaid frame. I frowned. Since when had such opulence been added?

The neck of the black dress came to a V that connected at the waist, and the skirt brushed against the tops of my toes. I tucked a stray lock of hair behind my ears. A small scar marred my right cheek. Strange. I'd never had a scar there before. My deaths had always left me without any physical wounds. The mental ones were countless. I ran my finger across it. It cracked and widened under my touch, traveling down my jawline. Chips of my skin fell off with the tinkling of glass. Mauve flesh peeked out from underneath. I shrieked and backed away from the mirror, covering my face with my hands. My forehead itched, and more flesh fell away. This couldn't be happening. I wouldn't be like her.

"Gabby, you have to get a hold of yourself. This isn't real." Esais's voice echoed through my head.

"Esais?" His name fell from my lips in a halting lilt.

I lowered my hands and caught my reflection again. My face had fallen away, supplanted by angular cheekbones covered with a pinkish hue. Black orbs replaced my once blue eyes. Two silver horns rose out of my forehead at the hair-line, curving inward. I wore Allegra's face.

I screamed again and grabbed at the mirror. It toppled over and shattered on the ground. The lights winked out, and I returned to the darkness of my stone prison. What little air that remained stifled me. I slammed my fists against the lid repeatedly, ignoring the burst of agony from my wrist. A light appeared above my head.

"Will you stop that wailing? It's damn annoying," Marge said.

I gaped up at her, my eyes straining against the light she held. Someone had come for me. I wouldn't lay here forgotten and alone. But I was a demon now, so it didn't matter. I sat up with my head hung low, avoiding her gaze. Why hadn't she yanked me from the coffin and proceeded to kick my ass yet?

"You're too late," I said. "You'll have to kill me."

"I would love to take you up on that offer just to shut you the hell up, but I just saved your ass."

"I've become a demon. Look at me."

She looked me up and down. "I don't think you'd say that if you were a real demon."

"It was a hallucination," Esais said. *"Ose got to you again."*

I pressed my fingers to my forehead. Smooth skin greeted my touch. My breath came out in a long whoosh. I still felt dirty inside, but there were no horns and my skin remained pale. However, even if I was a demon, no one would be able to tell from the body. I hadn't been forced to consume Menrazine, so I hadn't changed that way. Either way, with my last bit of humanity I would see the Van Helsings safe and Ose dead.

I climbed out of the tomb and ran through the door. Ose's treatment of me had taken its toll on the cemetery. Chunks of shattered gravestones lay strewn about the grass, but it was otherwise empty. A knot formed in my stomach. Adrian was gone.

"Ose has Adrian and Tres," I said. "We need to move."

"*Are you all right to do this?*" Esais asked.

Marge came outside. "Yeah, not seconds ago you were freaking out."

I shivered, still feeling Ose's touch brushing across my mind. He'd gotten inside of me. He knew my worst fears and how to play me like a puppet. But I couldn't let him do what he did to me to Tres and Adrian.

"Can you help me when I get to the hospital?" I asked.

"*I can try, but I don't know how much I can do,*" he said.

"Just enough to keep me going. We'll see you soon."

I walked to where Nancy's body lay and closed her eyes. The police would eventually find her body and bring her home. I retrieved my sword from near the lake and sheathed it. Adrian's talisman lay a few feet from the cars. Deep fissures covered the stone. It may be good for another direct attack but anything to keep me going. I slipped it over my head and exhaled as my mind cleared. No, I wasn't a demon. I hadn't died and gone to hell at all. I hadn't been locked in the coffin for very long. I grabbed Adrian's gun and tucked it in my waistband. He'd spent time creating it to use on Ose; it would be a pity if it was left behind.

"*You should hurry. I'm sensing something strange. I'm sensing—*" Esais's voice and the choir vanished from my head.

"Esais?" I called.

No answer.

"We need to go," I said.

"Just us storming the castle?" she asked.

I pulled out my phone and dialed John's number. "I'm calling for a little back up."

43

John stepped out of his car when Marge parked behind him. She pulled out her shotgun and strapped it to her back while I climbed out of her truck and walked to him. His brow furrowed as his gaze traveled from my face down to my dirty, torn clothing. He lingered on my arm, now bound to my chest in one of Marge's shirts.

"What happened?" he asked.

"Ose has the Van Helsings," I said. "We need to get them back."

He raised an eyebrow. "We?"

I held his gaze. "Will you help me?"

"You actually want me to help you?"

"Is he going to be of any use?" Marge asked. "I already have your crazy ass to deal with."

"I can handle myself." John pulled out a few vials of liquid. "I have holy water and a good throwing arm."

"Just don't get in my way." Marge turned and walked to the gate.

"Were you able to get anything to stop the hallucinations?" I said.

"Not enough time," he said.

I touched John's arm, and he tilted his head to me. I pulled the talisman from around my neck. I held it between us. John wasn't used to this kind of thing, but I needed someone to free the Van Helsings while Marge and I dealt with Ose. My throat tightened at the thought of Ose's hands on John. No, that wouldn't happen. I pressed the cool jet into his hand. Better me than him.

"It should help against the madness effect," I said.

He frowned. "I think you need it more than me. I'll be fine."

"No, take it. We can't all be crazy."

"I won't go crazy. Besides, there is Marge."

I snorted, a smile coming to my lips. The image of Marge as a pillar of support was absurd. I slipped the cord around my neck as John reached in his car and pulled out a flashlight and a handgun, which he stuck in a holster at his waist. He let out a long breath and gave me a thumbs up. I kept my smile, despite the twisting in my stomach. He did have a strong will; perhaps it would be enough.

"Ready?" I asked, and he nodded.

"Gate's closed," Marge said when we joined her. "We'll have to go over the wall again."

"You'd think this place would have more security," John said.

Marge smirked "They probably think all they need in this small town is the gate."

I walked along the wall to the corner and to the tree we'd used during our first visit. I chewed on the inside of my cheek as I stared up at its height. There weren't enough grips to scale in one-handed. John rested his palm on my shoulder.

"I got you," he said.

I raised an eyebrow. "And how do you propose that?"

"Marge, go first." He waved her in front of us before

turning back to me. "If I carry you on my back, do you think you can keep a grip with one arm?"

Marge snorted, walked past us, and began her climb.

"Maybe," I said. "But are you sure you can carry me?"

He grinned. "I think I can manage."

He hoisted me onto his back. I pressed my knees into his sides and wrapped my good arm around his neck with my fingers digging into the tender part between his collarbone and shoulder. He grunted and began his assent. John was a lot stronger than I had believed. After a few moments, and a couple of slips, he helped me get my footing on one of the stronger branches that ran close to the wall. Marge smirked back at us from her perch and hopped over into the yard of the asylum.

"I'll go next," I said.

I darted along the branch, leaped, and landed on the top of the wall with a soft thump. I stepped over and braced myself for the impact. The force jarred my legs and jolted to my arm. My fingers dug into the grass as my head swam. I gritted my teeth and breathed out through my nose. I could do this. There were miles to go and monsters to fight before I could rest.

After my arm had settled back to its dull throbbing, I scanned the yard and whistled. John came over and rolled a few feet. He came up panting and rubbed his left shoulder.

Marge nodded to the asylum. "No lights."

"They should at least have the flood lights in the yard," I said.

She shrugged. "Makes it easier for us."

I shook my head. "Or it means something is wrong."

She trudged up the hill. I motioned John to go ahead of me. I didn't want any nasty surprises sneaking up behind him. The windows in the doors had been broken. Glass lay strewn across the porch and the sidewalk. Marge bent down and peered in the dark hallway.

"I can't see anything in there," she said.

She pulled a flashlight from her belt and attached it to a plastic clip on her shotgun. She reached through the window to open the door. It swung inward. With her gun raised, she strode inside. I grabbed John's arm when he started to follow her and shook my head. If she ran into anything, I didn't want John in the middle of it.

She whistled. All clear. I gave him a nod and a gentle push forward. The welcome station at the front was empty except for a pair of legs stretched out from behind it. I moved around the desk. The orderly's head was twisted around backwards, and parts of his skull were crushed in.

"They've gotten lose," I said.

"Who has?" John asked.

"Ose's experiments. Whatever did this is very powerful."

"It couldn't be Ose?"

I shook my head. "He's strong, but not like this."

"I'll take point again," Marge said.

She kept her shotgun trained down the hall as she crept along. The thin beam of light from John's flashlight played over the floor and the ceiling. The tables of the visitors' area had been smashed. Splinters and plastic cushion covers were strewn about the floor. A nurse's body lay sprawled against the wall with one shoe hanging off of her foot. Marge checked for a pulse and shook her head.

"Let's keep going," I said. "Esais's room is on the second floor."

"Stairs?" Marge asked.

"Would be best," I said.

I tightened my grip on my sword, my heart pounding in my chest. Both Malantha and the alastor were destroyed. I'd killed the boy my last trip here. Still, how many of Ose's experiments roamed the halls? How many doors had been bolted on that floor?

Marge stopped again when we were ten feet away from the emergency stairs. Fragments of the door littered the hallway and the frame itself was missing pieces. Something had burst through. Marge moved the barrel of her gun, allowing the light to pass over the stairwell.

"We're clear," she said. "Ready?"

Goose pimples ran over my skin. The darkened portal yawned open before us. If the creature came up behind us, we would be trapped in that tiny hallway like a tomb. I took a slow breath to keep my throat from closing up. There were other doors we could get out of. Besides, I couldn't let my claustrophobia get in the way of helping the brothers.

"Ready," I said, and John nodded.

I led the way up the steps with Marge taking the rear. The remains of this door dangled from the hinges while several large sections lay on the steps. Whatever this demon was, it didn't like doors.

Muffled shrieks echoed through the hall. At least one person was alive up here. I doubted it was any of the Van Helsings. They wouldn't shriek like that. I peered in both directions in the hall, keeping my back against the side of the doorframe. No signs of movement. Esais's room was several doors down. I tapped against the door frame with my sword to motion for Marge and John.

The door to Esais's room remained intact. I let out a breath I'd been holding and moved into the room. The mattress lay half on the floor with the back end still on the bed. The two armchairs lay overturned.

"Looks like he put up a fight," John said.

"He's a Van Helsing," I said. "But I doubt it was with whatever is roaming the halls now."

"What now?" Marge asked.

A scream from the hall answered her. I pushed John to the back of the room and grabbed his flashlight. I moved behind Marge, where she stood in the doorway. Charlotte ran down the hallway at full tilt. A hulking shape closed in on her at a speed that belied its size.

"Looks like you get your first bit of action for the night," I said to Marge as I stepped into the hall.

❦ 44 ❦

Marge shone her light in the creature's face. It recoiled, rearing up until its head bounced against the ceiling tiles, and held its arm in front of its face. It glared down at me with beady eyes almost hidden by puffy cheeks and roared at us. Its hot breath ruffled my hair, and I gagged at the stench of rancid meat. I stepped in front of Charlotte and backed her into Esais's room. The hallway narrowed, and the creature took on an almost slow motion. All my aches faded to the rushing of blood in my veins.

"Stay there," I told her. "John, give us more light."

Marge's shotgun boomed, and the wall shook. I stood in front of her. The shots didn't keep it from coming at us. "What the fuck is that?"

"An abomination," I said.

"Can I kill it?"

"Only if I don't first."

With another roar, the creature charged us. Its muscles bulged in its arms twice the size of my waist as it used them to balance the gait of its stunted legs. It raised its fist to smash me into the doorway. I dodged under its arm and slashed the tendons. The demon faltered as its appendage constricted. It grabbed me with its other hand and tossed me. My right shoulder slammed into the wall before my head did. A star exploded into a supernova in front of my eyes, and I fell to the floor with a moan. I sat up and blinked, trying to clear the double vision in my eyes.

Marge fired her shotgun and caught the demon in its lower jaw and neck. Blood exploded out the back of its head. It staggered before it righted itself. Its eyes, now glowing bright red, focused on Marge. If the thing still had a mouth, it would probably be screaming at this point. Marge gaped at it.

"What the hell?" she sputtered. "That was iron shot."

"Demons don't need the human to be alive to use the body." I pulled myself up with my good arm and ignored the screaming in the other one. "It's bonded with the human's soul. It has to be using it as some kind of shield."

"So iron is useless."

The demon swung at Marge, missed her by several feet, and slammed its fist through the wall. It yanked it free and stumbled back to crash into the opposite wall.

"Not completely useless," I said.

Marge cocked the gun. "Then let's fill this asshole up."

Her shot boomed through the hall and filled my ears with a high pitched squeal. I darted forward and sliced through the muscles of the creature's legs. It tried to use its good arm to pull itself up, but slid flat on the floor again. Marge pressed the barrel of her gun to the back of the demon's head and fired. Its body jerked in several shot spasms before falling still.

John peered out from the door. "Is it dead?"

"One way to be sure," I said.

I hacked my way through the remainder of the neck. Even with the large hole in the middle, there was still a lot left.

When I finished, I stood and moved back into the room with Marge. John had wrapped the bed sheet around Charlotte. She sat in a chair and stared at the floor, rocking back and forth. I knelt in front of her. Her gaze remained unfocused, and her body trembled.

I snapped my fingers in front of her face. "Charlotte."

She blinked and looked at me with her teeth chattering. "G-Gabby?"

"Where is Esais?"

"I don't know. The whole hospital went down, and those things came out of nowhere." She covered her face with her hands.

I sighed and rubbed my forehead. They had to be in the third floor lab with Ose, and God knew what he was doing to them.

"All right," I said. "John is going to get you out of here."

"I am?" he asked.

"Wait, what about the others?" Charlotte asked. "What about Nancy?"

I bowed my head. "Nancy's not here."

"She's safe?" Charlotte's shoulders relaxed.

I bit my lip. The woman had been through a lot tonight. She looked on the verge of a breakdown. Would now be the best time to shatter the hope in those mascara-smeared eyes? Still, if I waited, it could make this worse for her.

"She didn't make it," I said. "She was becoming something like the thing chasing you."

"What do you mean?" she asked.

"I had to kill her." My voice grew softer. "I had no other way to save her."

Charlotte jerked as if she'd been slapped. Her head fell forward, and her shoulders slumped. I put my hand over hers, but she slapped it away. My head drooped as my chest tightened. What had I expected? She wouldn't want comfort from the one responsible for her cousin's death. I hadn't tried hard enough to save Nancy, and she knew it. With a sigh, I turned to John.

"Get her out of here," I said. "Marge and I will deal with Ose."

"I'm not leaving these people here," she said. "You can't be counted on to help them."

Marge snorted as she leaned against the doorframe with her gun trained on the hallway. I could imagine the smirk on her face. She had no conscience about the helpless bystanders that were hurt in the wake of demons. Except for the little girl. Marge had dropped everything to help her. There was hope for her yet. I turned back to Charlotte.

"You have nothing to fight these things with," I said.

She stood up and flung the blanket from her shoulders. "Then I suppose I will die. Better that than living as a coward."

I rubbed the bridge of my nose. Charlotte stared at me with narrowed eyes and her jaw firm. She wasn't going to give in. The minutes ticked away as I argued with her. More minutes Adrian and his brothers spent with Ose. The less time I had to save them from dying, becoming mad, or worse, demons. My stomach clenched.

"Fine," I said. "Where are these survivors?"

"Hiding in a doctor's office in Ward C. It's on this floor."

"Marge, go with them. Clear out the remaining demon hybrids. Charlotte and John can organize the survivors and escape. Does that sound good to everyone?"

"What about you?" John said.

"I'm going after Ose and getting the brothers back."

"Alone?"

"I won't be alone. I'll have the Van Helsings."

If they were still alive, and human.

❧ 45 ❧

I took the stairs two at a time. The faster I got out of the staircase, the better. The keys from one of the orderlies jangled in my hand as I unlocked the door. Darkness and silence greeted me as I entered the hallway. It was as if I'd entered a different hospital by climbing one staircase. Nothing had been broken or destroyed in the hall. The double doors stood open. I headed down the hall and used Adrian's key card. The metal door slid open into the wall with a swoosh.

I blinked as my eyes adjusted to the light. The smell of chemicals pervaded the room, and it traveled down my nose and throat, leaving a burning sensation. Three medical beds, each holding a Van Helsing, filled the center of the room. I.V. bags, filled with yellow liquid, were hooked to the boys' arms. I moved to the closest table, which was Adrian's, and began inspecting the leather straps. Adrian groaned, and his head rolled to one side when I touched him. His eye half opened before closing again. Ose's fingerprints had left a fading mark on his throat. I probably had a matching set. Esais's eyes fluttered open at the sound of his brother's voice. Tres didn't move. A yellow bruise decorated half of his face. None of them seemed capable of walking and I couldn't carry them before Ose found us.

"I'm going to get you out of here," I whispered to Esais. "Think you can stand on your own?"

He coughed. "Help my brothers first."

"Can you wake them?"

He nodded. I sheathed my sword, pulled a knife from my boot, and slit through the top strap of Adrian's bindings. My hand remained steady despite my heart trying to pound its way out of my chest. I slipped his gun in his hand and shook him. He groaned again, and peered at me, blinking rapidly. The door swooshed open behind me. I spun halfway around before a rush of air slammed me into the lab table on the opposite side of the room. Bottles broke underneath me, their shards jabbing into my back.

"You're supposed to be in the tomb." Ose clamped his hand around my neck. "I'll have to get another bed."

I reached back and grasped one of the glass bottles on the table. I threw it at him. He moved his head to the side, and the bottle flew past him. It shattered on the ground. Steam rose from the liquid with a hiss. Ose shook his head with a sigh. He raised me up and slammed my head into the table. The room spun, and I crumpled to the floor. I lay on the floor panting and trying to keep the contents of my stomach in place. Ose knelt over me and brushed my hair from my face with a soft caress.

"There's no fighting it. In a few hours, you will be my new daughter," he said.

"I already told you others have tried," I said.

"They were fools to think your curse would break you. You're too special. I'll do it in time for you to help me choose which Van Helsing to take as a host."

"You're not going to touch them."

"Yes, yes. You'll stop me." He waved his hand. "Now, which one? The one touched by fate or the one touched by inspiration?"

He looked over his shoulder at Esais. I struggled to sit up, but Ose laid his hand on my shoulder and held me to the floor. A sharp jolt raced through my arm, and I went limp.

"That one is dangerous. I should kill him now, but the idea of taking one an angel has chosen is delicious." His grin spread across his face.

"Your doctor is not going to be happy."

"He's outlived his usefulness. I have the drug perfected. I can take it to a bigger venue."

"So you can turn people into demons?"

"No, those are failures. You killed the perfected forms, including my daughter. But you will make up for that."

He took the talisman in his hand and squeezed. Dust poured out of the bottom. He grabbed my hair and yanked my head back. I looked deep into his eyes, and the world faded away to black. Only he and I remained.

The dark crowded around me until there was nowhere for me to go. I squirmed under him. I had to get out. It was too tight here. His laugh echoed in my ears as my fists pounded on his chest. I tried to turn my head, but my gaze strayed back to the depths of his eyes. I began to fall.

Ice crept along my skin, sinking deeper until my bones ached. I reached out, trying to find some surface to break my fall, but my fingers met air. I tried to scream, but the darkness reached in my throat and stole my breath. Allegra's laugh surrounded me.

"I always knew you would be one of us," she said. "You could have been great at my side, now you will just be a slave to another demon. Either way, I won."

Tears pricked my eyes again. Maybe she was right. I had chased her for over five hundred years. Every time I had gotten close, I failed. The exorcisms, the sigils—everything failed against her. Even with the sword I'd sought in order to kill her, I'd failed.

"And of course, you've gotten people killed," Allegra put in. "Innocents, your husband, your lover."

And now Esais, Adrian, and Tres would die as well. They would pay the price for my mad need to kill demons. I slid down the wall and turned my head in their direction. I choked back a scream. The brothers' forms had changed.

Tres's pretty face had peeled back to reveal his skull. The teeth had been replaced by fangs, and tiny spikes lined his cheek-bones. Two black ram horns curled around each side of his head. Tanned leather replaced his once smooth skin, with bony ridges running along his shoulders and forearms.

Adrian's face had elongated to that of a lizard with ridges running up both sides of his snout. Green-brown scales, like bog muck, covered his face until they reached the hair line. Course tufts of chlorophyll-colored fur covered his body.

Bat-like wings wrapped around Esais's body like a cloak. Some sort of black bone mask covered his face, coming down into a point at his chin. I sobbed, bringing my hand to my mouth. The drug already had them in its grip. I'd been too slow. I stood and walked to them, with Ose following behind me.

"So, which do you choose?" he asked. "I want the best host."

I stared down at Adrian's hands. Creator's hands, now covered in hair and long, jagged claws. I placed my sword over his neck. If I couldn't save them, at least I could free them to the best of my ability. Esais's blue-gray eyes stared at me from behind the sockets of the mask.

"I'm sorry," I said. "I did this to you. I always bring death to your family."

"No," Dimitri said. "You don't."

I faltered as my head started spinning. The world faded to nothing. Candle-light flared up, the only source of light in the dark. I reached toward it and found myself sitting at a small table. The tables around us had their chairs resting on them. The stage lay darkened and the black drifted on forever. We were the only two people.

"Do you remember this place?" he asked.

I nodded. "The bar in Paris. We met here. You thought the demon was a vampire."

He chuckled. "And you showed me different."

"Then I almost got you killed."

"Gabby, I almost died many times. And when I did die, it wasn't because of you."

He took my hand, and his warmth spread through me, easing the ache in my bones. My heart slowed to a steady pace, and for once, I felt at ease. I took a deep breath and wiped the tear from my eye.

"They can only win if you let them," he said. "Show them you have strength and can overcome this."

"I don't know how," I said.

He looked around. "You are already doing so. The sword is in your hand."

My sundang was still in my hand. I hadn't released it in all this time. I filled my eyes with Dimitri before I closed them. I stood over Adrian, beautiful and human again, with my sword at his throat. Ose stood inches behind me. I spun before the insanity caught a hold of me again, my blade swinging in an arc. A deep gash opened in a diagonal line across his chest. He hopped back in surprise before I could get another hit in. He looked down at the wound and laughed.

"You think you can still beat me alone?" he asked.

Then came Adrian's voice behind me. "Who said she's killing you alone?"

❧ 46 ❧

Adrian sat up and pulled the trigger. Ose dodged back in a blur of motion. He glared at his shooter, walking towards him. Not in the Seven Thrones of Hell. I intercepted him, my blade swinging in an upward arc. He sidestepped me, and my blow glanced off of his hip. Ose paused. He touched the wound and looked at the blood on his hand before looking up at me in puzzlement. He should have been fast enough to dodge that.

"I'm making him think he's using his speed, but he's not," Esais said.

Esais lay on the bed with his head lifted and his brows knitted together in concentration. Adrian kept the gun trained on Ose as he moved to Tres. The youngest brother winced as he raised his head. I dipped down to catch Ose in his calf. He spun his leg out of the way and ended facing me. Now would have been a good time for a comeback, but I had no words for him.

He grabbed for my wrist, but I dipped my hand back and out of his reach. His other hand darted forward to catch me in his favorite attack, the chokehold. I ducked, but he was too fast. He lifted me and tossed me into the desk in the back of the lab. The computer caught my fall. I bit back a scream as the shoulder of my wounded arm slammed into the edge of the monitor. I staggered to my feet, panting.

"I'm tired of being tossed into the scenery," I said.

Ose grabbed a scalpel off of the lab table. "Allow me a little bloodletting instead."

"Denied." Adrian stood beside a now freed Tres with his gun aimed at Ose.

The shot reverberated through the room. The air shimmered around Ose, and in a second, he was beside Adrian. He raised the scalpel and brought it down along Adrian's jaw. Tres grabbed the devil's arm with his right hand. Blood burst out as the flesh split open. Ose pulled his arm free and backed away. He looked from the two brothers to his arm, his scowl deepening. He still hadn't figured out what was wrong.

Tres slid to his feet and stood in front of the beds, putting himself between his brothers and Ose. Adrian moved to Esais to free him from the leather straps. I stepped beside Tres with my hand tightening on the grip of my sword.

"How are you feeling?" I asked.

"A bit lightheaded," he said.

"I know the feeling," I said. "We can rest later."

"There will be no rest for you," Ose said.

Ose came at me in a rush, but I still could see him move. Esais's trick seemed to work half the time. I ducked and cut the devil across his gut with my sword. His eyes widened, and he leapt back. Tres darted forward.

"Do you remember the boy you maimed after you killed his parents?" he asked.

Ose sidestepped Tres and grabbed him by his neck. "Still weak, I see."

"Not as weak as you think," Tres said.

He pressed his right hand to Ose's chest with his fingers

formed into a claw. At the same time, I attacked, aiming for the back of his neck. In another blur I flew through the air with Tres. We bounced off one of the beds and landed in a heap on the floor.

"You're supposed to be stopping that," I thought to Esais.

"I'm trying," he said.

He kept his gaze locked on Ose as he climbed off the bed with Adrian's help. Tres's weight disappeared as Ose lifted him in the air and slammed him on the bed hard enough to dent the metal. There was the sound of cracking bone and Tres's scream. Ose had twisted Tres's left arm back at an odd angle.

"I started with your back before," Ose said. "I think I'll just take the arm this time."

I scooted to him and slit open his ankle. He jerked his foot back with a yell and brought it forward to kick me in the face. I ducked. He yanked Tres's shoulder, and there was a loud pop followed by another scream from Tres. He dropped the boy and scanned the room with a frown. His eyes fell on Esais, who was staring at him with his brows locked in concentration.

"You are doing this," Ose said.

He slid the middle bed out of the way and stood beside Esais in an instant. He grabbed him by the face and lifted him. Adrian raised the gun, but Ose held his brother in front of him. Esais thrashed as the devil's fingers tightened around his skull.

"Your little trick won't work if you can't concentrate," Ose said.

He slammed Esais's head against the corner of the bed, letting the boy fall to the ground in a heap. He swung his arm in a backhand and sent Adrian flying. Adrian landed, and Ose was already waiting for him. He crushed the hand that held the gun. Adrian yelled. I had to get Ose off him.

"El Shaddai, Elohim, Elohi, Tzabaoth, Elim, Asher Eheieh, Yah, Tetragrammaton, Shaddai," I said.

Ose snapped his head in my direction, the veins in his skin bulging. He rushed me, but halfway he froze. His momentum sent him stumbling past Tres and me into the opposite wall. Esais stood, his eyes glowing a soft gold-white light. He moved to help Adrian to his feet. Ose snarled as he turned around.

"You should have stayed unconscious," he said.

He ran straight for Esais. On his way by, I slashed his calves with my sword, causing him to stumble. Tres leapt off the bed and grabbed Ose's shoulder, near his neck. The skin split, and more blood rushed out. The demon staggered forward, right in front of Adrian's gun, now held in his other hand.

"For my family," Adrian said.

And he pulled the trigger.

❦ 47 ❧

Yellow light exploded from the barrel. Ose tried to move, but his body seemed to refuse to obey, and he ended up making a stiff jerking motion. The bullet pierced the temple near his left eye. A sickly yellow light flared from his eyes and the wound. He collapsed, dead. Adrian stood over the body with his gun trained on it. Esais and Tres moved to stand beside him. They formed a circle around the body. I stood, rubbing my lower back. I threw my head back and took a deep breath. The room snapped into focus around me. The blurred effect of the lights disappeared, and the wall glared under their glow. The astringent smell of sanitizer lost the battle to the sulfur that now permeated the air. I hadn't noticed how hazy it'd become while I'd been under Ose's power.

"Mama, Papa," Tres said in Romanian. "Justice has been done."

"May your spirits rest in peace," Esais said.

They bowed their heads; even Adrian looked respectful. I inched away from the scene. This was their time. They didn't need an outsider like me intruding.

I moved to the table on the opposite wall. Several crates were stacked in two rows to the side of the table. I opened the lid of the top crate of the first row. I.V. bags of yellowish liquid lay on top of each other in neat stacks. The next crate held bags filled with little capsules.

"Find anything interesting?" Tres asked.

"Ose's drugs," I said.

He walked to stand beside me, holding his shoulder the entire time. Adrian and Esais joined us.

"He had quite a stash," Adrian said.

"So what are we going to do about it?" Tres asked.

"Destroy it," Esais said.

"So, another fire?" Tres asked.

I shook my head. "I don't know what burning will do to it. I'll have to take it to someone who handles things like this."

"You know someone that handles demon-made drugs?" Tres asked. "Does this happen a lot?"

I smiled. "Jonah knows a few people that handle cursed objects. I think this is apt to fall under that category."

Tres blinked. "Uncle Jonah?"

"He's a lot more influential than you think," I said. "Speaking of which, he'll probably want to see the three of you now that this has been taken care of."

"Why?" Adrian asked.

"About the legacy your father left you," I said.

I stepped out the door and into the hall. I breathed in and smiled. The weight I'd been carrying for centuries lifted. If I didn't know better, I would say I could fly. The boys had proven themselves capable. Together, they would be a force to be reckoned with. I could see Jonah's proud smile, though he would probably try to hide it behind a stern look.

Marge and John waited outside on the tailgate of her truck. Someone had managed to unlock the gate. I told them of the fight and Ose's demise. During my retelling, the brothers came out. Tres wore a sling over his left arm. He wouldn't be healing anyone for a while. I sighed. I was going to have to get my wrist looked at and take things the old fashioned way. Charlotte stood with a small crowd about twenty feet away. She and the remaining nurses surrounded the patients in a circle.

"Can you do something about them?" I asked Esais.

"They won't remember us when we leave," he said.

Tres walked to Charlotte and pulled her aside. From the look on her face, she was not happy about it. I updated Marge and John on what we needed done. Marge had taken out the two remaining demon hybrids stalking the halls of the asylum. We piled the bodies along with the crates in her truck.

Tres walked back over with a sigh. "Well, that's done. She doesn't want anything to do with us anymore. She said if she sees us again, she's telling the police everything."

I sighed and glanced over at her. Her gaze met mine with a look of cold fury. The numbness had passed, and it looked like she'd found someone to blame. Me. Us. I hadn't been fast enough to save Nancy, and it'd been my hand that had slain her. I felt bad it had to be done, but I couldn't bring myself to feel guilty over it. Death had been a better fate.

A blank stare replaced Charlotte's glare. She and her group began to sway in sync with each other. Esais turned from them and let out a long breath. John's car pulled up beside Marge's. The clouded sky rumbled above us.

"We should get these bodies burned before it starts to rain," I said.

"Who am I taking where?" John asked.

"I need to get my books and our car," Esais said.

We met in the woods outside of town. The bodies caught fire quickly, and soon a bonfire rose in the night's sky. I threw some angelica into the flames, and Esais said a prayer over the pyre. He was the best suited for doing it. After all, according to Ose, he'd been blessed by angels. I never trusted the word of a demon, but it made the most sense that Esais was an emissary of an angel from what I'd seen in the past week. He had a large purpose to fulfill with both his father's legacy and whatever the angel wanted.

My own purpose was still out there, probably screwing over another soul. Perhaps it was time I found her trail again. With Ose dead, my obligation had been fulfilled. I glanced at Marge, who kept her gaze on the flames. The shadows played over her face, giving her a look of primal vengeance. I had forever. She only had a few years.

"Have you thought about what I said a few days ago?" I asked her.

She stared at me for several minutes. "Sure. Why not. You're not that annoying."

"We'll have to drop the crates off first," I said.

"What are you talking about?" Tres asked.

"I'm going to help Marge find the demon she's after," I said.

"You weren't going to invite us?" Esais gave me a hurt look.

"Don't the three of you have bonding to do?" I asked.

"We can bond while helping Marge," Esais said. "We owe her for what she did for us."

"Besides," Tres said. "The family that slays together—"

"Don't even finish that lame ass line," Marge said.

"What do you say?" I asked her.

"Do I have a choice?" she asked. "If I say no, they'll probably just follow like little lost puppies anyway. Saying it's for my own good or some shit."

"Then we should be on the road," Adrian said.

I raised a brow. "Not going off to start your arms empire?"

He smirked. "I left once and look at what happened."

Tres snorted and walked to the car. John stood with his hands in his pockets, separated from everyone else. He gave me a ghost of a smile as I approached him.

"Running off to your next quest?" he asked.

"Duty calls," I said.

He ran a hand through his hair and smiled. "I should head home as well. I actually do have an article to write."

"With all of the good parts left out."

He laughed. I rose on my tiptoes and kissed him. Fire flooded through me, leaving me breathless. I pulled away with an ache lingering in my chest. He ran his thumb across my cheek with a sad smile. The first drop of rain splashed on my forehead.

"You should get going," I said.

He climbed into the car and started it up. "Don't be a stranger."

"I won't."

As if that was a signal, the rain began to pour. It sizzled in the dying embers of the fire. I turned back to the others as John drove off. Warmth spread through me, replacing the ache. The road may still have been my home, and these people weren't my family—they weren't Dimitri, but for once in a long time, I wasn't alone.

EPILOGUE

The sun gleamed off the silver convertible as he sped down Highway 10. "The Devil Went Down to Georgia" by the Charlie Daniels Band blared from the speakers, and he tapped his fingers with the beat. Some woman in Mobile, Alabama, had offered herself along with the car. He'd enjoyed her, then taken the car, which had been the best part of the offer. His cellphone chirped.

"Yeah?" he answered.

"How is your progress?" a sultry female voice asked.

"It's been handled. We have the drug, and Ose is no more."

"Do you think you can recreate the effect?"

"It should be simple."

"Excellent. We have a buyer who is interested. Get a perfected sample to New York."

Faust chuckled. "Big city lights, here I come."

"And Gabriella? I hope she wasn't too much trouble for you."

"She is still our tool, if that is what you mean."

"Excellent." The voice filled with a pleased purr.

"One thing, though, she seems to have developed friend-ships with the Van Helsings and Marguerite Devereux."

"That is unfortunate. It can interfere with our goals for her. Wasn't the Devereux woman one of yours?"

"Her mother made the deal."

"Then we should make these friends ours. Bring your puppet to trade me Devereux's soul."

So, Allegra wanted to raise her head out of the hole she'd been hiding in. This would be interesting, but it could inter-fere with his own plans. Allegra always complicated situa-tions. He passed a car full of a group of teenage girls. He nodded his head with a smile as he passed by.

"No need to get your hands dirty," Faust said. "I can handle this issue, and I'll continue to watch Gabriella. I know where she is headed."

"Be careful. If she discovers you—"

He laughed. "I know. But what's existence without a little danger? Ciao Allegra."

Amusement bubbled in her voice. "Very well. Good bye, Faust."

The End

Ready for the next book in the Van Helsing Organization?
Purchase A Dose of Brimstone now!

NOREE'S NOTES (A PRESCRIPTION FOR POSSESSION 2021)

Thank you so much for taking this journey with Gabby and me. I cannot express how much I appreciate that you decided to pick this book up and read it! You're still here, so I'm going to express a little more about me. I also have a short biography, but I wanted to get into what led to the creation of this series.

I have always had an active imagination since I was a child. From believing in fairies to having a multitude of imaginary friends and going on adventures with them. I could pick up hair clips and pretend they were people on adventures.

It's no wonder that I picked up a voracious love for reading from my mother. I moved from fairy tells to Science Fiction and Fantasy. In my teens, I discovered Urban Fantasy and fell in love. It didn't just stop with books. I also became interested in roleplaying. Especially, in a system known as World of Darkness. They had vampires, and I LOVED vampires.

To this day I still read when I get a chance, and I role play every Saturday. It's my stress relief.

So, it will probably come as no shock to you that the Van

Helsing Organization started out as a roleplaying game I played with friends. In fact, many of the main characters were inspiration from characters my friends played. I played Gabby, of course. I loved Gabby so much, when the game ended, I still wanted to play in her world. So, I started writing it.

Gabby is my tragic hero, still unwilling to give up. I plan to throw a lot at her as the series continues and I know there are a lot of unanswered question I left in this book. Who is working with Allegra to manipulate her? What will become of the drug? Who is Naamah? Why did they curse her in the first place?

There are still many trials and tribulations for Gabby to face in the upcoming books. I hope you enjoyed this one enough to continue.

I want to give special thanks to my husband Jayson. He is my brainstormer and alpha as well as an inspiration for Adrian. Without his support this book wouldn't be what it is today. I also want to thank my fellow role players Andrew, Chad, JD, Matt, and Jericho for the inspirations of the characters. Thanks to all of the fans of this book who have stuck with me over the years. I love you! I want to thank Rebecca Frank for her awesome job on my covers!

If you enjoyed this book, please consider giving it a review. Your kind words and encouragement help motivate me to write more. Reviews and word of mouth is some of the best ways for other readers to find my work.

Want to comment on the best hunter, weapon, or scene in the book? You can join Noree Cosper's Myth Maniacs, my reader group on Facebook.

As I said at the end of the book, you can sign up for my Newsletter for Midnight Magic, a collection of short stories, including Flower of Hell which features Gabby's first hunt with Dimitri Van Helsing. You will also receive news about the upcoming books in the series.

And again. Thank you to all my readers. Without you, I'd be nowhere.

Yours in Books,
Noree Cosper

ABOUT THE AUTHOR

Noree Cosper is a USA Today bestselling author. She loves writing about magic in the modern world, and while growing up in Texas she constantly searched for mystical elements in the mundane.

She buried her nose in both fiction and books about Wicca, religion, and mythology every day becoming an adventure as she joined a group of role players acting out her fantasies of vampires, demons, and monsters living among us.

Noree grew but never left her love for fantasy and horror. Her dreams pushed her and her hand itched to write the visions she saw. So, with her fingers on the keys, she did what her heart had been telling her to do since childhood. She wrote.

Her first published novel, A Prescription for Possession, was awarded the B.R.A.G. Medallion from IndieBRAG as well as Reader's Choice Award for Horror from the Blogger Book Fair.

Noree lives with her husband and two adorable cats, Mab and Nyx.

Visit Noree Cosper's Website